The Rebel Christian Publishing

Copyright © 2025 A. Bean

ISBN: 978-1-957290-66-9 (eBook)
Print: 978-1-957290-67-6

This is a work of fiction. Any references to historical events, real people, or real places are used fictitiously. Names, characters, and places are products of the author's imagination. Inclusion of or reference to any Christian elements or themes are used in a fictitious manner and are not meant to be perceived or interpreted as an act of disrespect against such a wonderful and beautiful belief system.

Cover designed by Valicity Elaine

The Rebel Christian Publishing
350 Northern Blvd STE 324 - 1390
Albany, NY 12204-1000

Visit us: http://www.therebelchristian.com/
Email us: rebel@therebelchristian.com

Contents

My Fellow American

A Christian Billionaire Romance
By A. Bean

A Rebel Christian Publishing Book

For America.

1

Jonah King

"Congratulations to the graduating class of 2025! You may turn your tassels."

Applause filled the room, accompanied by cheering and hugging and lots of crying. We'd finally done it. We'd earned our master's degree. The celebration was jovial and giddy, the air teeming with the sweaty smell of happiness. I could feel a smile stretching my mouth across my face, teeth showing, lips parted. I was almost happy.

My degree was in social work, a great disappointment to my dear mother. She said I wasted my time going all the way to college for a crap degree, so my joy at this graduation was not just for the accomplishment but for the salt I'd rubbed in my mother's wound as I turned my tassel. A tassel worth more than 20 thousand dollars, but still.

Despite the salt, my mother was here. She was even clapping for me, shouting congratulations like every other

1

proud parent in the crowd. I smiled and waved at her, my hand only coming to my shoulder. Not one of those over-the-head waves like I was flagging someone down. She didn't quite deserve one of those. Don't get me wrong, I wasn't cross with my mother, I just knew when the excitement wore off—by the next morning—I'd get another earful about my useless degree that would get me nowhere.

My mother only says these awful things because she has a doctorate in business administration and runs her own *very* lucrative business now. It started as a boutique selling exotic furs and all kinds of little odd things. Now, she has a fashion line and an actual factory of workers. She gets things imported, takes specialty orders, has an online store as well as one standalone store and one in the mall which carries her *affordable* designs. She's got the whole nine yards, and she isn't slowing down. My mother is amazing in her work, and as busy as she is, she still has time to criticize me for being soft and loving the community.

I can't help it.

When my father passed away, my mother was left as a single parent. I was 14 then, as opposed to my 24 years today. Back then, I didn't know my mother was struggling as much as she was, because she did it all with a smile. But now that I'm older, I understand that my mother struggled to take care of me and be there for me when I broke down. She didn't get to mourn. She didn't get to truly recover from the devastation of her failed marriage. She had to put her feelings aside and work until her store became something.

2

By the time I realized my mother's strength, I was in my senior year of high school and had designated in my heart that I would help families like my own. And through college, I did just that.

The 'My Fellow American Project' was the topic of my final paper for my English class in high school. I wrote about what it means to be an American and the opportunity we all have as one. That turned into a club my sophomore year of undergrad and my work there was my basis for my theses that carried all the way into my master's degree.

During undergrad, our club did a few charitable things, but the most memorable was the free tutoring we offered to students, and the annual mock job fair we held for neighboring colleges. The mock fair gained our group a lot of attention that has carried on through the years. Now, the few of us who've graduated are trying to take this project beyond a club. We want to get this program off the ground by applying for grant funding. It has a real chance at becoming a fundamental part of young American society. An organization that can truly make a difference.

So, I bet you're wondering what the *My Fellow American Project* is.

It's a nonprofit organization that began as a dream that is now manifesting into a real program to help urban communities and low-income households. The program doesn't give out money, but everything is free to those involved, which is why we need funding.

My Fellow American is designed to train young people,

single parents, and those who normally wouldn't have the opportunity to learn a skill or further their education for the workforce. It also educates people on loans, mortgages, bills, taxes, and life skills. Tutoring is available in a plethora of subjects which helps prepare our clients to apply for and even attain better jobs. Outside of this, we also do simple charity work like meal delivery, and nursing home visits. When we expand, we plan to establish an after-school program for kids.

Like I said, we don't give out money. We don't even offer scholarships. But everything we do offer is completely free and top quality. Our tutors and mentors are college professors and Ivy League graduates. Some of the classes we offer are for college credit or even for certification, like CPR training. Off-duty cops help with meal delivery to connect with the community, and on weekends they voluntarily lead self-defense classes for young women.

We are not here to pay anyone's bills. We are here to help prepare people to pay their own bills and provide a better future for themselves and their families. This is the new American Dream. It may not be as shiny as the one my parents and grandparents grew up with, but it's a dream, nonetheless.

So, My Fellow American is not a fancy boutique like my mother's, but it is good, meaningful work. To me anyway.

∧ ∧ ∧

"Jonah!"

"Yeah, Mom?" I called from my bedroom.

4

"How long are you going to sleep for?" She came and stood in my doorway; her long legs looked graceful in her casual black slacks as she leaned against the door frame. Unfortunately for me, I didn't inherit my mother's height or slender frame. I had short legs and sturdy hips, but I was blessed with an excellent metabolism that allowed me to eat whatever I wanted or however much I wanted without worrying. Secretly, I wanted curves like everyone else, boobs like everyone else, but why do I care about any of this? Because my mother does, and what she cares about, unfortunately, I cannot stop myself from caring about. Or rather, *worrying* about.

"Ma, I just graduated with a master's degree—"

"In something that doesn't matter." Her voice was crisp and clear. A pleasant voice. The kind you hear on old television shows with mothers who made family breakfast and wore big, pink hair rollers in their heads. She was fully dressed and smelled of perfume and fruit, her eyes rimmed in kohl, and her lashes fully extended. My mother was a sinfully, intimidatingly beautiful woman.

With a wrinkled nose, she said, "That easy degree couldn't have made you this tired."

"Right." I sat up from my blankets.

"Come on and get ready, I want to take you to one of the stores today." I sighed and my mother snapped, "Don't have an attitude, Jonah. I'm doing this for our future. I've let you do what you want all through college, now it's time to get serious. So hurry up."

5

She left and didn't wait for an answer or a response, which was fine because I wasn't going to give one. Not because I was offended by what she'd said, but because I knew it would be easier to just get through the day with a smile. Once the grants come through, I'm going right to my pastor to ask if I should pass up the opportunity and just work for my mom or pursue the one dream I've been chasing that was inspired by my mother.

I pulled on a skirt and a ruffled shirt to try to impress my mother, or really just to cool her annoyance with me. Grabbing coffee on my way out the door, Mom and I walked the streets of Texarkana (on the Texan side) to a shopping plaza where one of my mother's stores sat proudly. There were cars parked out front already, at seven in the morning. The store didn't open until eight, but the place was a big hit, there were always a few cars here early.

"Morning, Silvia," Ms. Anne called as we walked in. Ms. Anne was the first thing you'd see in the store, since the checkout desk was straight down the front of the entrance. A sparkling pink floor outline led customers right to the desk for questions or checkout, while mannequins with high fashion clothes modeled for you on either side of the pink outline.

As I walked up the center, Ms. Anne took one look at me, and a wide smile stretched across her chubby brown cheeks. "Well, I'll be! Jonah King has time for us today. Congratulations little Ms. Master's," she joked as she came around the desk and pulled me in for a hug. The smell of her plum perfume was unforgettable, choking me almost every

6

time we embraced.

"Thank you, Ms. Anne."

"How long until your doctorates?" She made a sly face, bumping me with her elbow.

I was going to respond, make a joke of the whole thing but my mother chimed in instead.

"Please, Anne, she's already run my nerves up with this silly social work mess. I don't want to encourage her any further. It's time Jonah got her head on straight."

Ms. Anne looked from me to my mother and back. Her gaze returned with pitiful eyes, but I forced a smile and casually changed the subject.

"So, Ms. Anne, now that I've got more free time, I'd like to finally start learning how to bake when you're free."

Her face lit up again and she said, "If your mother didn't work me so much, I'd have more time. But for now, let's start with the weekends."

"Sounds good."

She patted my arm and returned to the front desk. She was counting out money from the cash register when another familiar figure walked inside.

"Morning..." Regina stopped in her tracks the moment she saw me, an iced coffee frozen at her lips, ready for a sip. She was a few years older than me and wanted to break into the fashion industry, so she was starting her journey here. "Jonah!" she squealed before making it to the checkout desk in two seconds flat and crushing me in a hug. "Congratulations!"

"Thanks," I wheezed.

Reggie pulled back and beamed at me, her long faux lashes tangling in her curly bangs. She was one of the prettiest women I knew with her smooth skin and perfect makeup and subtle Spanish accent. I loved Reggie, but I didn't get much time to chat because Mom called from the back, "Alright, Jonah, you need to get back here so you can learn about management. Reggie, you need to get on the floor and learn some better folding techniques."

Reggie stuck her tongue out before shaking her iced coffee and taking that sip she never got. "She's a nut."

I snorted as I waved and moved through the store to the back rooms. The long building had plenty of space for offices, an employee lounge, dressing rooms, and of course the display floor for shoppers to browse through.

My mother was digging through her files when she waved for me to sit. "You like the chair?"

"It's very comfy," I said, setting my coffee down and taking a seat.

Mom laughed. It was an uncharacteristic sound that almost caught me off guard. Then again, we were in her shop. The only place she was ever truly happy.

She walked over and patted my back. I could see the excitement on her face as she waited for her computer to load. This was truly what my mother wanted for me. Her dream was for us to work together in the successful empire she was building brick by brick. She wanted us to be a power couple. A mother/daughter pair who took the business and fashion

8

industry by surprise, despite all the setbacks and hurdles we had to overcome.

This was her American Dream.

She didn't know she was imposing it on me. She didn't know her relentless ridiculing of my degree was weighing on me. My mother was not the horrible person she seemed like, she was just more than rough around the edges. She knew that this store, with its growing popularity, would be a definite career, something I could grow in and lean on for a long, long time. She wanted success for me, and here in this store, she could see it. But if it wasn't something she could see, if it wasn't something she could truly realize, then she pushed it away like some horrifying plague.

Did I have it in me to break her heart? To follow my dreams and not the ones she dreamed up for me?

The My Fellow American Project has been my dream for her, but she won't hear me out. She says it's nonsense, and I should pour my time into something that'll be worth my value in the end. But she doesn't know how much this program means to me. Walking away from The Galleria Shop would break my mother's heart but turning down the grant wouldn't just break the hearts of everyone involved, it would sever the lifeline we want to create for the participants. And above all... *my* heart would be broken.

God? I whispered in my heart as I nodded along to my smiling mother's banter. Her tan skin seemed to glow and her thick coils that she passed to me were tied away from her face, so I got a good look at her smile. I could remember the days

9

when that smile was forced, now she was genuinely happy.

I can't decide, please, set my feet on the path You've prepared for me. Help me to follow that path with no regrets. That's all I ask. In Jesus' name, amen.

2

Hudson Blue

I lounged in my chair as the disco lights flickered and women walked by wearing little more than glitter and heels. There was a dance floor full of people, a bar and a private lounge filled with drunks and strippers. I loved the party scene, but I loved even more that the scene and the party were all for me. My dad was finally bringing me into his business, The Blue Barn. A powerful company that steered the press in whichever direction we say. We're the guys that keep people investing.

Let's take recycling. We've got investors paying us to get their businesses supported. So, an investor makes a request, and we find the experts, celebrities, and journalists to tell the press that recycling helps because plastic is everywhere, and we need to do something with it.

Talking is our job, coming up with real solutions isn't. We just want the public to get into a frenzy every few months, so they spend some money investing in more recycling resources, and then recycling companies make money and we get interest off whatever money that company makes. It's an easy cycle, dealing with the press.

We make trends. We make things that are important disappear. Or we make unimportant things very, very important. We take advantage of the Mandela Effect to change brands as often as we need to. Some would say legacy companies like my father's *invented* the Mandela Effect, giving it a fancy name to stir up curiosity, interest, and conspiracy theories. Because nothing keeps the wheel spinning better than good gossip, and as long as that wheel is spinning, we are making money.

"Hudson! Man! Your dad sure knows how to throw a party," Jeremy boasted as he flopped into a chair beside me. We were watching the pole dancers shimmy and shake, occasionally coming off the pole to do a routine.

"My father's a good man," I said, raising my glass. It was filled with coconut brandy, Mendis' Coconut Brandy. A case of the million-dollar bottle was sent over as gift from a friend of the family. I was supposed to thank him, but half the party's passed out, and the other half is tipsy and too busy to slow down for thank yous and appreciation. So here I am, drinking and smiling and drowning in the gooey warmth of alcoholic glee.

"Tiff's here," Jeremy said as he lifted his own glass to sip from. His eyes followed one of the dancers, and when I traced his blue gaze, she seemed to be dancing only for him.

"You saw her?"

12

He glanced at me for a second and then back at the dancer with a nod. "She was looking for you. You should probably find her."

I chuckled, throwing my head back to take the rest of the liquor. "If I'm going home early, then I'm not going alone." I stood and grabbed his shoulder. "And I'm certainly not going with just one girl."

I could hear Jeremy whistling behind me as I stumbled out of the lounge and into the next room where the music boomed and vibrated through me. The first blonde I could find, I tossed an arm around her and whispered in her ear. She giggled when I told her what I wanted to do tonight and silently agreed to come with me. Thankfully, she had friends, so I didn't have to recruit anyone else. All I had to do was tell my driver I was ready to go home.

∧ ∧ ∧

Groaning, I sat up out of bed. There were three women in bed with me, each one naked. I pressed a hand to my head, trying to ignore the pounding headache as I called, "Reesha! Aveda!"

One of the girls exhaled, turning over with a smile. "Good morning," she whispered.

I ignored her as two of my maids stepped inside. They were polar opposites of the women in my bed. Large hips, thick shoulders and hair, and they were very brown. Dark skin, smooth as silk, richer than chocolate milk. They stood out in this house, in the company of Blue Barn, like they didn't

13

belong. If it weren't for the maid uniforms they wore, they probably *wouldn't* belong here.

I had nothing against them. It was not my idea to hire a certain race to scrub our floors versus another race to work with in the office. That's just the way my father ran his house and his business. I never questioned it. Why would I? This form of business has made us very rich. I don't see the need to ever change it.

When I walk outside, I see that format reestablished in almost every other area of my life. When I'm at work, everyone looks the same. When I go out to party, everyone looks the same. Only the dancers have vibrant, exotic skin tones. Like little dolls from around the world, set up and ready for me to pluck from the shelf.

At a young age, I learned that people who didn't look like me didn't live like me. I didn't mind that notion because the only people I saw who were different from me were the maids who changed my sheets or the women I threw money at when I went to the club. That was the extent of our connection.

They could iron my clothes. I could take them to bed for a few hundred dollars. But I could not marry one of them. I could not befriend any of them, not even the few my father was forced to hire to fill his diversity quota every year.

Blue Barn only sees the color blue. That's what my father said. It's what he *said*.

"Reesha, can you get my breakfast ready?" I asked kindly. "Aveda, can you get these girls out of my bed and sent home or wherever they need to go?"

14

"Of course," Reesha said as she nodded and turned to head back to the kitchen. Aveda stepped inside, gathering up the clothes of the women all over the floor.

"Mr. Blue called," she told me. "He said it wasn't urgent. Just to give him a call whenever you got up."

I sighed. "Thanks."

She nodded as she carried the clothes out into the hallway. "I'll be back to retrieve the ladies."

I never called Dad back, I hopped in the car after Reesha's breakfast and coffee and headed over to the family estate. I'd be moving back in there soon, so I was excited to head over anyway instead of calling. When I turned eighteen, I was put out of the house and made to go to college while beginning my father's grooming process.

I had to live with my uncle and work for his business, which was a press company that worked directly for The Blue Barn. Blue-Prints, that was the name of my uncle's business. I had to work my way up through college to become a manager and eventually a comprehensive partner of the company alongside my uncle. Even though I graduated two years ago, my father made me work those extra years until he deemed me ready to begin working in his company.

Thankfully, I wouldn't start from the bottom here. I'll actually come in as the co-president of Blue Barn, while my father worked as the president until he retired. Technically, I'm just shadowing my father for the next year or so until he's gone. It's been our tradition that sons of Blue take over the company when their father said so. With my father accepting me home again, and bringing me into the business, it'll only be a few months to a year before I am king of the billion-dollar Blue Barn company.

I stepped out the car once it pulled around the manor's circle. I eyed the beautiful home. Grey bricks built by my greatest grandfather when he finally made a mountain of wealth. The rows of green grass looked like waves, stirring just like the rippling water in the fountain out front. There were at least eighteen windows across the front of the house, along the width of the two-story home. The house was larger now than when it was first built, thanks to additional rooms constructed by the next generation of Blues. My father didn't have anything added, but I'd already thought of my own designs for an additional living quarter somewhere in the back.

Knocking on the freshly painted black door, I waited on the steps. The old door opened without a squeak and a young woman peeked out. "Can I help you?" A southern drawl sat on the ends of her words with a voice as sweet as candy. It made my heart wrench as I stared at her.

For all 24 years of my life, I was never allowed to have a serious girlfriend. My father had to approve, vet her family, and make sure the relationship would be fruitful to the Blue name. It was way too complicated. Even more egregious was my taste in women.

The young girl before me was beautiful and small and had eyes that held the world. She worked for my father, so she clearly had a good head on her shoulders. Ambition. Drive. All the things my father would approve of. But she didn't work in

16

his office, she worked in his home. That meant she was off limits unless I wanted a quick moment of satisfaction, rolling around in my bed tonight. She was good for nothing more than that.

In a trance, I stared at her evenly toned brown skin, I admired her dark hair pulled into a curly puff, and I wondered what exactly she was doing here. How did she end up in a maid's uniform, cleaning up the mess of a grown man?

"Excuse me, sir? Can I help you?" the sweet girl asked again.

Clearing my throat, I realized I'd been staring. "What do you mean, can you help me?"

Her dark brows raised as she looked over her shoulder into the house. I got to sweep my eyes over her lovely neck and tiny frame while she was distracted. When she looked back at me, I found it in me to produce a scowl, though, I was more intrigued and bewildered than anything. No, she wasn't an animal to gawk at, but she was a beauty to be knocked off your feet by.

"I'm sorry, sir. I'm not sure who you are, and Mr. Blue doesn't want a lot of visitors. Especially not right now."

"Do you have any idea who you're talking to?"

She snorted and tried to hide her smile as she said, "Sir, that's why I'm asking if I can help you. Because I don't know who I'm talking to."

"You little—"

"Mace? What's taking so long at the door?" A familiar figure came into view. Large and thick, just like Reesha and

Aveda. Her hair was completely covered by the white headwrap that most of the maids wore. "Mr. Blue! I am so sorry about this," Erma said as she grabbed Mace's arm. "Macey here is very new, so she's still learning."

I eyed Macey who, to my surprise, was eyeing me back. The staff were usually very respectful. More respectful than Macey, at least. None of them have ever eyed me before, so I didn't know how to respond except to slowly blink at this insolent girl.

"Mr. Blue?" Erma said nervously.

I looked back at the woman who'd basically raised me and managed to compose myself. Erma was older than all the rest of the house staff, built like an experienced ox. Always working. Always trudging forward, dragging the rest of the staff along with her. She was good at her job, and she loved my father, so I loved her. It was hard not to when she cooked all my food, ironed all my clothes, and taught me to tie my shoes as a kid. Erma was, in many ways, my mother.

"I suppose that's alright, then," I said, unwilling to make Erma uncomfortable.

"Please," Erma waved me in, "come inside."

I nodded as she closed the door behind me then watched her rush to Macey's side and pinch the young woman. Macey yelped, rubbing the spot that hurt.

"Go on back to the kitchen and finish up that food," Erma instructed. "And apologize to Mr. Blue."

Macey held her arm a little longer, her brown eyes flicking over my frame before she said weakly, "Sorry."

"*Macey*," Erma snapped, "like you mean it."

She sighed and dropped her arm. "Sorry, Mr. Blue. I didn't know who you were, but I should've treated you with more respect."

I nodded and she ducked her head before turning for the kitchen.

"Hudson, I'm sorry about that," Erma apologized.

"How new is she?"

"Macey?"

I nodded, still watching the young girl drift down the hall. She was almost at the kitchen when she glanced back, a shy smile on her lips before disappearing beyond the swinging double doors. I reached up and straightened my tie, desperate for something to do with my hands. And I also needed an excuse to touch my chest, to make sure my heart hadn't beat out of its cage.

When I returned my focus to Erma, she had a raised brow. "She's been here two weeks." Erma glanced down the hall, as if wondering what I was still staring at.

"Then she has much to learn."

Erma chuckled lightly, but I didn't miss the knowing look she passed me. "Well, Hudson, we're excited to welcome you back next week."

"Have you missed me?" I offered her my arm as we walked through the foyer.

Erma laughed. "Oh, it's been six long years. You have been well missed."

I patted her hand. "I missed you, too."

19

"I know you did when you had to learn how to do your own laundry."

We shared a laugh, stopping right in front of the large white staircase with a winding black railing. "Is he free?" I nodded up the stairs. "He called me this morning."

Erma looked troubled, but she bunched her shoulders. "If he called, then he wasn't expecting you to come in person. Let me go up and get him. He had a real tough morning after staying out so late."

I laughed as we unhooked arms. "Was he cranky?"

"Very." Erma grabbed the railing, but I called out to her.

"Hey, Momma." I'd always called her that since my biological mother passed away when I was young. The name pulled her to a halt, and she turned like a cow spinning around to face me. It was a slow movement, accompanied by the groans of a tired, aged woman. But when she looked at me, Erma wore nothing but a smile. She loved me, this lovely, old, fat woman. She loved me.

"Has he changed at all?" I asked

Erma raised a brow as her left hand held onto the railing. Slowly, she understood my concern and she nodded. "You worried about moving back in?"

"Is it obvious?"

"I'll tell you one thing; your father's appetite has changed. Changed like you'd never imagine."

"He's hungrier?"

She smirked. "The hungriest I've ever seen. Have to find all kinds of things for him, particularly sweet things."

20

"Wow," I whispered as I glanced down at my freshly shined shoes. My father had never been one for sweets. Hearing he had a sweet tooth now almost made me concerned, but it could be a phase with him. "Well, I'll hang around while you grab him. I'll be in the living room."

"I'll go get him right away."

3

Hudson Blue

"How was your first night back at home?" my father asked as he sipped dark coffee. I watched his wrinkled lips pucker as he placed the mug against his mouth. He looked old, and I wondered when that happened. Was it during the last six years? All the time I'd been gone.

A week ago, I came to see my father, but Erma sent me away saying he wasn't ready for visitors. Now, I suppose he's finally gotten himself together. His hand slightly trembled as he held his cup. There was no steam rising from the mug, meaning, he was drinking it lukewarm. Tepid at best.

Who is this man?

Father always took just one cream, and two sugars. At least that hadn't changed. I could tell from how dark the liquid was in his cup. Erma had said his appetite had changed, but so far, it didn't look any different from the dark roasted blend that suffocated the entire kitchen just the way it always had, even when I was a child.

I forked some eggs into my mouth and said, "The welcome was great. Though you were missing."

"I wanted to greet you today—"

The front door crashed open, and loud rushing footsteps made my father and me blink at each other in confusion.

"Mr. Blue?" the voice of that sweet girl called out. It had only been a week, but so much happened in preparation for my return home that I'd completely forgotten her name. As she rushed into the room, however, I realized I had not forgotten her face at all.

She had a pink duffle bag in her hand that matched her skintight pink dress. It stopped above the knee, revealing dimpled thighs and beautiful skin. Her round hips made the tight dress ride up even further. They were the kind of hips that weren't made for childbearing, just for holding. My eyes continued to trace her frame, picking out the things I liked— which was everything—while simultaneously forbidding myself from making eye contact.

Too late. When my eyes finished trailing her frame, I found her blinking at me. My heart began to beat wildly again. Just like it had when I first saw her.

How could *she* make me so nervous?

"Macey?" The concern in my father's voice was alarming. Normally, he'd freak out and fire a worker for interrupting him, especially for her indecent attire. However, Macey was still fairly new, so it was possible my father was going easy on her.

"I'm sorry, Mr. Blue," she paused and looked at me again,

23

"and Mr. Blue, for being late. I know your son, Mr. Blue," she nodded at me and my father raised his hand.

"Just call him Hudson."

Macey's nervous eyes reached between both of us as she spoke in her sweet southern voice, "I know that your son, Hudson, had his welcome home party. You wanted the entire fleet there, but I couldn't make it back in time and I'm really sorry, Mr. Blue and Hudson."

"You missed my son's welcoming," my father said calmly. We had matching green eyes, but his thick black hair was greying now, while mine was only getting shinier. A tired hand went to my father's weathered face. Years of hard work had taken a toll on him, and I made a silent vow to never let that happen to me. Though, with my father's new greying hair, the tired look was working for him now.

Now, he looked like what women called a *silver fox*. He still had the chiseled jaw he passed to me, the dark brows, and confidence that those same brutal years of work ironed into him. I just wish he had good health to match. Who cares about your square jaw if your coffee cup trembles each time you try to take a sip?

"Yes, sir, it was my mother again," Macey explained. "She's too sick for me to take care of and work here. So, I had to send her back down to Louisiana so that my sister and uncle can take care of her."

My dad nodded. "She went by plane?"

Macey shook her head. "By train."

"A train all the way back to Louisiana when she was sick?"

24

"That was all I had enough money for." She paused, fiddling with her fingers in a nervous manner. "Not that the pay is bad. I only had one paycheck to work with, and I had other expenses, too. So, it was—" She looked embarrassed as my father raised his hand again.

"Macey, I want you to understand that you work for me," my father said sternly, and Macey nodded. The tension had begun to build, and the next sentence from my father lifted the top off the simmering pot to cool it. "Which means you can come to me anytime something happens with your family. You are part of my family now, so in a way, your mom is extended family. Got it? I need you working and doing your best when you're here, and worrying about your mom won't help."

"I-I understand."

"Good. Is that your bag?"

She nodded. "Mr. Blue, I'm going to be moving into the service quarters."

"Excellent to hear. You go get settled in and don't worry about missing the party. Right, Hudson? You weren't upset that she missed your welcoming, were you?"

My eyes met Dad's, but I had no idea what he was thinking. Looking back at Macey, she had a pleading look on her face and I said, "Right. It's alright. I'm glad your mom's okay."

Macey nodded with relief.

"See, it's all alright. Now go ahead and get settled in." My father waved a dismissive hand toward the door.

"Thank you, Mr. Blue, and Hudson."

We both nodded. Macey turned, and I swallowed thickly

25

as I caught a glimpse of her hips swaying. *She's so* … I shook my head, looking over at my father and hoping he hadn't caught me. He hadn't. He was watching Macey walk. And … he was smiling as he watched her.

I almost choked on my seltzer water.

"*Dad*," I said forcefully.

His eyes were half lidded with a lazy smile on his face as he glanced over at me. He shrugged and said, "I think she's a really good girl. Erma gave her the job when she went shopping for me a few weeks back. Said she overheard her asking for a job application at the store and asked her to join my fleet."

"When did you start letting Erma choose girls?"

"It's only been a few times." He grabbed his coffee and took a shaky sip before he checked his watch. "I've got to head to the country club to get your initiation information submitted."

"Want me to go with you?"

He shook his head and stood. Slowly, he pulled a hunter green jacket from over the back of his chair and slipped it on. "It's fine. I want you to start getting settled in. I'll have more for you to do tomorrow, so enjoy this day off." I caught the glimpse of the wide square diamond on his little finger. That was new, but my father was a man who believed in finer things, particularly jewelry.

"Alright I'll get settled in."

Dad nodded and patted my shoulder on the way out. I waited until I couldn't hear his footsteps anymore before I left the room.

26

When I got to my bedroom door, it was cracked. Hesitantly, I pushed it and stopped. Macey was sitting on my bed in her hot pink dress. The buttons were undone all the way down the middle. I gulped, feeling an immediate heat swelter in the room.

"What are you doing in my bedroom?"

"I'm sorry, Mr. Blue." She stood and shook her head. "Sorry, *Hudson*. I know we were all supposed to be here for your party, and I didn't make it, but you still covered for me. So, I just wanted to thank you."

I nodded, glancing away from her. I wanted to look at anything but her. "You're welcome."

"Well then, Hudson, if you need anything you just let me know and I'll—"

"Stay away from me and stay out of my room," I said quickly. Hatefully. Angrily. *Who is this girl and why is she doing this? Why does she have my attention?* "Do you understand me?" I snapped. "We don't have to do each other favors. You *work* for me."

I watched her stiffen, wilting in her bright demeanor. My words were harsh, even to me. I didn't mean to snap at her, I just didn't like the way she made me feel. I didn't like that *this* girl was attractive. I hated it, but the best thing I could do to avoid mistakes was force her to leave me alone.

"Of course, Hudson." She nodded, stepping by me to move for the door.

"Macey," I called.

"Yes, Hudson?"

27

"Put a title on my name from now on."

Another pause.

"Yes, of course. Mr. Hudson."

∧ ∧ ∧

Two weeks passed and Macey had done her best to avoid me. That was working out well for me, keeping my mind focused on the beautiful women Jeremy brought around for me. When we hung out late, he wouldn't let me go since there were two girls there, but they both wanted to leave with me. Unfortunately, I couldn't get hammered because I had a breakfast meeting with my father, and I had no idea what his rules were about women in the house just yet, so I held off on taking anyone home. We had an image to keep up. Having tons of girls in and out of my father's house wouldn't look good.

Moving through the dark hall, the sensors for the lights didn't pick up my presence, so they didn't flick on. I stumbled into the wall, hitting something that fell over and shattered.

I swore under my breath as I heard Macey call out, "Mr. Hudson? Is everything alright?"

Now the lights flicked on, and I saw Macey standing at the opposite end of the hall. I'd walked right into a mirror.

"Why is there a mirror here?" I wasn't drunk enough to reach out and touch the splintered glass, but I was tipsy enough to stare and sway on my feet, my emotions too confusing to sort out. Should I be angry that I'd broken this? Or distracted by Macey and her silly little dress and her wide, curvy hips. I

28

couldn't sort my thoughts or my words or my feelings, so I burped and sighed and said, "I broke it."

"Your father said to leave the rest of your things outside your door."

Right. I'd forgotten I just moved back into my father's massive manor. The Blue Estate. That's why I'm here now. 'Cause I live here.

"I live here," I said to Macey, as if she didn't know and this information would somehow impress her. When she didn't smile, I rolled my eyes which made me a little dizzy. "Why are you here anyway?" I snapped as I unlocked my door. "Didn't I tell you not to bother me?"

"Yes, but, Mr. Hudson, I was the only one available—"

"I don't care!" I said quickly. "You don't follow orders. You run around here with your too tight uniform, and your hair is never fully covered. You don't follow the rules."

Macey glanced down at herself. "I didn't know my uniform didn't fit properly. I just saw the other ladies—"

"Yeah, well, you're not them. Your uniform is all wrong. *You're* all wrong. Everything is wrong." I stepped over the broken glass, shoving my way into my room.

"I'll get this cleaned up, right away," Macey said behind me, and that just pissed me off even more.

"No. Get someone else. I'm tired of seeing you."

"Mr. Hudson..." Her voice sat on the edge of tears, tilting into anger and sadness. "I don't know what I've done to hurt you or offend you, but I am so sorry."

I whirled around, my anger besting me. "Pack your things

29

and go."

Her eyes widened as a tear rolled down her cheek. She said nothing, but dipped her head, standing from the mess on the floor.

Slowly, my words fell from my mouth like drops of acid sliding off my tongue. "You think *you* can insult me or offend me? You work for me. I *own* you. That means there is nothing you can ever say or do to offend me."

She nodded, her eyes still focused on the floor.

"Raise your head and answer me clearly."

"Yes, Mr. Hudson, I understand."

I grinded my teeth together as I listened to her shaky voice. I was reacting out of confusion. I was angry at myself for liking Macey so much. This was all wrong, it went against everything I knew.

"You don't have to leave permanently, but after you clean this mess up, I don't want to see you anymore. So, you better avoid me. Again."

"Yes, Mr. Hudson. Thank you."

I turned to go inside again, but I stopped and looked over my shoulder. Macey lowered herself to the floor, and I watched her trembling hands pick up the broken pieces of glass. I felt so bad, so annoyed with myself. But I didn't feel bad enough to do anything about it.

Whirling around, I slammed the door shut and flopped down on my bed. I sat there, staring at the floor, listening to Macey cry outside my door. I rolled my eyes, erupting to my feet. It took just a few long strides to cross my room, once I

30

did, I ripped the door open to find her cradling her hand.

"Sorry, Mr. Hudson, I was just—"

"You can't do anything right, can you? Follow rules, wear your uniform right, clean up a mess." I sighed. "Get up."

"But I—"

"Get up!" I shouted as I reached out and yanked her up by her wrist. She tripped into my bedroom, and I checked the halls to make sure no one was there to witness this. I couldn't hold back any longer, I couldn't ignore the way Macey made me feel. But the only way I could express it right now was through aggression. It was my default. My defensive reaction to anything that made me uncomfortable.

"You wanted my attention, didn't you?" I accused her.

She shook her head, but I didn't believe her. I couldn't believe her. There was no way this was one sided. No way I was the only one who felt something here, so I tried to prove it.

Snatching her by her thick curls, I shoved my mouth over hers. Surprisingly, Macey didn't fight me. She didn't push against me. In fact, she melted into me. Fighting desperately to kiss me *back*.

I was right. She'd wanted this too.

I lifted her up and carried her to my bed. "You knew I liked you all along, didn't you?"

"I wasn't sure," she said, panting. "But I was hoping so."

I squinted. "You … you like me?"

She blushed. "Mr. Hudson, don't make me say it."

"I mean… Do you like me, even though I'm not…"

31

I couldn't really say it. Didn't know how to say it, really. That was the confusing part of this attraction. Macey wasn't just another woman I wanted to roll around with in my bed. Although, yes, I had every intention of doing that in a moment, but it wasn't the only thing I wanted from her. I liked Macey. I genuinely liked her. And I wanted to be with her, even though she was everything my father would not approve of.

She was a housemaid. And she came from a poor family with a history of poor health, if her mother was any clue. And she ... she didn't look like me.

"I ... uh…" I searched my mind for words. "Do you like guys from other cultures?"

Macey looked at me now with a confused pout. Her pink lips were aching to be kissed but I needed to know this before I went any further.

"Mr. Hudson, I thought you weren't sure about me because I'm just the hired help," she said. "I didn't think you really cared about things like that."

"Things like what?"

"Like my race."

She looked away, but she wasn't shy anymore. She was uncomfortable. Disappointed. Of course she was disappointed. It's 2025. Who on earth cared about interracial dating?

My father did. He cared an awful lot.

"N-No, Macey," I stammered. "My father cares. Not *me*. I just—"

"You just thought that I was like him. Because he doesn't

like me, I don't like him. Is that it?"

I stayed quiet, thinking for a moment.

My father wasn't a racist. He didn't *dislike* anyone. He just had a way of doing things. We all did. And it wasn't because of our skin color, it was because of our class. Our reputation. Our legacy. Being part of Blue Barn meant we had to maintain a certain image. That image was a green-eyed, dark-haired man with a beautiful blonde-haired, blue-eyed wife.

That was the image of a successful American couple. There was no room for women who looked like Macey. Not unless she was wearing the uniform I'd slowly stripped from her body. Not unless she was lying in my bed late at night. Like now. But I wanted to change that. I thought I could. With her.

"I'm sorry, Macey," I whispered. "For everything, and for yelling at you today. I didn't mean to make you cry."

She shrugged. "You kissed me and made it all better."

My eyes dropped to her lips immediately. Could a simple kiss wipe away the differences between us?

"Can I kiss you again?"

"Yes," she said.

"Can I … Can I do more than that?"

She bit her lip in a lustful smile before she whispered, "Yes. Yes, please."

4

Jonah King

Mom wanted me to go into the office today, but she let me off the hook when I told her I wanted to meet up with some friends. She doesn't know these friends are actually part of the My Fellow American Project. I invited them to lunch because I got a strange piece of mail yesterday, an envelope from the Association of Grant Resources. This will tell us if we've been accepted into a grant program, along with funding information.

I took a deep breath as I read the envelope over again while I waited for Carlos and Juanita. I met Juanita my freshman year of college, and Carlos joined the official My Fellow American group on campus during our junior year. He really stepped up when my boyfriend (now ex-boyfriend) Dante dropped out of college in pursuit of his artistry dreams. He never really cared for the group anyway, and our breakup was less than hurtful. We weren't that close, though we'd dated for three years of college. My campus work kept me busy, his artwork kept him traveling. We grew apart and were totally fine with breaking up. He called every now and then just to check in. He even called on graduation day, told me congrats for making it for the both of us.

As I stared at the envelope, I wondered what he would think of this letter. I wondered if he'd be proud of me. Probably more than my mother has been, that's for sure.

My hands trembled, gripping the letter. I could hardly wait for Juanita and Carlos to get there. If I stared any longer, I'd end up opening it, and if I held onto it any longer, my hands would sweat through the paper and blur all the words before we'd even read them.

With a sigh, I stuffed the envelope back into my purse and tapped the table in rhythm with my nervous thumping heartbeat.

"Joey!"

I looked up and saw Nita waving her hand wildly as the waiter tried to speak to her. I'd asked my friends to meet me at a local diner. The pretty blonde waitress gave up and let Nita pass with a smile. Nita's long slender legs carried her over to the table in her white lace summer dress. She looked adorable; her skin as dark as the night seemed to glow beneath the bright colors she always wore. Pastel pinks, baby blues, bright greens, and mellow yellows. Nita always wore her tight coils in some new style. It never ceased to amaze me that she found so many ways to make natural hair look easy to do. Ringlet coils, finger coils, satin scarves tied around a small afro, Nita was my inspiration. One day I'll have more time for my hair, but right

35

now I had it pulled back in a sloppy ponytail that desperately needed moisturizer and a detangling brush.

"Joey! I missed you," Nita called as she tossed her arms around me. The smell of peach lotion filled my nostrils, and I squeezed her, too.

"It's only been a few weeks since we've seen each other, Nita."

"I know, but weeks are long without you."

"I love you too," I joked as she held my hand and sat beside me.

"Neat place you picked." She looked around; the black wire table with metal seats and the red umbrella in the center made the outdoor scenery of the small restaurant feel comfy. All of us were still working and couldn't really afford something fancy, so Chick-n-Other Things was the finest place we each could afford.

"I thought it'd be a nice change of scenery versus our normal grille."

"Where Mr. Taquito always gives me free taquitos?"

I snorted. "I forgot about Mr. Taquito. He looks just like Carlos." I shrugged. "Date him."

She stuck out her tongue. "Carlos is cool, but he's not the same as Mr. Taquito."

"Yeah, he doesn't have that ridiculous beard."

"Hey, that beard is sexy."

We both laughed as the blonde waitress came over with Carlos. "Your third party member has arrived. I'll be back in a minute to take drink orders."

"Thanks." I waved as Carlos came around the table and hugged me, then Juanita.

"Ladies," he said, taking a seat. "What's going on? It's been too long since we've seen each other."

"Not you, too, Carlos," I complained.

Nita exclaimed, "I said the same thing, Carly!"

Carlos laughed, tan cheeks pulling into a gentle smile. His brown eyes found mine and I glanced away at Nita as she said something silly about three weeks of no meetups could no longer happen. Then the waitress returned and took our drink orders and lunch orders. When she left, I decided to finally tell Carlos and Juanita about the grant envelope.

"So…" I glanced between the two of them. "I'm glad both of you could make it today."

"Are you dying?" Nita asked with wide eyes.

"No?"

"You're sounding really serious all of a sudden."

"Yeah," Carlos chimed in, his words always ended with a purr because of his Spanish accent. "You got real serious out of nowhere, mama."

"That's because of this." I reached into my purse and set the envelope on the table.

Juanita and Carlos both leaned in and then gasped as they read the front together.

"What does it say!?" Juanita squealed.

"Shh!" Carlos hissed.

"I haven't opened it yet. I wanted you guys to be here."

"Well, open it!" Juanita clapped.

Carlos set his hands on the table, and like we always did, Juanita and I both grabbed one of his hands and clasped ours together. Bowing our heads, we said a prayer, thanking God that He brought us this far, and no matter the outcome, we would stay together and continue to give Him the praise.

"In Jesus' Name, amen," we all said together.

I picked up the envelope, turned it over, and opened it. Each rip made my heart pound harder until I pulled the paper out.

"Are you guys ready?" I glanced up and the two of them nodded in silence then grabbed each other's hands and held my shoulders as I unfolded the letter and began to read aloud. "Dear Jonah King, representative of the My Fellow American group. We are pleased to inform you that the My Fellow American Project has received three grant offers. Please see the information below for the grant officials showing interest in your project."

"Oh my goodness!" Juanita screamed as she jumped to her feet. "I can't believe this!"

"Three!?" Carlos held up three fingers.

I didn't respond. I couldn't speak. I was still reading the letter, repeating each word over and over in my head, trying to make myself believe that what I read was real.

"Jesus, let this be real," I breathed.

"It *is*!" Juanita cried.

"Read the rest!" Carlos pushed.

I nodded. "The first grant official is located in Arkansas, they're offering a hundred thousand dollars to help with startup costs, and they're offering a facility for us to begin in."

"Please tell me this is a dream." Juanita covered her mouth as tears began to form in her eyes. Carlos grabbed her hand again and I continued.

"The next place is in Minneapolis, Minnesota. They're offering seventy-five thousand dollars for startup costs, and a crew to help us get started. There's also a list of buildings they've looked into that would charge us cheaper rent, and they've spoken to a school that's willing to put our information in their take-home folders as free advertisement."

"It's less money, but more incentives," Nita said.

"Ok, the next one." I paused, eyes scanning the words. When the silence went on for too long, Carlos spoke up.

"What is it?"

"This one is in New York City."

Juanita gasped, clutching her chest.

"And they're offering us a building. A high-tech facility that was a school investment, but the school ended up moving to a different facility. It's a vacant building and this company just … owns it. They need to fill it and they're offering it to us. Plus—"

"*Plus?*" Carlos was close to biting his nails.

"Our relocation expenses would be covered. Up to six months of rent at fifteen hundred dollars a month for up to four people. And we'll be assigned an agent to set up our project as an official nonprofit while putting us into a database for charities which will allow more grants to flow our way. And there are two more things."

39

"*Two?* Who are these people? They sound too good to be true," Nita said with a worried look.

I kind of agreed. I knew rich people and big businesses had millions to spare. I knew they freely gave away crazy amounts of money just to write off on their taxes, not because they actually cared. But this seemed excessive. This seemed unreal.

I glanced down at the paperwork and found the name of the company. "The Torn Veil." I covered my mouth. "Th-They're a Christian organization that funds other Christian projects. Here's the comments they left below: **We believe in everyone having a chance because God gives us a chance every day to get things right through Jesus. We want to extend that to Christian organizations that believe in second chances.**"

"That's literally us," Carlos said, nodding. "We believe that people shouldn't be left out just because they're poor or because they're foreign or because they have a criminal background. Jesus leaves the ninety-nine." He nodded again. "So do we."

"In our grant applications and all the query letters we sent, we mentioned that we were Christian." I set the letter down. "Remember we were all afraid because we thought no one would take us because of our faith?"

"Yes," Juanita sobbed. "God, I thank You!"

"Thank You, Jesus," I whispered as I wiped my own tears.

Carlos reached across the table and squeezed my hand. I squeezed his back and gave him a small smile. "You did it, mama," he told me.

40

"God did it."

He laughed and erupted in a string of Spanish words which I recognized as worship. I'd been around Carlos long enough to know when he was praising God. Honestly, worship sounded awesome in Spanish. I loved when he did that, so I sat and listened and prayed in my heart until we were calm enough to speak again.

"Let me read the final par of their offer," I said. "They have partnered companies that have the sort of clients we would work it. They're offering to test run through the program with us, along with a team of developers to help us shape the project. Their final piece of the offer package," I paused as I read the number, "is five hundred thousand dollars for startup costs."

"There's no way this is real!" Carlos exclaimed.

"It's real, and we're taking this investment." I stopped as I stared at the city again. "It's in New York City."

"That's the big leagues." Carlos laughed.

"That means we have to move," I said stiffly. Suddenly, the heat of the summer's sun seemed to burn, and the excitement was sapped from our table.

"What about your mom and her business?" Juanita asked quietly.

I blinked around the table. "I don't know. B-But no matter what, you two have to take this offer. We can't let our dream die."

Carlos looked pained as he said, "We can't do this without you, Joey. This is *our* project, sure, but *you* started it. This has

41

been in your heart for so long, it wouldn't be right to do it without you."

"It wouldn't be right not to do it, either," Juanita said. "This means something to everyone, and we've got organizations that believe in what we believe in. God is giving this project an opportunity to change lives. We can't pass it up."

We sat in silence, mulling over everything and feeling every confusing emotion until the waitress came over with our sizzling food. "Sorry," she said cautiously, "am I interrupting?"

"No," I smiled up at her, "we just needed a change of pace."

∧ ∧ ∧

We made it through lunch, not willing to talk about a decision. We had time to respond to the offers. The deadline was the first of August, and we were just a week into June. However, I didn't wait, I *couldn't* wait. I called up Pastor Izzy and asked him to meet me at a coffee shop on Saturday. He agreed and I had to wait a full week to tell him the good news.

Pastor Izzy stepped into the coffee shop wearing a black shirt and casual slacks. His youthful face was deceiving since he was actually in his early forties. Grabbing a chair across from me, Pastor Israel gave me his winning smile.

"Thanks for meeting me," I said.

"Of course. You seemed a little stressed."

"I am." I pulled out the envelope and set it on the table.

He blinked at it and then blinked up at me. "It's either very positive or very negative."

"It's very positive, but there's negativity in the air."

He nodded and opened the envelope for himself. I watched him as he read it over in silence before setting it down. I'd marked the Christian organization as the one we wanted to accept.

"So, you're leaving me to go to New York City. I'm very proud of you, Jonah," Pastor Izzy said warmly.

"Thank you, Pastor Izzy. But I'm having a problem with moving. It's my mom."

"Right." He made a face that let me know he knew exactly what my problem was.

My mother didn't attend church with me, I've been going on my own since high school. Mom used the church as her personal, free version of babysitting, even though I went as a teenager. She would drop me off on Sunday mornings and for Bible study services, then drive off to enjoy her life as a single woman and entrepreneur. Twice a week.

I ended up enjoying church more than she thought I would, and that really made her happy because she didn't have to worry about me 'getting too wild' when I was in high school. Once I graduated, going to church became my responsibility. It was up to me to maintain attendance, so I got rides with friends and caught the bus. I did everything I could to make it to the one place I felt at peace.

During my freshman year, I began confiding in Pastor Izzy about getting my mom to join the church. He told me to be

43

patient with her, but since going to college, and earning the dreaded degree in social working, my relationship with my mother has been pretty shaky.

I told Pastor about that, too. He's been helping me through the years, so Pastor Izzy knows all about my mother and the store she wants me to work and take over.

The news of her being a problem for this grant didn't surprise him. He took a deep breath as he scratched the scruff of his chin and said, "Well, how badly do you want this?"

"Does it matter? I can't leave her."

He squinted. "Tell me, what do King David, Samuel, Abraham, and Jesus have in common?"

I sighed with a shrug, tapping my finger against my black mug of overly sweetened coffee. The quaint little coffee shop had a homey feel to it with creaky wooden floors, and couches and chairs as décor that really looked like home furniture.

"They all left their families," Pastor Izzy answered for me. "You know God specifically instructed Abraham to leave his kindred? Samuel didn't even have a say in where he stayed. His mother had given him up to the Lord before he was born. And David? He had always been alone. Protecting the sheep, fighting bears and lions and giants with his faith in God."

"Jesus didn't leave His family."

"He left His birth family to preach the Gospel. They came to visit Him from time to time."

"Yeah, but the Disciples were more like His family, right?"

"In a way, but those weren't the people I was talking about."

I raised a brow, and he explained further.

"Jesus left God, His *Father*, to come to Earth for us. He couldn't accomplish His mission in Heaven with God, He had to come here. Then He left His earthly family to return to God to finish His work. So, you see, everyone who works for the Lord experiences movement and changes. And a lot of times, they are moved from location to location, doing what God called them to."

I sat back in my seat and thought it over. "But what if God wants me to stay here? What if this isn't His will for me?"

Pastor Israel smiled, reaching out and taking my hands. "I've watched you grow for so long, Jonah. I knew this day would come long ago, and God prepared me for it."

"For what?"

"For sending you off. You've been like a daughter to me."

My breath hitched. Pastor Israel lost his wife and daughter fifteen years ago in a car accident. He continued to preach, and a few years later I joined his church as a high school kid. Four years later, he began counseling me one-on-one. He's been something like a father to me too, but better.

I blinked back the tears in my eyes as Pastor Izzy said, "I had a dream three nights ago. We'd been working to get your wings attached. Finally, the moment they were attached, the phone rang, and it was time for you to go." He released one of my hands to tap the letter. "The phone has rung, Jonah. Time to answer the call."

45

5

Jonah King

August was around the corner, and I still hadn't told my mother that we'd accepted the grant. Juanita and I were going to share an apartment since there weren't that many places to rent at 1500 bucks a month. We were able to find something at two thousand a month, which the organization sponsoring us said was fine since there were only three of us. Carlos got his own place, a studio half the size of our place for nearly the same price.

Things were coming together, except for the problem with my mother. I've been working at her store nearly every day while spending Fridays and Saturdays with Carlos and Juanita doing some program planning. But now, we'd be moving soon. Across the country.

I'd have to tell my mother.

Slowly, I began packing things up, stacking boxes in my closet, getting rid of lots of things I didn't need or didn't want to drag to New York, especially since I'd be sharing a place. I didn't want to overcrowd the small space. Mom had noticed me getting rid of big bags of garbage. She never asked what I was doing, just told me to hurry up so I wouldn't be late for work or a meeting. Now, I'm all packed up, and plan to leave Texarkana in two and a half weeks.

This was cutting it too close. I kind of knew how the conversation would go. I knew I'd likely get put out or at least receive the silent treatment, so I had plans to stay with Juanita until the big move.

"Mom, let's stay in tonight," I said as I sat on the couch with my purse in my lap. We were supposed to be going out, but Mom wanted to pregame first.

"Stay in? Today's new display was a hit! We need to celebrate." She poured a clear liquid into a fancy glass and twirled the stem between her white polished nails as the happy juice started working on her. If it wasn't for this business, I was certain my mother would be a wine head or just a plain ol' alcoholic. She drank a lot when Dad first passed, but once the business took off, she cut back a little. Now she's a social drinker, which isn't a problem unless you love to socialize ALL. THE. TIME. Which my mother certainly does.

"I know," I agreed with a nod, "but there's something I've been meaning to talk to you about."

"Can't it wait?"

"Mom, everything always has to wait."

She set her glass down with a raised brow. "Excuse me?"

I sighed. "I don't mean any disrespect."

47

"Yeah, you'd better watch your tone."

"I'm not five," I said weakly.

"Then act like it and stop talking back to me. I'm your mother and you're not going to sit in my house and disrespect me."

"Ok." I fought to control the whine in my voice as Mother eyed me darkly. "Can I please tell you now?"

"Hurry up." She waved her hand and raised her glass for another sip.

"I'm moving to New York City," I said with my eyes closed.

Complete silence.

My heart hammered as I slowly opened my eyes. Mom was standing there looking at me like I'd said something foreign.

"Jonah, how and why and when are you moving to New York City?"

"It's for my," I paused. She might've been happy if I told her I just wanted a trip with Juanita but telling her I was moving for my organization would devastate her. Still, I didn't want to lie to her. Slowly, I started over. "I'm moving for my organization. We've got a grant, and they want us to fly out to New York to establish the program there. It's a really good program and I—"

"How dare you," she hissed. "How dare you live off of me to make your little project work. And then when you're ready, you just up and leave."

"Mom—"

"I *couldn't* leave!" she screamed. "I had to stay here and take

48

care of *you*! Just so you can walk away?"

"I'm sorry," I apologized as I stood from the couch. "I'm not running away, I just, I have to find my own path. And I have to answer God when He calls."

"Stop it." She shook her head. "You've never supported my business while I've tried to support you in everything you've done."

"Support me?" I blinked. "When have you ever supported me? You've ridiculed me since high school about majoring in social work! And even when my dream project become something, you couldn't even tell me you were proud of me. Never once."

"Oh, do you want a pat on the back? You're an adult doing what you want. You've got all the world patting you on the back while I'm fighting to make this business into something."

"You think it's been easy for me?" I whispered.

"Cry me a river." My mother's voice was flippant. "I'm not going to sit here any longer for this foolishness. Go unpack those boxes you thought you were hiding from me in your closet and then get down here. This discussion is over."

"You went through my things?"

"This is my house, Jonah. Everything in here is mine, including you. Now go unpack."

I balled my hands into fists, clutching my purse strap, and closed my eyes. I prepared myself to defy my mother for the first time in a long time. "No," I said softly.

"Excuse me?"

"No." I raised my chin.

49

Mom snorted and fanned the air as she laughed at me.

"Please don't be foolish, Jonah. Go upstairs and unpack." She paused, her smile gone, only a tight frown present. "Right now."

I shook my head. "I have somewhere I need to be, and eventually those packed boxes are going with me."

"You think you get to walk out my house?"

I didn't answer. I glanced down at the floor as the anger in my mother's voice twisted into a calmness I hated to hear. I wanted her to understand, but the tension in the room was a brewing storm, and I knew my mother would never understand. Not now, and not in the future.

"Answer me," she grated out.

"Mom, I can't stay."

"You walk out that door, you don't get to come back."

The callous words I'd feared for so long flooded my mind as my eyes found my mother glaring at me. She was so angry that she couldn't stop me, that my mind had been made up. She was so angry that I wasn't giving up on this... but I just couldn't.

"Is that what it's come down to? My future or yours? Is there no room for both?"

"Were you thinking of both when you decided you wanted to take this non-paying job? When you decided you wanted to abandon me? Your *mother*?"

"Yes!" I finally snapped. "I thought only of you! If it wasn't for God, I wouldn't even be going!"

"Don't bring God into this like He's *making* you do this.

50

You've never wanted to work with me."

I stammered, "M-Mom, you can't be serious? I've done nothing but try to make things work between us. Even when I had my own goals and aspirations, I never stopped pursuing your goals, too."

"Like I said," she crossed her arms over her chest, "you walk out that door, Jonah King, you're not welcome back here."

I chewed my lip, tears filling my eyes. She'd made this her career versus my career. I couldn't walk away from the calling on my life. But I didn't know if I'd be able to find my footing after walking away from my mother. Now, this was about my mother or God, and I had to choose, right now.

I reached for the golden doorknob and glanced around the house before my eyes fell back to my mother. Her eyes were stretched, complete shock taking over her face. For so long, she'd ruled over me, forcing me to believe in her dreams and goals and ideals. For so long, I cowered to her. I let her belittle the things I loved, and I let her tear apart the things that were important to me because they weren't important to her. She wasn't an evil woman, but she had her own set of rules, her own way of seeing things, her own tunnel for her vision. She didn't just block out distractions, my mother blocked out everything and everyone she didn't agree with. We were all wrong in her eyes, and I would never be right until I did exactly what she told me to do. But even God lets us grow up and make our own decisions. So, why couldn't she?

"I'll send someone to mail my boxes." I hoped this

wouldn't be permanent, yet I was afraid that it was. So I took a deep breath and looked at my mother, held in the sight of her angry face. I wanted to tell her I loved her; in case I wouldn't get to say it later. But she would only turn that confession into another argument, so instead I said, "Goodbye, Mom." Then I opened the door and stepped out without looking back.

6

Hudson Blue

"What do you think about the gun laws?" my father asked as he cut into his steak. He sat across from me, at the opposite end of the long white table between us.

"Well, I heard you say that Americans need guns, and they shouldn't be—"

"Not what I said," he lifted a piece of red steak to inspect it, "what do you *think.*"

I gulped, setting my fork and knife down. Dad and I had been having these kinds of conversations a lot. He would ask me about a controversial topic and then criticize my answer until I told him what he wanted to hear. An answer that would make the company look good.

Over the last six months, I've learned that my feelings need to align with what my father feels, but I have to say it in my own words. To take over Blue Barn, I need to have the mindset that my father and forefathers had. That's how we've stayed on top, even if I didn't believe the way they did, it wasn't really about me. It was about preserving our name, maintaining our connections. My father went through the same grooming process he's putting me through. Changing my mind to be like his is supposed to be a privilege, but it's just a burden to me.

Since moving back in, the only peace I've had was when I was with Macey. Yes, the physical part of our relationship was wonderful. The best I'd ever had. But there was more to it than that. We enjoyed late-night talks that helped ease the tension and stress of my workdays. Macey listened to me. She offered me her best advice, lots of stuff she learned from her home in the south. Sometimes she admitted the old wives' tales she'd heard were nutty, but I liked hearing them anyway. No matter what we talked about, Macey understood me. She understood that I didn't want to become a copy of my father. Like ice, she wanted to preserve who I truly am, which was possibly the sweetest thing I'd ever heard.

I relied on Macey to preserve the part of me still left inside when I'm done with work every day. I needed Macey to remind me of who I really was after hours pretending to be the man my father is. I could be the man Blue Barn needed me to be, but what about the man Macey needed me to be?

That didn't matter because Macey and I would never have anything more than casual sex and late-night conversations. My father made it clear long ago that women like Macey had a clear place in this world. She did not belong at my side; she belonged in my kitchen. In my office to empty the trash. In my room to warm the bed or change my sheets. Or both. I could use her however I wanted, but I could not have her. Not as a wife.

The very thought angered me. I had obeyed every rule my father had ever given, but that was the only one that made me pause.

"I'm waiting," my father's voice brought me back to reality.

I cleared my throat. "America instituted the right to bear arms when the country was birthed. Through the years, we have struggled to make that happen, especially after so many public shootings. So ..." I paused, trying to pick the answer my father wanted me to deliver. Whenever he'd been put on the spot, he would always say he believed Americans should have their guns. Honestly, I wasn't sure if he truly believed that, but that was what he was *supposed* to believe because others in the country club did, and so did many of our work partners. We were taught to believe in the society we'd created through our business, and we needed to be a certain kind of person to do that. Only one person could do it, so we've all become copies of someone in my history who got Blue Barn the fortune it has now.

I sighed. "I view this subject the same way I view rebellious teens."

My father tilted his head to the side.

"Telling a teenager they can't do something only makes them want to do it more. Even if they know what they're doing is wrong, rebellious people never think something bad will happen to them. So, I think the best thing to do is let them have what they want."

He smiled. "Let them have guns."

"Yes, Father."

"And when they hurt themselves, then what?"

"Then you get to say, I told you so." I reached for my drink. "Well, not in those words exactly, but letting them screw up provides the perfect avenue to implement the ideology we wanted from the start. We use their own mistake as an example of why they should've listened to us from the start."

"Very good." His smile stretched. "So, what if all this backfired?"

I raised my eyebrows.

"If the media exposes us for backtracking."

"We're allowed to change our minds—"

"Not when you're rich." His voice hardened. "When a business as large as our takes a stance on a controversial matter, we don't get to change it. Not without losing the trust of our consumers and investors."

I sat quietly. Thinking.

"Try again, Hudson."

I cleared my throat. "Fine, we don't change our minds. Instead of using their mistakes to push for more gun control, we would use it as a learning experience."

He nodded slowly.

"We can take advantage of the situation to launch programs that would teach gun buyers about self-defense and preservation. Give them guidelines and cautions. All funded by Blue Barn, to make it look like we care." I smiled as I said that last bit, because that was the answer my father was really looking for. He didn't care one way or the other about gun control. His interest was in money and how he could make more. If the public wanted more guns, we'd find a way to support it. If our investors were against it, then we would be too. Our feelings didn't matter because we weren't allowed to have any. That's the way it was.

My father eyed me for a moment before his tense face dropped into a wide grin. "Very good, Hudson. I think you're the best of us, really. Blue Barn is going to be in very good hands."

"Thank you, Father. It's your teaching that's really helped me."

He laughed. "Believe it or not, you're naturally gifted at this work."

Gifted? I laughed within. I'm a liar with no face of my own. No words of my own. I don't know what I believe about guns, but I know Macey doesn't like them. She said a lot of people from her community were against them, largely because of gang violence but also because of the alarming increase of school shootings and other public shootings, a few of which were racially motivated. That's what hit me the hardest when we talked about gun control, but she assured me it wasn't as simple as I thought.

"Not everything within our community is about race," she'd laughed one night, drawing circles on my bare chest. "Some Black people like to hunt too or go to the shooting range. Some of us want to keep our guns for the same reasons as everyone else. Recreation and protection."

That was interesting. Whenever someone talked about

grabbing a gun for protection, I imagined a masked man breaking in and trying to steal from a hardworking family. But what did the man beneath the mask look like? What did the hardworking family look like? If I asked my father that question, I know exactly what he would say. He pretty much summed it up as he reached for his glass of wine and took a long pull, lips puckered.

"Criminals have had guns for so long. I don't care if they kill their own people. I don't care if they tear their own neighborhoods apart."

Every time he said *they*, I thought of Macey and Erma.

My father sipped his wine again, sucking the flavor from his teeth before he said, "If they act like animals and kill each other off, fine by me. But once they start getting into *our* neighborhoods," he tipped his glass toward me, "that's a problem, Hudson. We've got to push for this."

I wanted to argue with him, if only to defend Macey and to tell my father that she was different. She didn't believe in gang violence and senseless shootings and destroying anyone's community. Macey was more than my father ever thought she could be. But there was no way I could say that to him. Not without losing everything I'd worked my entire life to get.

"Besides," I said, trying to steer the conversation, "I've heard there's been a big investment in metal. With the rising demand for weapons, The Builders Hub has had a big uptick in their production. And I read yesterday that America was looking into reworking their talks with Taiwan who's been producing gun parts for us. The increase has benefitted the

58

whole country. We've got to move in on this."

My dad slapped the table with joy. "My boy! You've got every aspect of this business covered. I'm proud of you, Hudson."

"Thank you, Father."

He rang the little silver bell beside him. "Are you interested in dessert? I think it's peach cobbler tonight. Erma makes the best."

"Sorry, Mr. Blue," said a feminine voice across the room.

I looked up from my plate, panic and relief washing over me as my sweet little Macey walked in with a black tray. Her eyes skipped to mine for a second, but that look could've lasted me a lifetime of peace. She focused on my father, her brown legs extending fully as she strutted over to the table. Macey had been my best kept secret, and that's what made her more alluring.

The other maids were older women, mostly out of shape, with tired faces and a mother's touch to them. But Macey was young and vibrant. Barely legal, she'd finished high school and came up here to New York to find a job and live on her own until her mother got sick. Since her mother lived alone and Macey didn't want to leave her job, her mom traveled to New York to live with her. But money got tight, Macey needed a second job or a *better* job, and that's when she found this one through Erma. Normally, my father didn't hire young girls, not *this* young, however, he made an exception at Erma's recommendation.

Now Macey's here, making the old grey and white maid

outfits look skimpy and attractive, paired with heels instead of the white shoes my father issued to them. No one stopped her. I was positive even if my father didn't say it, he at least thought Macey was kind of cute. He was particularly nice to her, and when I asked about it, Macey said my father told her that when I lost my mother, I took it hard—which was true—so he had compassion towards her.

"You'll have to eat my peach cobbler tonight," Macey explained, still holding that tray. "Erma's ankle is swollen again, she said it's nothing, but I had her go to the hospital."

My father touched his chest, wide hands pushing into the white shirt he'd skipped the first few buttons on. "Goodness, I'm glad you sent her, Macey."

"Of course, sir."

"Are you alright?"

She nodded, and an earnest look veiled her face. "Yes."

"Well, I don't want to put you through anything extra. Can you have Velma bring a bit of cobbler to my room? I think I'll retire for the night."

Macey held the empty tray against her chest, completely ignoring me. We'd done this for so long, it was child's play now. "Did the news of Erma ruin your appetite, Mr. Blue? I'm plenty sorry, sir."

"No." My father shook his head. "I'm glad you told me. I'm getting old, Macey," he teased, and it made her wary look change into a soft smile as she chuckled.

"In that case, please rest up for the night."

"I plan to."

My father gave her a smile, a really kind one. This was the same man who'd just told me we needed to protect ourselves from thugs. I didn't know how to feel, but I guess I should've felt nothing since Macey was where she belonged in my father's eyes. He could be nice to her because she was a maid and she did what he said, but that was the problem. My father liked her because she knew her place. If he knew how I felt about her, he would have her removed from the house. Because housemaids don't eat at our table, they only clean them.

When my father left, Macey began to clear the dishes.

"I'm finished as well," I said to her.

She glanced up, her eyes flicked to me and then down to my plate. "I'll clear that right away, Mr. Hudson." Crossing the length of the table, Macey stopped beside me, and I watched her slender frame as she cleared the plates and glasses. When I shifted in my seat, she didn't look at me. She raked my leftovers onto one plate before stacking it and kept working like I wasn't there.

"Pardon my reach, sir," she said as she grabbed my glass.

I inched closer to her in my chair and slipped my hand beneath the table, brushing her thigh. She gasped, looking over at me before glancing around to see if we were alone.

"Finish clearing the table," I said firmly. My grip on her leg shifted from a gentle brush to a desperate clutch. "Finish quickly."

"Yes, sir," she replied.

Her eyes wouldn't dare find mine. Toying with her was always my favorite thing to do whenever I could.

61

"I'll be excusing myself." I let her go.

"Of course," she said politely.

Standing from the table, I glanced around before I wrapped my hands around her waist. She held in her giggles as she turned in my arms for a kiss. "Mr. Hudson, we'll get in trouble."

"I don't care," I whispered, then I pressed my lips over hers. I could feel her smiling into our exchange as I pushed her against the table. The glasses clanked together loudly, and Macey pulled away snickering.

"Shh," she cautioned.

"Sorry." I laughed. "I missed you today."

"I missed you, too."

"You're free tonight, right?"

She nodded, a loose curl bounced with the movement. "I've got to call my mom and then I'll be over."

"Okay," I said as I grabbed the plates she'd stacked and carried them to the tray. I helped her finish clearing the table before I kissed her once more and then headed to my bedroom.

It usually took Macey about two hours after dinner to make it to my room since she still had chores and called her mother every night. Tonight, though, it took her only an hour before she knocked on my door. When I opened it, I found her smiling and I couldn't help but smile back. Macey had changed into a bathrobe. Normally, she just wore her maid uniform or something comfortable but tonight was different for some reason.

"Everything alright?" I exhaled, staring at her negligée.

She pushed me inside and kicked the door shut behind her. I stumbled back, unable to produce any words as she untied her robe and dropped it to the floor.

I stared.

Macey wore a winter white lace body suit with fishnet stockings. She looked like a sexy doll, or just a sex doll. I couldn't decide. She'd never worn lingerie before.

I sat on the edge of the bed as she crawled into my lap and draped her arms around my neck. "So, when are we going public?" she asked.

"Public?" I ran my hands along her fishnets, feeling the odd pattern beneath my fingertips.

"You said you didn't care if we were caught." Macey shrugged. "So, when do we go public?"

"Oh…"

Macey's brown eyes had been lit up the entire time, but now they were dimming.

"Mace … You know I care. I have to care about what happens if we're caught."

I could lose everything. I'm sure neither of us wanted that to happen, but the look on Macey's face said she might have been willing to risk it.

She leaned back, brows pinching together. "That's not what you said before."

"I know—"

"You said you didn't care."

"I *know*," I told her, annoyed. Was this the reason she

63

arrived all dolled up tonight? To celebrate our relationship going public?

I frowned. "Mace…" How could I tell her I'd been caught up in the moment?

She shook her head. "We've been together for six months now. When do I stop being a secret?"

"You know things are complicated."

"But we love each other. That's not complicated at all."

I sighed. "You're too young for love, Macey. This is fun, but we can't do this forever."

"I know, which is why we should go public." Loosening her grip around my neck, Macey climbed off my lap. "I don't understand how you could change your mind like this."

"Macey, come on. I haven't changed my mind. You know I do love you, it's just—"

"Then act like it. Act like you love me." Her eyes began to water. "Act like you want me to stay here."

I squinted. "What are you talking about, *stay here?*"

She shook her head, eyes falling to the floor. "My uncle called two days ago. Mom is really bad. She doesn't want me to come down there, but my uncle says there's not much time left until she passes. I was thinking about going, but," she looked up at me and I felt my heart cramp in my chest. "I don't want to watch her die, and I don't want to leave you, either. I was going to stay, and go home when I could, maybe just for the funeral. I didn't want to see her like that anyway. But now, I don't know."

I walked over to her and grabbed her small hands, I kissed

64

them and said, "Stay with me. I promise to make things right for us."

She looked at our hands. "I can't stay for a promise, Hudson."

"Macey, come on. You know you're the only one for me. We're perfect together. Things are just complicated."

"Then do something, tell everyone that you love me!"

"I *can't*." I dropped her hands. "I can't, Mace." I watched her tears begin to fall, breaking my heart as they dripped from her chin. "I've wanted Blue Barn for so long, I can't just give it up."

There was a pause before Macey nodded. Her heels clicked against the wooden floor as she leaned down and grabbed her robe.

"I thought you understood me," I said. "I thought you understood what this was. What it was supposed to be."

She looked back at me as she grabbed the door handle. Streams of black tears rolled down her cheeks as she said, "I thought so, too."

And just like that, Macey left.

7

Hudson Blue

One Year Later

It's been a year since Macey left. A week after she stopped seeing me, she told my father that her mother was gravely ill and needed to return home. He got her a flight and asked if she'd be coming back in the future. Macey couldn't give him an answer. She said there was a lot to work through with her mother's property and whatnot. My father told her there would always be a place for her here on his team.

On the day of her departure, Macey thanked my father, squeezed a tearful Erma, and exchanged kisses, hugs, and tears with the other girls. But for me, she merely nodded. She didn't mutter a word. Didn't even shake my hand when I extended it to her. It was a painful goodbye, one that was silent between the two of us.

I've never forgotten that day. I'd somehow let my father

down and hurt Macey at the same time. I couldn't live up to my father's standards, but I couldn't become the man Macey wanted me to be. Though she'd been everything I'd ever needed. I didn't know it a year ago, but I think I had truly fallen in love with Macey. Sure, the sex was blinding, but she kept me grounded, rooted in someone I was proud to be. Rooted in individuality, not just a copy of my father and every Mr. Blue before me.

Now, I've taken office as the head of Blue Barn, and it gets harder and harder every day to remember the guy that Macey fell for. She was young and vulnerable, only eighteen at the time. There was a six-year gap between us, but that never bothered us because, to Macey, none of that mattered. Not my age, not my race, not the fact that she was working for me. She loved me and all the problems I came with, and slowly, I'd fallen in love with her too. I was going to do things differently. I was going to be Macey's hero. I was going to be my own hero. But I failed.

I swore I'd spend every second of my life making things right so I could go and bring Macey back. However, all I've managed to do is sink further and further into the cast of my father to forget myself.

When work was over, I grabbed my things from the office and went home. Jeremy had invited me out for drinks, but I just didn't have it in me today. Not on the anniversary of losing Macey.

"Good evening, Hudson," Erma said as she greeted me at

the front door of my home.

"Evening, Erma. No dinner tonight. I just want to sleep."

She gave me a small smile as she collected my briefcase and coat. "Of course."

My father was out of town, it seemed like he was always gone now. He'd retired but still checked in on me. Every now and again he showed up to overlook deals with larger businesses, but for the most part, my father stayed in his part of the manor and kept to himself. I think he's truly enjoying the retired life.

Pushing open the door to my bedroom. I kicked my shoes off and threw my suit jacket onto the lounge chair. Loosening my tie, I trudged over to the bed in the dimness of my room when a voice said sweetly, "Welcome home, Mr. Blue."

I stopped and glanced around. A woman was sitting on my bed. Vibrant brown skin and eyes that had once lost their glow.

"Macey?"

She smiled as she stood and clicked my lamp on. "I'm back, Hudson."

My heart almost beat out of its cavity as I raced to her. Sweeping her off her feet, I kissed her deeply, only pulling away to ask in a gasp, "When did you get back?"

"A few hours ago. Erma let me wait in your room because I told her I wanted to talk over the details of my return. She doesn't suspect a thing."

"I can't believe you're here," I said, cupping her face. "You're here, aren't you? I'm not dreaming?"

She giggled, and the memories of her flooded my mind,

making me warm all over. Pressing my lips to hers, I kissed her relentlessly until we fell onto the bed. I was stripping her before I knew it. Tearing at her clothes to feel her warmth again, to let her envelope me in a desire I'd been starved of since she left.

No one compared to Macey. Not a single woman. I hadn't been satisfied in so long, I was afraid I'd be too rough with her. But she didn't mind. Welcoming me back with ease and delight. I think Macey missed me as much as I missed her.

When it was over, she laid on my chest as I looked up at the ceiling. "Mace?"

"Yes?"

"What took so long for you to return?"

She was quiet.

"Mace?"

Sitting up from my chest, she pulled the blankets over herself as she adjusted beside me. "Hudson, I returned because I'm engaged now."

"What?" I sat up and blinked at her.

She looked away, shier than she's ever been. "I'm getting married in six months."

"Then why are you here?" I snapped.

"Because I haven't stopped loving you since the day I left." Macey's shoulders began to tremble as she dropped her face into her palms. "You're the only person I've thought about since I moved back home. And even after meeting my fiancée, I couldn't stop thinking about you. So I came back. I wanted to see if maybe things had changed."

"Changed? How?"

Slowly, Macey lifted her face from her hands. Brown eyes spilled tears as she stared at me in awe. "I guess things haven't changed."

"You can't show up on my doorstep and expect me to tell the world I'm sleeping with you! You don't get to do that!"

"And you don't get to keep me as your pet! I'm no one's secret, Hudson." Her words were venomous as she glared at me. "I don't want to be a secret. I don't want to only know these four walls. Your bedroom isn't good enough. My fiancée," she looked down at her hands, and I traced her vision to a ring I'd been too occupied to notice. It was a small diamond, one that would've been pocket change for me. "He loves me so much. He wants everyone to know that I'm his. This little diamond, he saved up for it." She smiled as she extended her hand, holding it up for me to see. Because I wouldn't see it otherwise, it was barely a wink on her finger. "I love him for the life he wants with me. So why," her tears began again, "why is it so hard for you to love me?"

I didn't answer. I stared at the small rock on her finger, realizing the weight of my own mistakes. A ring that small was going to take Macey away from me forever. Love, *unashamed* love. It was such a small thing to this world, but when you're living in a realm that rules the world, love is not so small. *Love* doesn't exist—opportunities do. And if there's a woman who can extend The Blue Barn's fortune, I'd be forced to marry her. To shower her with huge gifts and loads of money. But Macey wouldn't have wanted any of that. All she'd wanted was for me

70

to tell the world that I loved her. Even if I did lose everything, Macey would've been there to help me find a new fortune.

The sheets rustled as she leaned over and kissed my cheek. "I hope that one day we'll find love like this with someone else. Hopefully this marriage will bring me closure, and I'll finally see that my fiancée loves me the way I hoped you would." She grabbed my hand. "I hope there's a woman who can bring out the real you, no matter the consequences."

"Mace," I said quietly. She stopped moving from the bed and waited for me to speak. "I'm … I'm so sorry."

"You'll be saying that to yourself in a few years if you never change, Hudson."

I wouldn't forget Macey's words for the next century. She warned me that I'd live in regret if I didn't make a change. I'll never find the peace I had with her, the *love* I had with her, if I don't start making changes. It's just that it wasn't as simple as she thought it was … Was it? Losing it all. How do you start over when this is all you've worked for? This is all I know. Can I really start over again?

Watching Macey dress, I toyed with the idea. But I was a coward, and I would never really know if I could start over. As I watched Macey leave the room, I decided I didn't want to know. I was fine with the way things were.

71

8

Jonah King

Five years later

"Juanita! Carlos! Come here!" I called down the hall. The Torn Veil raised its rent six months ago. We've been maintaining our overhead, especially since we've gotten more sponsors every year. Since we're part of a program, we can get sponsorships, but donations cannot exceed the amount of sponsorship money we receive. If it does, then our sponsorships are limited the following year. Last year we had that problem, so we've been forced to have less sponsors this year so that other groups in the program have the chance to receive sponsorships. But that made our donations go down while prices increased. Holding out for another six months was impossible, so I had Carlos apply for some grants and I just heard back from one of the grant companies.

Clicking through my email, I opened the grant maker's

email but didn't read it until Carlos and eventually Juanita came inside.

"What's up?" Juanita asked as she leaned over my desk. Carlos took a seat across from me and I scrolled down the email and began reading out loud in a shaky breath.

"Dear Applicant, thank you for applying to Blue Barn's Grant Program. We are pleased to inform you that—"

Juanita screamed, ripping Carlos from his seat for a jumping hug as I went on.

"We are pleased to inform you that your charity, the My Fellow American Project, has been selected for our grant. You will receive a donation from our company along with the following; a full year's support from Blue Barn."

"A *year* of support?" Carlos asked as he peeled away from a grinning Juanita to sit again. "What does that mean?"

"I don't know." I searched the email and began reading again. "The support will include press coverage of events, and Blue Barn's own employees will spend time volunteering at your charity. This package also includes a banquet at the end of your grant year to honor your charity. The banquet will allow investors to show their support as we present you with the donation."

"Wait, so we've still got a dilemma," Carlos said. "We won't get any money for an entire year."

"I know." I leaned my head back against the chair.

"Well," Juanita chirped, "it may not be all bad. How much is the grant worth?"

I sat up and scrolled. "Goodness!" I shouted.

73

"How much?" Juanita squeezed behind my desk to read over my shoulder as I highlighted the number. "A million dollars!" Her grip tightened. "A *million* dollars!"

Carlos stood straight up from his seat. He had no words, just silent shock on his face as he stared between us.

I turned the laptop so he could see for himself. "We won't need a single sponsor for an entire year with this grant. And their own investors will pour money into us."

Juanita began to fan herself as she moved to a seat. "This is ridiculous. A million dollars?"

"Plus, the investors," I said.

"*Plus,* the support," Carlos added. "If they're promoting us in any way, we'll likely be getting even more donations."

"Guys, this is what we've been praying for! A huge financial breakthrough, one with longevity. This grant can put us on the map for all kinds of donations and investments so we can get out of this sponsorship program." I clasped my hands together and silently thanked God.

"You're right!" Juanita exclaimed. "I can't believe this."

The excitement erupted from me in shout to the ceiling. "Thank you, Jesus!"

Carlos and Juanita joined in, clapping along until Juanita broke out in a hymn. We sang along, praising God for this breakthrough. Even though we'd have to figure things out for the next six months, we still had grants we'd applied to and were waiting to hear back. Not only that, since we didn't get that many sponsors this year because of the limitations, we'd be able to get more money right at the beginning of the year which would get us through the six months before our grant from Blue Barn was issued. Then we could use the one million dollars to get us out of the program.

"My mom would be so proud," I said, flopping into the fat living room chair. Juanita sat on the couch across from me. We still lived together in our apartment, living off the small salary we'd established for each of us. There were a handful of full-time employees, including Juanita, Carlos, and I who worked off of a salary from our nonprofit. It's small for most of us with Juanita, Carlos, and I individually earning about thirty-five thousand each year. The program was thriving, however, it hadn't thrived enough to make much profit for ourselves. I was tired, but not worried. We weren't in it for the money, we've been in this for the progression of low-income families and marginalized groups.

"Are you kidding? Your mom would laugh and ask if you've woken up from your daydream and are ready to work." Juanita threw a hand at me.

I laughed. "You're right. I guess I still want her to be proud of me."

"We're all proud of you for sticking it out. You walked away and have never gone back, Joey. That's a huge commitment."

"God wanted me to do it, and I wanted to be here, too."

"But you loved your mom equally." Juanita leaned forward and grabbed her mug from the table. "Carlos and I owe you."

"No, you don't." I waved a hand. "You guys helped just as much as I did."

"Maybe." She took a sip from her steaming mug. "But I know that you'd like it a lot if Carlos paid you back."

"What?"

Juanita grinned over the rim of her mug, staring into the open kitchen. Carlos was still sitting at the table, rereading the email we'd just celebrated. "Don't act like I haven't noticed you two digging each other," Juanita said slyly.

"We don't!" I shot to my feet.

Juanita sipped more of her tea. "Whatever."

"How do we…" I pulled my shoulders together and forced the words out, "*dig* each other?"

"I see the way you two watch each other when one of you isn't looking."

"Carlos watches me?"

"Does that matter?"

Not really. Carlos was handsome and he believed in the My Fellow American Project. He loved God as much as I did. It didn't matter at all if he watched me. I'd been watching him too, enjoying all the time we spent together, admiring his infectious joy, dreaming of his smile, and the way his words always rolled off his tongue. Carlos was a great guy. But that didn't mean we had to start dating.

I shook my head, pulling my gaze from Carlos still hunched over the table in the kitchen. "I'm going to bed," I said.

"Already? It's only nine."

"I'm tired." I walked into the bedroom and closed the door.

∧ ∧ ∧

The next morning, Carlos joined Juanita and me for breakfast as usual before work. He lived right across the hall from us and the only thing he didn't do here was shower or sleep. We spent nearly all our time together and, surprisingly, we never really got tired of each other. But Pastor Izzy, who I kept in touch with, said it's because our team was anointed to work together. God pulled us together to bring this project to life, He wouldn't let us fall apart now that it's here. He still needed us, so we still had to get along.

That was part of the reason I ignored the way Carlos made me feel inside. I didn't want to give life to anything that could jeopardize our unity and harmony. Juanita said she sees the way Carlos and I look at each other, but she doesn't know that I've noticed the way she tries not to let it bother her when Carlos and I share a laugh or do a project together. Love was too complicated for us, so it was better to live without it. I was fine with that.

"Morning," Carlos said as he sat down for breakfast. "Are you going to respond to the Blue Barn company today on our decision?"

"I don't know. I don't want to seem too desperate."

"But we are desperate."

"Shut up," I laughed.

Carlos smiled, chuckling along with me as Juanita carried over a skillet of sizzling bacon. She always made us breakfast, and Carlos and I swapped nights on dinner.

77

"Regardless, we only have two weeks to respond, we might as well do it sooner rather than later. If we wait too long, we'll seem like we don't care enough to check our email, or like they're our second option," Carlos explained.

"That could work for us, maybe we'll get a little extra money," Juanita teased. I fanned at her as she placed the bacon down and went to grab another skillet of eggs. Our homey apartment with a wooden circular table and three chairs in the shared kitchen and dining room made everything seem like a dream. Money had been tight, but I wouldn't have wanted to struggle with anyone but these two.

"I promise, I'll do it before the end of the week."

"Good," Juanita said as she took a seat between Carlos and me. "Then we'll celebrate with seafood and sushi."

Carlos snickered as we all grabbed hands.

"Sounds perfect." I smiled at both of my best friends. "Let's say grace."

9

Hudson Blue

"Mr. Blue," Lolita called from outside my door.

I sighed as I threw the papers down onto my desk. "What, Lolita?"

"May I come in?"

"No," I said flatly.

"Please?"

I couldn't stop myself from rolling my eyes. "Come in and be quick."

"Yes, sir," she said as she opened the door. A woman in white pants and a mangily green shirt with matching green heels stepped through the door. She was older, like fifty-five, but Lolita was a really good assistant. She'd been my father's assistant for twelve years and was passed to me when I took over Blue Barn.

"We received a response from the charity, they've accepted the grant. We'll need to schedule a day for us to visit their facility for an initial meeting, and then a presentation day."

"What charity was picked?"

She lifted a paper and squinted. "The My Fellow American Project."

I frowned. "My Fellow American Project? What kind of sappy political bomb did you just set off in this office?"

She laughed as she lowered the paper. Red lips pulled into a grin as she replied, "I'll be happy to let you know that this organization is not politically charged. They're actually a Christian organization who's helping lower income people and other marginalized groups."

I rolled my eyes. "Who picked something so shallow? There are a million programs just like that. Toss them out and pick another."

"Sir, we can't," she said dryly, "they've already accepted the grant."

I shrugged. "They accepted *my* money. But I changed *my* mind."

"You know it doesn't work like that, Mr. Blue."

I threw a hand. "Then fire whoever decided to throw money away on a copy of a program that's been around for decades."

"We can't fire an automated system," she said without looking up. She was writing something down on her notepad. I remembered when I had Lolita put in the AI system. I was tired of reading the proposals, so I had all of them dropped into an algorithm to pick out one for us based on the highest needs.

"Didn't I open the suggestions up to our office?"

"You did, sir." She kept writing.

"Then fire whoever put that name in if it wasn't a proposal."

She looked up finally. Dark hair was cut into a pixie cut with thick bangs and a little fluff on top. Lolita wasn't a bad looking woman, especially not for a woman in her fifties. "Technically, this was both."

"Both?"

"A proposal came in, and I also recommended the charity."

"So, it was in there twice? You rigged it."

"To be fair, I didn't know they'd already submitted a proposal when I recommended them. I've been putting their name in for the last two years."

"Why?" I frowned.

"Because they helped a friend of mine get back on her feet when I couldn't." She looked off, eyes searching for words, like she could find them on my office wall. "My friend was just out of rehab. She needed a job, or anything to keep herself busy. My Fellow American stepped right in. They helped her find a place to stay and covered her rent for six months while helping her get a job and learn some skills. Now she's a painter." She laughed as she looked back at me. "I had the money to help her, but I couldn't give her what they did. I couldn't put her feet beneath her, but that project, those people, they cared enough to get her head on straight. Every person that walks through their doors is not just a number in their system. They're just as I said, a person, and their specialty is helping

81

people."

"So, you wanted to help them as a way to thank them for helping your friend," I concluded.

"I didn't know how else to say thank you."

"Must be a very close friend for you to feel this way."

"We were raised as sisters until she moved out with her boyfriend. He wasn't a good guy."

"Was he the source of her drugs?"

She hesitated but nodded. "She started smoking with him, which eventually turned into snorting with him. Then stealing for him to get more money. After a while, they disappeared, and like magic, she showed up one day on my doorstep. Begging me for help." Lolita paused, swallowing hard. "I took her to three different rehabilitation centers. She broke out the last one and got arrested. Then she was forced into rehab. I'd tried everything, but I couldn't help her. So, I'm very thankful to everyone who has helped. She needed it. Badly."

Lolita played a bigger role than she knew in the fluidity of Blue Barn. Since my father's time, she has been vital to our functionality, and she has never once complained or asked for a raise. She loves her job and does it well. Took my father's crap in stride. And takes mine now too. When my father hired her, she was a young and passionate assistant. Rumors spread like wildfire about a fling between them, which I ignored because it ultimately didn't matter. Today, she's like a mother I should have had. A strong figure filled with years of knowledge worth more than any donation I could give. I couldn't ask for a better assistant, and hearing this story made my shallow heart feel something for the first time in a long time. No matter what, I'd make this work for Lolita's sake, I'd even make sure our top investors cut big checks to this place as a thanks to her. But she would never know. So, I kept my frown and furrowed brows as I said, "You know I should fire you for rigging the system and using company funds for your own needs."

She chuckled, glancing back down to her paperwork. "Yes, I know."

"You don't seem bothered."

"I'm not." She looked up and her normal smile had returned.

"You think I won't fire you?"

"No, I believe I'm on even thinner ice with you than your father. But I've got twenty years on the job now. I was an assistant for your father for twelve. I've been your assistant for six years, but before I was an assistant, I was a janitor here for five years."

"What?" That was news to me.

"Your father fired his secretary. I was there when it happened, something about not keeping secrets well enough. I was just cleaning up like I always did, when he turned to me in the middle of their fight and asked if I could keep a secret."

"You're kidding me. Dad's never told me this story."

She smiled. "Because it's chaotic. I only agreed because I felt I had no choice. I thought your father was just looking for some support in his argument. The next thing I knew, he was telling me I was starting Monday as his secretary. He slapped a

83

stack of papers in my hand and asked me to read through them all over the weekend, and I'd be transferred in the system." She shrugged. "I was supposed to be a temporary assistant, but I suppose I'm good at what I do."

"And you learned everything on the job?"

"I was flying by the seat of my pants."

"How did you survive?"

"I have no idea. Thankfully, your father also said I'd get to count those five years of janitorial work as part of my years of work here. Since I worked only part-time then, they were condensed to two and a half years which puts me at just over twenty years."

"So that's it, you're just here for the money?"

"No. I'm here because I want to watch you grow and change, as much as your father did even in his older age. When I look back now, I wish I would've valued that more. But I got a second chance. I don't want to miss out."

Her words made my heart swell almost too much. I looked away. "Well, I guess I won't fire you. But only because you're not a bad assistant. Not because of your sob story."

"Thank you, sir."

"Pick a day." I bunched my shoulders. "I don't care which one. Just pick a day to do the meet and greet or whatever."

"And for their introductory day?"

"I don't care, just make sure my schedule's clear."

She nodded as she jotted things down again. "I'll get right on this.

∧ ∧ ∧

Lolita really did get right on that stupid meet and greet day, because it was only a week later that she and I traveled to the heart of Brooklyn to find a surprisingly nice facility. It was tall with the American flag painted across the front of the entire structure. Lolita and I stepped inside and were greeted by a cute blonde with crystal blue eyes—that was my favorite eye color on a blonde. Green just looked too weird.

"Good morning," she said, "can I help you?"

"Yes," I spoke before Lolita could but was cut off when a voice from the winding glass staircase spoke clearly.

"Can I help you?" The voice belonged to a woman as dark as the night sky. She was in a yellow pants suit which made her tight afro and dark skin more noticeable.

I raised a brow. A lot of organizations helped underprivileged people and marginalized groups, but I hadn't expected the program itself to be run by those same people. I glanced back at the blonde who worked the front desk; would it be so bad to admit I expected their roles to be reversed?

As the woman approached, I let Lolita talk. "Hi," she extended a hand, "I'm Lolita Ramirez from Blue Barn, with our president, Hudson Blue."

"Oh my goodness!" Her voice echoed through the entire facility. "I've got to tell the others. Jess," she called to blonde, "can you get Jonah and Carlos?"

"I'll page them right away."

"Please follow me," the dark-skinned woman said as she

85

waved us on. We began an exhausting tour through the facility as she introduced herself. "My name is Juanita Williams, I'm a cofounder of the My Fellow American Project, and I am also the director of our teaching program."

"That's right," Lolita chimed in happily. "You guys teach people skills and things?"

She smiled over her shoulder. "Actually, we have a GED program. We offer college courses that count for credits taken with adjunct or retired professors. There's also our skills institute, that's for people who just want to focus their studies on one area, like a trade school."

"Wow." Lolita was charmed. "That's amazing."

Juanita agreed with a nod and continued on, leading us through the bright facility when she stopped to wave over a man. "Sorry I'm late," the man said as he extended a hand to Lolita, "my name's Carlos Bloom, I'm a cofounder and director of marketing."

They shook hands, and when Carlos turned to me, I held in a sigh and shook his hand too. His pants were a little too big for him, and his shirt was wrinkled and didn't really match. He looked like someone the organization was helping, not a cofounder.

"Carlos, this is Lolita Ramirez and Hudson Blue from Blue Barn."

"It's a pleasure to meet you both, we really appreciate you."

"I can tell," I said flatly.

Lolita passed me a dirty look before she said, "Where's Jonah? Should we wait for him?"

"Oh." Juanita chuckled lightly with Carlos. "Jonah is a lady. She's the third cofounder, but she's the one who spearheaded the whole project. She started it in high school, and it blossomed through college, and the last six years, into what you see now."

"Goodness, I'm sorry for calling her a man."

"Everyone always says that." Carlos shrugged. "It doesn't bother her. All Jonah cares about is this project. She really loves helping people."

I started tuning them out when they got sappy. I wasn't in the mood, and we didn't need to be sold. We already promised them the money; they didn't have to try to amp it up. But I suppose that's what every organization does. It just bothered me that this organization was run by wrinkly-clothed kids and people who looked like they needed as much help as Lolita's crackhead friend.

I suppressed an eye roll as we began walking through the facility again. Lolita was visibly excited, gushing with questions and laughing at their friendly jokes. She fit right in with them. She'd started as a janitor, mopping my father's floors. She had no formal education. English was not her first language. And she had friends who bought and abused drugs. She looked like she belonged in this program. Maybe that's why she liked it so much. Maybe that's why *all* of them did. It was a bunch of minorities helping minorities. Maybe they liked giving handouts to their own kind. I don't know, but the donation made Blue Barn look good, so I wasn't going to fight it.

We took an elevator up, and when the doors dinged open,

87

I froze.

"Jonah!" Juanita exclaimed.

She was as stunning as … Macey.

"Sorry I took so long," she apologized. "I was just tying up loose ends on a phone call and I couldn't get them off the phone."

"No worries," Lolita said as she stepped off the elevator. "I'm Lolita Ramirez, this is Hudson Blue, president of Blue Barn."

I stood there staring at her. I was winded by her beauty. A slender frame with ebony skin that glowed from within. Her hair was pulled back into three thick braids that were tied off, so the ends were pulled together in a curly puff. Almond eyes and pretty pink lips made my mouth dry as I remembered the first day I met Macey. She wasn't all smiles like this woman, she was shy and confused, but when she did smile, she looked just like Jonah. Maybe they weren't replicas, but there was something genuine and sweet about this woman. She was as beautiful as Macey, taking my breath away in an instant, the way Macey had.

"Mr. Blue?" Lolita called.

I snapped my vision to her. I hadn't realized I'd been staring at Jonah long enough for there to be a stiff silence around us now. Jonah's hand was extended, it was as small as Macey's. Reaching out, I took it. "Sorry, I got lost in thought."

"And I got lost in my own building," she laughed. Her voice was womanly, cunningly even, but there was something pure in there. She could talk me into anything, probably even into bed if she didn't remind me so much of Macey.

I nodded, finally releasing her hand.

Jonah glanced around the group. "Do you guys want to continue the tour, or we can sit down and talk about—"

"I don't mean to cut things short," I interjected, "but I forgot about this meeting with my father." I looked at Lolita, she kept her composure like a good assistant should. "It slipped my mind."

"Ok." Jonah nodded. "We can just finish this at the presentation next week."

"I can stay," Lolita said, her eyes piercing me. "Mr. Blue, you go home."

"Right. Thanks, Lolita." I glanced around the group, stopping at Jonah who only blinked up at me. She looked exactly like what I'd assumed Macey would look like as she got older. She still had an air of youthfulness around her, though her voice was womanly. "Thank you for your time."

Jonah extended her hand again. "No, Mr. Blue. I'm sure you're very busy, so I appreciate you taking the time to come out today."

I nodded and shook her hand once more before turning and leaving. I couldn't get out the building fast enough, only breathing once I made it into a taxi. I'd left the company car for Lolita; it was the least I could do for her since she covered for me.

When I got home, Erma was there as always. By then I'd found it in myself to calm down and push away the thoughts of Jonah and Macey. I'd spent the entire drive trying to figure out how to tell my father that we had a *diverse* charity. I knew he'd be against it, and I was thankful I wouldn't have to spend the next year frequenting their events, pretending this wasn't a problem. Not just because it was clearly a handout to our cultural friends, but it was also a charity with *that* woman as the head of it.

"You're home early," Erma said as she met me at the kitchen counter. I'd shooed everyone out to get water while she paid the taxi for me.

"I had a rough day."

"You want to talk about it?"

"Where's my father?"

"Busy," Erma said slowly.

"Are you hiding something? You're acting funny."

"No." She shook her head. "But you are. I haven't seen you this distraught in five years." She walked by me to the fridge. I knew what and who she was talking about. Erma knew about Macey and me. She told me one day when I'd snapped at her for spilling my drink. It was back when Macey had first left, I was snapping at everyone, honestly. But only Erma connected the dots and figured out why.

When I confessed to sleeping with Macey, she said she'd known all along. Macey and I both changed at the exact same time. And our subtle glances were obviously not so subtle. Erma's been the only one to see through me. But even then, I still don't recognize the person she tries to pull out of me. That part of me left with Macey and never returned.

"You hungry? It's just after lunch," Erma said, standing by

the fridge.

"Yeah," I answered weakly.

"Can the fancy Mr. Blue eat common food like a sandwich?"

"Erma, I'm not in the mood."

"Sandwich it is."

She cut thick slices of bread and stuffed meat between them along with cheese, pickles, and raw onions. I watched her toast it and slather the inside with mustard, then she passed it to me and took a seat at the small table. Technically, only the staff ate inside the kitchen. Erma was supposed to serve my food to me in the official dining room, but I wasn't in the mood to eat there and I doubt she would've brought me the food if I'd left.

We sat in silence as thumping rang out above us. Erma and I both looked up, and when my gaze dropped to her, she quietly stood and left the kitchen.

"Erma?" I called.

"Stay right there!" she called back.

I obeyed, waiting in the hall between the kitchen and the dining room. The thumping stopped after what I assumed was Erma's intervention. A few minutes later, I returned to the kitchen as footsteps came down the stairs and entered the kitchen behind me. Surprisingly, it was my father and not Erma. He was in his white bathrobe, his hair pulled back into a bun.

"Dad? Is everything alright?" I picked up my half-eaten sandwich and took a bite.

He looked unbothered, in fact, he raised a brow like he was shocked by the question. "Why wouldn't it be?"

"I heard thumping. Then Erma freaked out and ran upstairs." I shrugged. Took another bite. "Thought you'd broken a hip trying to reach for your reading glasses."

He chuckled as he looked around the kitchen, spotting the sandwich supplies Erma left out. In silence, he slapped two pieces of bread together around half a pound of ham and bit into his salty lunch.

I watched him chew, waiting for a response.

"I had an outburst, alright? The stupid television wouldn't work."

I snorted. Sounds about right. My father has never had great control over his temper. "Why was Erma so upset then?"

"Because I broke a television last week, and she didn't want me breaking another one."

"Dad," I sighed, feeling only a twinge of relief since that charity was still on my mind. "You've got to stop losing remotes."

He laughed. "I know. But, change of subject, why are you home so early?"

"Crazy day. I took the rest of it off."

"What happened?"

"I think I'm going to have to cut this charity loose."

"Why?"

I paused. "The charity helps marginalized groups, but it's *run* by marginalized groups. Everyone there is…" I picked at the crust of my sandwich, trying to find a nicer way to say it.

"Everyone's like Erma."

My father shrugged.

I stared at him. "Dad, it's a woke program focused on helping poor people. A *woman* is in charge."

"Crackheads and minorities need help too, Hudson. Don't be such a bigot."

I was shocked. Who was I even talking to? My father was the man who taught me that *other people* were beneath us. Because of him and his elitist ideology, I was forced to sneak around with Macey because she wasn't good enough to be my wife. The man who beat those beliefs into my head now stood in his staff kitchen calling me a bigot.

"Are you feeling alright?" I asked.

My dad took another bite of his sandwich and spoke around all the ham in his mouth. "I'm just saying that it looks good for Blue Barn to be part of this project. We have to do these charities every now and again. I had to do a few myself. I know it's a chore but get through it. Give most of the work to Lolita, and it'll be fine."

Blowing air threw my lips, I hung my head. *I don't think I can see her again. I can't face Jonah.*

10

Jonah King

"He seemed weird, didn't he?" I asked as Juanita, Carlos, and I sat around our tiny dinner table eating fried rice and grilled vegetables.

"Who cares?" Juanita shoved a piece of broccoli into her mouth. "The dude's loaded and his loaded company is giving us a load of money."

I pressed my lips together and turned my attention to Carlos. "He was weird, right? The way he just stared at me on the elevator. And then he just left."

"His poor secretary was issuing apologies nonstop after that." Juanita laughed.

Carlos's dark brows raised before he scooped a third serving of rice into his white bowl. "You're a pretty girl, Joey, maybe he was caught up."

I chomped down on my fork, the metal clanging between my teeth in shock. Juanita leaned forward and made kissy noises like a child.

"Why would you say that?" I snapped at Carlos.

He looked up from his rice, confused, like he hadn't said something loaded. Sometimes, I wondered if it was all in my head that there was something stirring between Carlos and me. Most days, Carlos was totally oblivious to the things he said that made me squirm with nerves.

"I'm just stating the obvious. You're striking, and maybe he just was knocked off his feet."

"Or maybe you're strikingly ugly," Juanita added.

I took the piece of broccoli she was going for, leaving her to whine as I munched on it. "We should just be careful. He doesn't seem bad, but I don't know if we should trust him or his company. Did anyone get the details on Blue Barn?"

"Yeah, but not much is online about them besides the information Lolita sent you in that email."

I pulled my phone out and tapped around until I found the email. Reading it over quickly, I said, "The company description is so basic. A news outlet that takes reporting to a new level. With a promise of truth and dignity to our clients, we report only what's true."

"But the Blue Barn Company itself isn't a news outlet. It *owns* a bunch of news outlets," Carlos said.

I slid my phone onto the table in distress. "What if we just signed a deal with the devil? Why were we idiots who did no research before signing the dotted line?"

"Goodness, Joey, you're such a worry wort." Juanita snapped her chopsticks at me. "We're already locked in place

95

with Blue Barn, why even fight it?"

"Because we can't make deals with the devil."

"Relax. Our charity is about to be on the map like never before." She aimed her chopsticks at me again. "Don't go messing things up with researching and your weird way of coming up with horrifying scenarios."

Sighing, I leaned back in my chair and hung my head over the back of it. Everything was perfect, but I couldn't help but feel that something was off. Maybe I was just thrown by Mr. Blue's weird introduction. Juanita was right, I shouldn't let this get to me. Besides, God wouldn't let us walk into a trap. He didn't before and He wouldn't now.

"Come on," Juanita slapped my belly, and I sat up abruptly.

"*Nita*," I hissed as she laughed.

"We've got bigger things to worry about for next week. Like the presentation we'll have to do for Mr. Blue."

"That's right." Carlos scooped vegetables off the tray in the center of the wooden table. His silver chopsticks glinted in the retiring sunlight as he stuffed a pepper into his mouth. "We've got to let Blue Barn know what we're going to be doing with their money. Or at least give them an idea."

"What exactly are we going to do with the money?" Juanita asked.

"Expand, of course. Our facility needs some minor updates, so we'll do that, but we need to expand and make room for the children's section. We've got to hire folks, do screening processes and whatnot, so that'll take a big chunk of our money."

96

"What about a pay increase for us?" Juanita shrugged sheepishly.

I knew we were all wondering about that, unfortunately, I didn't have great news to report.

I winced. "Since we're getting out of the sponsorship program, we'll probably have to take a pay cut."

"What?" Carlos lowered his bowl, chewing slower now that the biggest news was out there.

I sighed as I laid my chopsticks down. "I looked over the files today. Once we're out of the program, we'll have to allocate as much money to staying out of the program as possible. Acquiring our own grants, pitching ourselves to get enough sponsorship yearly."

"We're scraping by now." Juanita tossed her crumpled napkin onto the table. Her radiant dark skin didn't have a single wrinkle in it until today. With her pinched brows and tight frown, Juanita looked more stressed than I'd ever seen her before.

"I know things have been tough, but this sponsorship helps. And with the investors from this company, we'll probably have enough to sustain us."

"So, then what? We get jobs?" Juanita shook her head. "Jonah, we can't work, there's no time for jobs outside the project."

"The project *is* our job," Carlos muttered.

"I know," I said, "but we'll figure it out, we always do." I reached for her Juanita's hand, but she stood from the table, excusing herself to the bedroom.

I dropped my head when the door slammed.

"She'll get over it," Carlos said.

"I know, but I also know how she feels. Don't you ever wonder if we've made a mistake?" I looked up to see Carlos wearing a smile filled with concern.

"I don't have to wonder, the evidence is right in front of us every day that this was the right move. This is a dream; we've just got to tough it out through the harder times. It'll get easier."

"We're six years in, and it's still hard, Carlos." I dropped my eyes to my bowl of half-eaten rice. "This doesn't feel anything like a dream."

I heard the chair squeak against the floor as Carlos moved. He sat beside me, taking one of my hands and kissing it. Normally, my heart would race with my hand in his. Carlos could restart my heart with a single touch if it ever stopped. However, tonight there was nothing but a feeling of defeat burning in my chest.

"What are we going to do?"

"Joey, we've trusted God all this way. Why stop now?"

"I know, but the situation is—"

"Just a distraction from the real blessing in all this. Just you watch." Carlos squeezed my hand. "God's going to turn this whole situation around."

I agreed with a nod and took a breath. "Thanks, Carlos."

He grinned, pulling his hand from mine and wrapping an arm around me. He pulled me into him, and I took in the smell of fried rice suffocating the fading scent of his woody cologne.

"We'll leave things to God," he whispered as he held me. "He'll figure things out for us."

I was hardly listening as I forgot my problems to indulge in this moment. Carlos was comforting me, holding me, and somehow everything felt like it would work out.

∧ ∧ ∧

Juanita stayed in a funk for the rest of the week. But on the day of the presentation, she was back to her normal self. Rushing around our conference room, setting pens and prints down at each seat. There would only be seven people attending today. Mr. Blue and Lolita, of course, a few investors partnered with Blue Barn, and others that I guess are just tagging along. Lolita wasn't very clear in her email.

My phone buzzed and I checked it. Carlos had texted and said Blue Barn Company members were in the building.

"They're here!" I said to Juanita.

She tensed immediately. "Is my hair okay? Do I look ugly? Goodness, I should've eaten something light. I'm bloated and they're not going to take us seriously!"

"Nita, calm down." I began to laugh. Her nerves always calmed my nerves because Juanita freaked out more than she needed to. Whenever it was something important, she couldn't find it in herself to stay calm, so I had to for the both of us.

"You look stunning," I said as I rubbed her shoulders. She really did. She was wearing a blue dress with a pretty orange pattern. It wrapped around her body like plastic wrap, fitted

99

and sexy like this wasn't a professional meeting. Juanita always dressed like that for business. Outside of the office, she wore flare skirts and coral pink. Anything girly and bubbly. Office Juanita was very different from regular Juanita.

I wished the same could be said for me. I wore a black skirt and white button down. Nothing flashy like my friend. I kept my hair pinned back while Juanita wore her tight coils free. We were opposites but it worked for our dynamic.

I took one more sweep of the pale blue room. There was an oval table in the center, ash grey with similar colored chairs. A royal blue folder sat in front of seven spots with pens and yellow notepads for everyone. With a deep breath, I lowered my head and said a prayer in my heart for peace and a good time.

The door opened and Carlos entered and held the door as the Blue Barn Company members filed in. A few men in expensive suits and blazers stepped inside, followed by two women and then Lolita came in waving. She was happy to see us, and I was happy to see a familiar face. An older man walked in behind her, he looked similar to the man that followed him—Mr. Blue. Walking in last, he wore a black suit tailored to hug his frame and tug on his broad shoulders, making his warm ivory skin look creamy. Beneath his suit jacket, he wore a crisp white shirt, while the smell of his expensive cologne made me weary with the masculine scent. Somewhere between expensive and *extremely* expensive is what Mr. Blue smelled like. It's what the room smelled like, honestly.

Blue Barn was rich. Even the employees were rich. I

couldn't imagine what it'd be like to have that kind of money. I didn't know what the company did with all their cash, but they had a million dollars and a lot of resources to throw away every year.

Mr. Blue sat beside the older man, and his eyes were like a hidden forest beneath his dark brows. Green as the grass within the forest, hiding something in plain sight, the way the forest hides its animals to protect them from the hunters. I couldn't get myself to look away, like I was searching for something within his eyes.

"Jonah," Juanita elbowed me, and I snapped my head towards her. "Say something."

"Right." I shook my head to clear my thoughts, and also to avoid Mr. Blue's eyes as I looked back at the group. "Good morning, everyone, and thank you for joining us today. My name is Jonah King, this is Juanita Williams, and that is Carlos Bloom. We are the owners of the My Fellow American—"

"Who picked that name?" Mr. Hudson Blue asked before the real introduction had begun. The older man beside him frowned as he looked over at Mr. Blue Senior, but the young business owner ignored the dirty look from the old man.

"I did," I responded.

He raised a dark brow. "Why?"

"Because we're all Americans, and I thought—"

"Who is *we*?"

Now *I* raised a brow. "That's exactly why I called it *My Fellow American*. Because anyone with an American citizenship is American. No matter their race or gender, the amount of money you have or don't have, we are all fellow Americans. If we dropped the labels, it would be clear as day."

"What labels?" he challenged.

"Black Americans," I said matter-of-factly.

He blinked like he hadn't expected that response, little did he know, I'd been waiting all week for this challenge.

"Black Americans, Mexican Americans, Chinese Americans. We get singled out as if we're foreign. But we aren't. We are American just like you, Mr. Blue, and we deserve to call ourselves that without the extra label attached. You take a group of Americans to a different country, they're not going to pick us apart, they're going to call us *all* Americans. So why do we categorize each other here on our own soil?"

"I like that." The older man nodded beside Hudson Blue who looked at the man, hiding the shock on his face. Unfortunately for him, he couldn't hide the way he went rigid at the man's words.

"My name is Olan Blue," the old man said. "I'm the retired president of Blue Barn Company. This is my son, Hudson Blue, who I'm sure you met last week."

"I met him very briefly." I extended a hand across the table. Olan stood and took it, giving me a firm shake and smile before sitting. His eyes slid from mine to Juanita. He looked her over, his eyes lingering before returning to me as I said, "Hopefully, that was enough background about our company." The group laughed and nodded as I went on. "My Fellow American is a not-for-profit organization that helps marginalized groups and underprivileged families get the same opportunities as their

102

more fortunate fellow Americans."

"When you say the same opportunity," a woman asked at the opposite end of the table, "what do you mean?"

"We mean that we've been told we all have the same opportunities in life, and I believe that is true. But I don't believe those opportunities are within reach for everyone. Some people are born with opportunity clutched in their infant palms." I shot a glance at Hudson. "While others have to fight for that opportunity every day, and they're fighting against so much more competition." I stopped to check my notes. "My Fellow American is a Christian program. We believe the only opportunity in this world that is truly free and equal to all is salvation through Christ Jesus. Everything else needs a little extra help. That's what we're here for." I smiled proudly. "Our program is not a pity party or a system of handouts. We aren't here to say that minorities have it hard because they're Black or Asian. In fact, we focus very little on race. My Fellow American is here to help those who need it. No matter their race or circumstances. Our program strives to equip anyone who walks through the door with the ability to reach that opportunity of betterment no matter where they're standing in line."

"Tell us about some of your programs," Olan said as he flipped through the folder. "This is very well crafted."

"Thank you." I nodded. "I'll let Juanita take the stand to explain everything." I stepped aside and let Juanita stand at the head of the table. Olan looked attentive, nodding along with the activities Juanita described. However, Hudson Blue sat with folded arms, almost nodding off.

I watched him from the corner of the room. His lids became heavy as he tried to stay focused. Drowsily, his eyes found mine, and for a second, he didn't look so indignant. His chiseled jaw was relaxed, his dark lashes fluttered until he sleepily blinked away.

Olan glanced Hudson's way and smacked him in the chest. Hudson jumped, and Juanita blinked in confusion before Olan issued her an apology, and Hudson too. Adjusting in his chair, Hudson folded his arms again and stared angrily at Juanita as she spoke.

"Excuse me," Lolita chimed in.

"Yes?" Juanita answered.

"Your program works with rehab centers, doesn't it?"

"It does." Juanita looked to Carlos, and he stepped forward.

"We have a partnership with a few rehab centers that sends people who finish their programs to us. We help them transition back into society."

Lolita lit up, her red lips parting to smile and say, "A good friend of mine went through your program. She's doing very well now."

"Really?" Juanita asked excitedly.

"Yes. Do you remember a woman named Jay Johnson?"

Juanita's smile began to melt, and Carlos looked ashamed in the awkward silence. Lolita stiffened too, trying not to let it bother her that they didn't remember her friend.

"She's really outgoing, right?" I asked as I stepped forward.

"Dark curly hair, tanned skin, pretty smile?"

Lolita's glow returned as she nodded.

"I remember Jocelyn, but everyone called her Jay," I said. "We don't always get to interact with everyone who comes through the doors since there are so many of them now. But the people I do meet and talk to about their progression each have an impact on my life. Jocelyn's got a bright future."

Lolita looked like she would cry, unable to form words.

"How beautiful," Olan chimed in. "To treat each person not like a case, but like an actual human being. That is what charity means to me."

I smiled. "That's what it means to all of us, Mr. Blue."

11

Hudson Blue

"Hudson," my father called as he stood in the doorway of the charity's conference room, "are you coming? These kind people have prepared lunch for us."

"I'll be there in just a moment. I had a question about something, if Ms. King doesn't mind waiting for me to ask."

Jonah looked from my father to me, she was hesitant, but gave a slow nod. Turning to her cofounder, Juanita, she said, "Can you host while I answer Mr. Blue's question?"

"Of course, take your time," Juanita said.

My father's deep green eyes focused on me for a tense second. I could feel the warning in his look but glanced off to disregard it.

"Well," Juanita chirped, "if you'll follow me, Mr. Blue—"

"Please," my father waved a hand, "we'll be working together for a year. Call me Olan, dear."

Juanita smiled and nodded, guiding my father out of the

room. Carlos nodded at Jonah before exiting and pulling the door shut behind him. I watched him through the door's window, jogging down the carpeted hall to catch up with the rest of the group. Once I was sure he was gone, I slammed the folder I'd been clutching onto the table.

Jonah jumped, taking a small step back.

"Who do you think you are?" I growled.

"I'm sorry? I don't—"

"Shut up," I hissed.

She listened, her mouth sealing shut immediately. In the silence, I stalked around the table and stood over her, leaning down so that I was eye level with her. "You think this stupid project impressed my father, but it didn't impress *me* in the slightest bit. It's a coverup to hand out money to the people you choose. You want to use tax dollars and my company's money for your own gain."

She shook her head. "Mr. Blue, you've got it all wrong."

"Don't you dare—" I cut myself off. My voice was rising, and I needed to calm down. I sucked in a sharp breath, working my jaw, searching for the right words before I looked back at Jonah. My anger fizzled out the instant my eyes came back to hers. Brown and misting, Jonah looked frightened, but she was trying her hardest not to break. Standing there, battling me in her silence, Jonah looked identical to Macey.

I stumbled backwards, shaking my head, trying to remove the image of the woman I'd loved from my mind's eye. I'd come too far to back down, but I couldn't stop seeing Macey. The way Jonah looked. So fragile, like if I said one more thing,

107

good or bad, she'd break into tears. Macey cried the day she realized I was good at keeping secrets, *too* good. Before that, she was all smiles, but I'd broken her. *She* had broken me.

"Listen," I said to fill the air with something besides silence, "I'm not going to pull the funding, but I don't like this little innocent act you're trying to pull. It's just like you said, we all have the same opportunity. Don't try to act like this group isn't any different from all the charities that are only interested in helping people who look like them. It's the same thing— with scriptures slapped onto the flyer header. I won't be fooled."

She cleared her throat. "I don't appreciate you disregarding all the hard work we've put into this organization."

"I don't care what you appreciate, Jonah. You need to understand something if you're going to be begging for my—"

"Watch what you say, Mr. Blue." Jonah's voice was rigid, yet quiet. She'd lifted her chin, and her tears were starting to fade. "We have never begged for a single dollar. God alone has provided for this company. No one else. Don't you ever tell me that my organization has begged." She stepped forward, all her shyness fading. "We have never begged in the past, and we aren't going to start today."

"Are you challenging me?" I took two steps to close the gap between us. Jonah was looking up at me, not cowering away like she had been before. I'd hit a touchy spot when I told her she was begging. It was almost cute, seeing her get so angry, like she could do something to me. I was one of the richest

108

men in this city. If I said the word, she would disappear, and it'd be like her company never existed.

"Call it whatever you want," Jonah said confidently. "I don't care. But don't you ever forget that God is the provider of this organization. Not you. Not anyone but Him."

I chuckled, slipping a hand to her chin. She tried to jerk away, but I cupped her face, holding her firmly. "See that?" I said in a low tone. "You can't beat me. I've got you by your weakness, God or not. So next time we have a meeting, I suggest you remember this little demonstration. You've got no power. You have nothing over me. Don't make me shut your organization down, got it?" I shoved her away and glanced around the room. "When you do get my money, get a better conference room. This place looks like you bought everything at Target." I snorted as I turned and opened the door to leave. "Come on," I snapped, "I don't know where this silly luncheon is at. You need to take me there. And don't go there looking all disheveled." I fanned at her as she tried to recompose herself. "I don't want my father asking questions."

"What kind of questions would I be asking, Hudson?"

I snapped around. My father stood halfway down the hall, a hand in his pocket, a dark frown beneath his white beard. I glanced back at Jonah, who was coming forward now. She looked like she was ready to explode. If she said one wrong thing to my father, I could be pulled from my chair as the owner of Blue Barn.

I tried to formulate words as Jonah stopped short of the door. She closed her eyes, took a breath, and when they

109

opened, I was amazed at her calm demeanor. Three short strides brought the Macey reincarnation to the door, just before my father made it.

"Mr. Olan," she said happily, "Mr. Blue and I were discussing the funding. He wanted clarity on the mission. He's all cleared up now." She looked up at me, and I felt relieved, but a very familiar, twisted pain shot through my chest. *Why did she just save me?* It was like the roles had been reversed. I saved Macey after she missed my move-in day at the estate. Today, Jonah saved me, sparing me embarrassment and my job.

I peeled away from her smile, a genuinely broken one. The same one Macey wore the last day I saw her. She was disappointed that I hadn't changed. Came all the way back to leave her fiancée for me, but all I had for her was more secrets. Suddenly, I was less thankful for Jonah's kindness. It made me angry, reminding me of Macey, someone I let go of six years ago. What was the point of bringing her up again? Jonah did nothing but make me remember the things I didn't want to. She thought her kindness would get her far, but it wouldn't. She might have covered for me, but she'd better remember the warnings I gave her today.

"Ah! Well, my son was a very rude guest today," my father said, almost cheerily. "Falling asleep during the presentation just to ask questions later on the things he missed." He shook his head. "That is unusual for him, I promise."

"Please don't worry." Jonah's smile held strong. "I'm sure Mr. Blue's just had a rough day."

"You are far too kind." My father extended a hand to Jonah, and she shook it. "I'm looking forward to working with you and this wonderful organization, Ms. King."

"Me too."

"Hudson," my father's voice lost all of its joy when he addressed me, "let's go."

I glanced down at Jonah, giving her a stony look. She continued to smile at me, even when my father's back was turned. I wanted to snap at her; to tell her to stop smiling, but instead, I only grunted and followed my father down the hall and out of the building.

Sliding into the back of a black truck. My father's door was barely closed before he snapped, "What is wrong with you?"

"Why are you yelling?"

"Because I heard you yelling at her!"

I blinked. "You heard that?"

"Yes!" he exclaimed, throwing his hands up and shaking his head. "Hudson, I told you, we don't hate anyone who has less than us. We don't associate with them because they're not like us. They're not smart like us, and good at things like us. We're not on the same level. But they are not bad people." He took a breath. "Well, these ones aren't bad. We have to work with them because the public does not like *racism*." He made air quotes like race had nothing to do with this but we both knew that it did.

My father continued, "They don't understand the difference between us and them. They don't get that we are the elite. We don't associate with people who aren't on our level.

111

If they were on our level, then it wouldn't matter. But it does, Hudson. Do you understand?"

I nodded.

"It's simple," Father explained, "but the world doesn't get it. Until they do, we are working with this organization. Got it?"

I frowned, clenching my fist in my lap. "Got it."

Father sighed and shoved his hair back. He cracked his window as our driver finally pulled off. "I know that sometimes we get frustrated because we want things we can't have. Jonah is very nice looking for a poor city girl. But you know our code."

It took me at least ten seconds to realize what my father was suggesting. Turning in the seat, the cream-colored leather exhaled with my movement as I faced my father. "Dad, I don't like her. I don't like women like her at all. They're disgusting." I bunched my shoulders, trying to sell the act.

"I was preparing myself to have this conversation with you." He wrung his hands. "Since ... you know."

"No, Dad, I don't know."

He gave me a slow blink. "Do you think I'm stupid, Hudson?"

"No—"

"Did you think I had no idea you were sleeping with your own staff for months?"

I swallowed. "What does that have to do with this?"

He chuckled. "She looks like her. That pretty Black girl you were yelling at. She looks just like Macey."

112

"I don't like Jonah," my voice was a growl. "And this has nothing to do with what happened with Macey. I don't want Blue Barn getting scammed into handing out money. That's it." I leaned back into the leather seats. "And it doesn't matter to me that Jonah is Black. She's pretty, Dad. You could have left it at that."

My father's eyes crinkled in the corners, but he said nothing. He tried to pretend that nothing ever had to do with race but we both knew that was a lie. For my entire life, the only women of color he ever exposed me to were Erma and the maids. Hard working women with calloused hands and feet, ashen ankles, and sweaty head wraps with dirty aprons. They were big women, old fashioned, ugly, and single. Always single, as if to say, women like them couldn't find a mate. They weren't good enough for marriage.

It wasn't just my father who taught me this. I saw it everywhere around me. Ivy League schools, country clubs, country *music*—movies, shows, and media reserved the roles of beautiful, innocent women for girls with pearlescent skin and golden hair. Wonder Woman, Charlie's Angels, Princess Leia. Even in a galaxy far far away, iconic, beautiful women did not look like Jonah.

What kind of impression do you think that left on a growing boy, discovering his likes and dislikes, crafting his taste in women? It taught me what beauty was supposed to look like. An image that closed the door on the possibility of love ever blooming anywhere else or in any other fashion.

But Macey rewired me. She reworked every part of my

113

brain and left me confused. Most days I was able to ignore it. But now, with Jonah and her demeanor replicating Macey, I was having trouble believing the things my father had told me for so long. Macey was beautiful. Just as beautiful as the women my father preferred me to enjoy. I loved her body and her personality, and I loved that she loved me, regardless of our differences.

I think I fell for Macy *because* she was different. She didn't fit the description of what I'd been told about women like her. And that had been fine. My father hadn't cared that I'd slept with her or discovered beauty in new places. He hadn't even cared that I'd loved her because Macey was supposed to be one girl, six years ago. She was supposed to fade, and I was supposed to move on. But that wasn't what happened.

Macey was a memory I was still trying to forget, while Jonah was a new dream I'd fall asleep in the day to experience.

12

Jonah King

I didn't tell Juanita or Carlos about the conversation I had with Hudson Blue. I decided it was best to just let it go, sweep it under the rug like it never happened. But it *did* happen, and it's bothering me. The things he said were nasty. They knocked me off my feet. What could I even say? I stood there like an idiot, holding back tears instead of chewing him out. And then I covered for the guy. Why? Why did I reward his behavior with an act of kindness? Because I had to. If I hadn't covered up the argument, Hudson could have retaliated and pulled funding for the project. What would Carlos and Juanita say if they found out I lost this deal because I was a big baby?

I sighed as I laid on my bed now. I've had the same purple comforter for the last six years. I was supposed to have someone come back and grab my boxes from my mother's place, but she wouldn't let my movers in, so I had to forsake most of what was left. I was able to sneak into my bedroom window and take a few boxes two nights in a row. But Mom must've noticed the boxes getting thinner in my room and locked the window.

Rest in peace to my favorite comforter and bedroom set.

"You've been sighing a lot lately," Juanita said as she came over to my bed. She pushed me over, making room for herself to sit. Surprisingly, Juanita and I were small enough to fit. We'd shared her bed when we first got here because I didn't get to bring my furniture with me.

"Just tired," I said, aimlessly scrolling through the emails on my phone.

"You're tired because you're always working, Joey." I felt the bed shift when Juanita stood. She was back across the room, digging through her drawers.

"Are you going somewhere?"

She looked over her shoulder, wearing a devilish grin. "I've got a date."

A date? The news made me roll over and sit up. Juanita was still grinning as she turned back to her drawer, doing a little dance. The drawers had been white when we moved in, but Juanita couldn't stand the color, so she painted it sherbet orange and it looked amazing. Her side of the room was beaming with color. She changed her comforter set with the seasons; the summer always warranted yellow or peach while autumn would have rouge or rustic orange. In contrast, I always grabbed a neutral color, but since the store didn't have any, I took the only twin size one left on the shelf. It was this horrifying purple blanket. I've been meaning to get a new one but there's hardly any time for shopping trips. Let alone extra money.

Juanita shoved the drawer shut and went to the closet. "What about this?" She held up a dress. The base color was turquoise but the different fruit on it made it pop with color. Paired with Juanita's dark skin, she would glow all night long in the cute dress.

"It's a little short, but I think it's cute."

She pressed the fabric to herself and looked down. "I think the length is perfect." Squealing, Juanita tossed the dress onto her bed and flounced away to the bathroom.

I got up from the bed stood over her dress with my arms folded. "Who's the guy?" I called. Our bathroom was right across the hall from our bedroom, and she'd left the door cracked because she knew I had questions.

"It's kind of like a blind date. I think."

I squinted. "Juanita, what does that mean?"

"I don't know."

I could hear the buzzing of her electric toothbrush from the bedroom. Marching across the hall, I ignored the creaky boards of our floor and took up post in the bathroom doorway. Juanita was hunched over, spitting into the white sink. After two rinses, she finally looked up at me in the mirror as she patted her mouth dry.

"Why do you look so disapproving?"

I hadn't noticed my reflection; brown skin with a dark brow lifted, eyes focused on her like she'd done something wrong. It didn't help that my arms were folded over my chest.

117

Sighing, I dropped my arms and ran a hand over my hair. It'd been smoothed back into a puff because I was too lazy to actually style it.

"I'm not disapproving you. It's not a crime to go out on a date. I just think the details are murky."

"Murky at *best*." Juanita tossed the towel over her shoulder with a grin as she left the bathroom.

"Why are you okay with this?"

"Because we work all the time, and this man is," she blushed, looking at the dress on the bed, "he's forward—to say the least. He approached me so carelessly." She giggled now as she moved for her underwear drawer.

Everything was getting murkier by the second.

"It's just nice to get out and do something fun. So I'm going on a spontaneous date. Who cares?" She shrugged. "Come on, Joey. Don't be a grouch about it."

"I just want you to be careful. It's New York, a really crowded and big city." I lifted a shoulder. "And we've never really dated, let alone dated *blindly* with a forward *man*. Not a guy."

"We've got to start somewhere, and we're too old for *guys*. We deserve men, Jonah. Once you get out there yourself, you'll see the difference and never go back." Juanita patted my shoulders. "I'm going to shower and finish getting ready in the bathroom. I don't want your stick in the mud mood ruining mine."

I flopped onto the bed as Juanita gathered her things and left the room. I debated going to see Carlos, but Juanita was

118

only one problem. I was still struggling with Mr. Blue's conversation three days ago. Not to mention my worry over the rent and our possible pay cut. I had a hundred problems; Juanita's date shouldn't matter so much.

Rolling onto my belly, I grabbed my phone and scrolled until I found Pastor Israel. I made sure I checked over my shoulder before dialing. The shower water was running at full strength. That was good. I didn't want Juanita and Carlos knowing about Hudson just yet. I wasn't sure how they'd feel, and I definitely didn't want to hear them siding with him indirectly by telling me to ignore his rude remarks.

Pastor Izzy picked up on the second ring. "Hello?"

"Hi, Pastor," I said glumly.

"Hey, Jonah, how're you doing?"

"I'm alright."

"Just alright?"

"I don't know what to do. Someone really offended me, and I just don't know how to handle it. And I'm doubly angry because I almost cried right there when it happened."

"Did Carlos reject you?"

I gasped. "Pastor!"

He laughed into the phone, and my mind summoned his boyish grin. Pastor Izzy and I stayed in contact once I moved. I haven't been home to see him in the last six years, but I call him at least three times a month if not every week.

"You kids still haven't figured yourselves out yet."

"Pastor Izzy, I'm having a *real* problem. Not a boy problem."

119

"Alright, alright," he said, and I could tell he was switching from the father I never had to my pastor. After some shuffling on his end, like he was finding a seat, he said, "Tell me what's really going on, Joe. Why're you so upset?"

I shook my head. "We got an amazing sponsorship—a big business has given us a *million* dollars, but they've attached a headache to it. The boss is a jerk and he's kind of," I paused, afraid to go down that road. When you looked like me, you lived on a very thin line constantly teetering between victim and perpetrator. If I acknowledged who Mr. Hudson Blue really was, then I would be pulling the *race card*. But if I ignored it, then I'd be another victim of his derogatory elitist attitude. I hated this. Never allowed to complain but also expected to fight like a warrior. To stand up for justice. But what was justice in a world that blamed victims and rewarded monsters like Hudson Blue?

I swallowed my fears.

"He said things that bordered the line of racism." I tried to say it quickly. I know I didn't have to be that way with Pastor Izzy, but I was so used to making sure I didn't pull this card, even the word *racism* felt itchy on my tongue. Sometimes it felt like the goal in the world was to exploit racism, not to bring it to justice. The goal was to stir up controversy and conflict, not to unite people. If I wasn't careful, I could easily cross into the territory of conflict, and that wasn't a place I wanted to be.

"Racism," Pastor Izzy said almost to himself. We'd never had a conversation like this before. Between two Christians, it never came up. Yes, Pastor Izzy had blonde hair and blue eyes, and was almost too handsome to be a dad. And I was Black with thick kinky hair, brown skin, a bulb nose, etc. We were totally different yet made and perfectly designed by the same God. We had never discussed race because it wasn't necessary. God didn't see race; He only saw the Blood of Jesus.

"You know, we're all different on purpose, not by accident," Pastor Izzy said. "God wanted a family, and He created one. A mixed family, so that everyone could bring something different to the table. It's why He gives us all different gifts and talents. Take one look around in nature and you'll see that God loves color. Why wouldn't He give color to His people?"

I stayed silent, blinking up at the white ceiling.

"We all are equal in God's eyes, no matter what."

"Well, tell that to him, not me. I've never had a problem with anyone."

"Which is why this hurts so badly. You've been godly, you've been kind. I'm certain you didn't do anything to warrant those kinds of remarks."

"I didn't." I swallowed, feeling my mouth go dry as I replayed the conversation in my head. "And then he told me we were begging for money."

"What did you say?"

"That we weren't."

"Good."

I rolled my eyes. "Why does it feel like you're scolding me?"

"Because you must always remain a Christian, no matter

how someone treats you. I don't mean that you cannot stand up for yourself. I mean, sometimes the only light of Christ someone will see is in you. So, even though this hurts, you must continue to show this person kindness."

"But why? He was so obnoxious! Didn't God strike Miriam with leprosy for being racist?"

"And didn't Jesus die on the cross for every racist person?"

I sat up. "That's not fair."

"It is," he said. "Do you know why we are light bearers?"

"Because light exposes darkness," I said begrudgingly.

"Because light shines *through* the darkness, exposing our mistakes so that they can be corrected. Being kind is a pathway to light. So even when someone offends you, they can see that light shining through you. They can see that God loves you, no matter what, no matter your skin color. What is God?"

"Our Father."

"A Spirit," he said, and I could feel him smiling. "He's a spirit and not a person for a reason. If God had been a person, everyone would feel like whatever race He was is the best race. I'm sure you've seen how much confusion there is over Jesus's skin color." He sighed into the phone and I did too. The war over the minute detail of whether Jesus's skin was black or white literally made people stop going to church altogether. Calling Christianity the 'White man's religion,' or saying the Bible was written by a bunch of old White men. Which just screamed no one has ever read their Bible. The Bible, first written in Hebrew and Greek, was not written by a bunch of White people. It was written by Hebrews.

122

"People don't realize that Jesus needed to look common." Pastor Israel had started again, drawing my attention back to the conversation. "If He was a Black man, everyone would hail Black people. If He'd been a White man, or a Hispanic man, or an Asian man—whatever race He had been would have placed that race on a pedestal in the minds of men. But God sent Jesus as a Jewish man. One of the smallest cultures in the world that has *always* been small and overlooked until recently. Jesus was common, yet He saved the world. And it had nothing to do with His skin color." Pastor Izzy went on, "So, I'm telling you all this for you to realize that God sees you in this trouble, Jonah. But He expects you to do the righteous thing and let your light shine. You've heard the saying, kill with kindness? You ever wondered if that applied to Christians? Because it does. Let the light of Christ be a gentle love that knows no bounds, granting kindness to those you come in contact with so their flesh will die, and their spirit awakens. It's up to you to offer the other cheek."

"How do I offer the other cheek *and* defend myself?"

"Bring everything to God," he explained. "And since you know you'll have to encounter this person again, you turn the other cheek by continually offering God's love and grace to this person."

"I don't want to turn the other cheek," I muttered, and Pastor Izzy laughed.

"I know, Jonah. But I promise it'll be worth it in the end."

Dumping all the air from my lungs with an exaggerated sigh, I decided to accept what Pastor Izzy said. "Turn the other

123

cheek."

"And forgive him."

I pressed my free hand to my forehead. "Fine. I forgive Mr. Hudson Blue in Jesus's name."

"All better?"

"All better. Thanks, Pastor."

"Of course, Jonah. Make sure you call with updates, alright?"

I laughed. A man of the cloth and the drama. "Ok, I will."

"We'll talk soon."

"Bye, Pastor."

"Bye now."

13

Hudson Blue

"Two blondes, six o'clock," Jeremy said beside me. He'd called me out for drinks right after work since he never had anything to do. Jeremy's father doesn't trust him to take over the company, which was no surprise. The guy wasn't sober for more than an hour on the weekends, and his weekdays were spent hopping from bed to bed. You'd think he'd stop after catching syphilis, and herpes—twice. But the guy won't calm down. I've got no advice for him. I have goals to reach so my head stays on straight. Jeremy's just coasting with nothing better to do than spend his dad's money.

"You take them both," I said as I threw back the rest of my drink. "I've got a date tonight and I don't want to mess things up with this girl."

Jeremy's blonde brows twisted, and a frown gripped his face. "What's this? You finally found a girl you like?"

"No. But this girl's got a dad who's interested in investing

125

in Blue Barn. This little date would be a good arrangement for our company."

Jeremy's frown sagged and he rolled his eyes. "Could you at least lie about things like this for once?"

I snorted. "I'll find someone eventually."

"Take big Erma. She's always around, isn't she?"

We both fell back in laughter, slapping the counter hard as I reeled. "You've got to be kidding me."

He shrugged, before a vicious look twinkled in his eye. "Whatever happened to that hot maid your dad had?"

I clutched my empty glass, staring into it, willing it to refill. "I think she left over some family junk."

He nodded, never noticing my stiffness. I stared at my glass, the blue lights of the bar sparkling off the rim and the leftover ice in the bottom as he went on in a dreamy voice. "Man, I would've loved to be with a girl like that."

It took me a second to realize that Macey was not only *hot* to Jeremy, but she was a woman he would've wanted to be with. To sleep with. To date. To have. To love.

I looked up from the glass to see him waving over the half-dressed waitress. He wasn't fazed at all. He ordered something, casually asking me if I wanted anything. I shook my head, and the waitress left us for a second, returning right away with his drink. He pulled a hundred-dollar bill from his wallet and stuffed it between her fake breasts before turning back to me.

"What?" He blinked.

"You said… You just said my maid was someone you wanted to be with."

He shrugged. "So?"

"But…" I licked my lips. "They … They're not like us. We can't be with them. Not seriously, at least."

Jeremy burst into laughter. "Old man Olan got you good, didn't he? I always thought it was weird that he only hired Black women to clean his house." He leaned over the table between us, his voice conspiratorially low. "Did he seriously do that on purpose? Raise you to think *other* people were beneath you?"

I blinked as he snorted.

"I always knew Olan was different."

"What's that supposed to mean?" I gripped my glass.

He stared at me. "Are you serious?"

"Do I look like I'm joking?"

Jeremy sighed and finished his drink, licked the spit from his lips before he replied, "Everyone knows your dad is an old fashioned, racist fart. Everyone except you." He looked me up and down. "Did you seriously take all of his brainwashing to heart? Uphold that garbage superiority thing he's been living on since the Civil War."

I didn't reply.

"So… You've never had a different kind of woman?"

I turned away, shifting uncomfortably at the lie I was about to tell. "I actually have a business to uphold."

"We all do. That's why we have secrets. You can't tell me your father's never had one."

"He hasn't," I snapped. "He's very upfront and strict."

Jeremy smiled. "I completely agree."

"You don't understand."

"I do. I get that people below us are different from us, but I don't think they're different because of their skin color, you idiot. I think they're different because they're poor and stupid." He waved the waitress over again, licking his lips as he watched her walk. "I'm not going to pass up a beautiful woman, no matter what my father thinks."

"So, you'd marry a housemaid?"

He passed the waitress another hundred-dollar bill and frowned. "No."

"But you'd sleep with her."

"Of course. We all would. But sleeping with someone isn't the same as giving them your family name."

"Are you kidding me?"

"It's not that deep, Hudson. When you find a pretty woman, enjoy her. They're all dying to have us anyway. Who wouldn't be?"

Jeremy had always been smug. He was handsome with big shoulders and a strong physique. The brute on the football team but dumber somehow. His words reminded me of my own smug comments. I'd said something similar to that woman, Jonah, three weeks ago. I'd told her that she was begging for my money. It's not exactly the same, but I can't get her stupid broken expression out of my head. She was genuinely offended and hurt. I could've cursed myself for the look she'd given me, but she wasn't worth a curse.

"I've got to go," I said as I threw some money onto the table.

"Leaving already?"

"Date, remember?"

He gave me a sneaky grin and I slapped his shoulder as I left. "Later, Jeremy."

"Later," he said back.

As I waited on the valet driver, I contemplated skipping my date tonight. There was no way I'd make it through dinner thinking about the chances I'd missed with Macey. But what would I tell my father? He'd arranged the whole thing for us to snag this new investor. We don't need them, we're a billion-dollar company. Anyone investing now just wants to leech off connections. Maybe I'd make that clear to Dad, skip the date, and sulk for the rest of the evening.

Did I really want to sulk?

I had five seconds to make a decision because once I got in the car, I had to pick a place and get there. With a huff, I settled on the date. The valet driver stepped out, passing me the keys and I gave him a tip as I got inside. I sped off, zipping down the street to make it to my dinner date. I really didn't care to be there on time, but I could hear my father antagonizing me for the next seventeen days if I screwed this up.

Speaking of screwing, that couldn't happen tonight. Tonight was not a safe night. I was so messed up, I feared calling my date by another name. That's actually happened to me before, I mixed up two different women while we were cuddling. If that happened tonight and I called Macey's name

129

instead of my date, I'd lose everything. The investment. My dignity. My father's trust.

When I arrived at the restaurant, paparazzi were waiting. I was the son of a billionaire; they were always waiting for me. People screamed and lights flashed as I stepped out. I was used to the crowds and had learned to ignore them years ago. I marched straight through the mass and into the lobby where I was met at the door by a waiter dressed in a black tuxedo.

"Good evening, sir. Reservation?"

"Blue."

He nodded and checked something off on the tablet in his hand. "Right this way."

"Is my guest here?"

"No, sir. She called about five minutes ago to say she was running late."

"Perfect."

They'd given us a cozy table in the quietest part of the restaurant. The whole thing was designed to mimic the ocean; shimmering blue and white lights filled the place; the carpeting was royal blue against black floors that glistened with seashells taken from the Indian ocean and sealed into the tiles. All the tables were glass except the silver booths, like the one I was in. The glass tables reflected the lights, making it look like they were made of water and not glass. The booths were soft; the shape of them replicated an oyster's shell.

I took it all in as I waited for my date. I was checking my watch when a woman strolled in with wild red curls dangling around her shoulders. She walked on pale legs that stretched from beneath her knee length dress, capturing every pair of eyes in the room. She was cute with freckles scattered across her nose, but she wasn't my type. I was not the redhead kind of guy.

"You must be Hudson," she said, extending her hand.

I took it.

"It's a pleasure, Kressa."

She slid into the booth. "The traffic was absolutely dreadful."

"Indeed."

She wore red fur over her shoulders, as she set her purse aside, it slipped down her arm to reveal a spaghetti strap dress that was deep rouge color.

"Do you like it?"

My focus shifted to her, a sensual look in her blue eyes.

She repeated herself. "Do you like it?"

"Your dress is very nice."

She didn't say anything else for a while, just wore a grin as she scanned her menu. This was unnecessarily boring. I was ready to go home and sulk instead of sit through empty conversations for the next hour or so. At least we'll be getting a new investor when this was over.

The hour passed, and like clockwork I got the bill. I was still aching to go home. We'd talked politics, policies, work, investments, and business. She was trying to corner me with her questions, testing my knowledge of my own company and then her father's. I didn't care; I hated business dates. However, Kressa seemed to be enjoying herself. At first, I thought she was just being polite until she suggested that we drive home together.

"We can share a car," she said as she clutched my arm.

"Unfortunately, Kressa, I do have other business to attend to before the night is over. But the evening has been wonderful."

"Then we should do it again sometime."

I forced a smile. "Of course."

Freeing me of her grasp, she stepped out and waved at a taxi pulling up. The yellow car pulled over and I grabbed the door for her. Leaning inside, I passed the man a few bills, "Get her home safe."

"Of course!" the driver exclaimed as he counted the money.

"You grabbed the bill, and my taxi." She raised a shoulder. "I think you might like me."

Playing the part, I left one hand in my pocket and used the other to raise her chin. "Good night, Ms. Lion."

Her eyes glistened with lust and desperation, but I let her chin go and turned away. The car door closed and when the taxi finally pulled off, I unbuttoned my suit jacket to breathe.

"Valet! Can you get my car?"

"Yes, sir.

∧ ∧ ∧

I was exhausted. I'd made it to the heart of Brooklyn, cruising through the streets with my windows down. That was where I spotted that charity's building, the My Fellow American Project. There was a woman standing out front, she looked lost, glancing back and forth. I recognized her as Jonah. Without a second thought, I whipped out of traffic and pulled over to the curb right in front of her.

"Hey," I called as I rolled down the window.

Wide eyes blinked emptily at me until recognition hit. "Mr. Blue? Sorry, I didn't recognize you behind the wheel."

"It's alright. Where are you heading?"

"Home."

"This late?"

"Long day," she said curtly.

I know she didn't have a clue why I was pulled over here, and I really didn't have a clue either. I came over without a plan. Now we were sitting in an uncomfortable silence.

"Well, I'd better get going." Jonah turned away.

"You want a ride home?"

That was stupid. I only asked because I was feeling guilty for snapping at her and then letting her protect me.

"Oh, no. I can walk. It's good for me."

"Let me take you home," I said a little more firmly. Jonah was such a pushover. She nodded after only one more try, opening the door and sitting down like a child being scolded.

"Sorry," she muttered as she pulled her large bag into her lap, "I've got a lot of paperwork."

"Busy, I understand that."

We pulled off. Neither of us spoke during the ride, except for Jonah mumbling her address. She had to repeat it twice so

I could put it into my GPS. After that, the car was quiet as a tomb. Felt like one too.

I'd sneak glances at her, peeking at the side of her face. Jonah looked straight ahead, watching the traffic crawl along. She really was beautiful. Even brown skin, and lovely curls just like Macey's. Up close, I could see that she wasn't a complete replica of Macey. There were definitely differences, but she reminded me so much of her. The way she was compliant and quiet. Macey had more backbone than Jonah, but at the very least Jonah did stand her ground when I told her she was begging for my money.

The memory tugged a sigh from my lips that caught Jonah's attention.

"Sorry," she apologized immediately, "I know I'm stuffed with my bag."

"You're fine." I motioned out the window. "It's just … traffic."

She nodded.

"Listen, Jonah, your presentation day was good. I was just having a bad day, and I took it out on you."

She didn't say anything. She just continued looking straight ahead which angered me.

"Did you hear what I said?"

Now, she looked over at me, "I didn't hear an apology. Just an excuse."

"Excuse me?"

Jonah glanced back out the window.

Anger brushed against my heart. "No, you don't get to say

that and look off like I did something wrong. Who do you think you are?"

"Who do you think *you* are?" She looked back at me, brows furrowed. "You said nasty things to me and then told me I was *begging* for your money. And even after I covered for you, you sit here and can't issue me an apology?"

"I'm driving you home! That *is* the apology!"

She grabbed her bag and yanked on the door handle. The door flung open, just *barely* missing a car that swerved around us.

"What are you doing?" I shouted in a panic. The tires screeched as I pulled over to the curb, ignoring the honking around us.

"I'm walking home like I intended," Jonah huffed.

"You'd better not—"

She stepped out and I reached across the seats to grab her by the arm.

"Let go!" she snarled.

"Get in this car!"

She grabbed my hand, prying my fingers from her shirt sleeve. "I will not let you treat me any kind of way. Why can't you just apologize!"

"Why do you people always think someone owes you something? You're getting *my* money. You're in *my* car! What more can you ask for?"

Cars honked, swerving around us as we held up traffic even more. I'd glanced away for just a second, and when I looked back, Jonah had a tear rolling down her cheek which infuriated me because I caused that tear to fall. I had no control over myself with her. This anger was familiar. It was the kind of anger I'd had with Macey the day we slept together, but I wouldn't let myself remember those feelings.

"Get in the car," I growled.

She yanked her arm free and stumbled back. "We're withdrawing our application. You can give your money to someone else."

"You're kidding me." I took a breath. "Jonah, get in the car."

She didn't move.

I burst into anger. "GET IN THE CAR!"

She slammed the door shut so hard, I jumped. Then she kicked my car. She kicked it over and over until someone honked at her and she lost it on them, screaming that she wasn't going to be treated poorly ever again.

I grunted, shifting gears and racing off through traffic.

By the time I got home, I'd calmed down a little. Sitting in my car at the front of my house, I took a deep breath. *Jonah would get over herself, and…* my thoughts trailed off as my father ripped open the front door and stormed out to my car. He was red as an apple.

I opened my car door. "Evening, Father—"

He didn't even speak, just whacked me over the head.

"What's your problem!" I shouted.

He threw his phone at me. It bounced off my chest and clattered to the cobblestone driveway. When I stooped to pick it up, I glimpsed the short email he'd received.

Due to unforeseen circumstances and behavior, the My Fellow American Project will be withdrawing their application from the sponsorship of the Blue Barn Company.

Thank you for your consideration and time.

Jonah King.

"That little—"

"What did you do!?" my father screamed. "Do you know how much this will hurt our reputation?"

"Dad," I tried to speak but he snatched his phone from my hands and threw it at me again.

"We've got to print our own failure in the papers for the world to see. Thanks to you." He turned away, heading for the house as I stared at his phone on the ground.

I lifted it to read the email again, sighing with regret.

14

Jonah King

I was tired as a dog... All I wanted to do was rest and wash off the grime and stress of the day. But then I unlocked my apartment door and found Carlos sitting at the table with his hands folded. Juanita was beside him.

I glanced between them as I kicked the door shut behind me. There was no food on the table, so they weren't having dinner, and they both looked angry. Really angry.

"Guys?" I asked, setting my bags down. "What's going on?"

Juanita's face wrinkled and twisted, the ugliest I've ever seen her. Her expression took me by such surprise, I barely registered her words as she said, "Don't act like you've got no idea what this is about."

I blinked. "Huh?"

With a huff, Juanita unlocked her phone and slid it across the table. That's when it all hit me. I didn't have to look at the phone to know what was going on. While waiting for my bus, I crafted a short email to the Blue Barn company, but I forgot that my work email automatically CCs Juanita. I have to manually remove her when I don't want her on the email chain, but I was so angry and in such a rush, I'd forgotten to do that. Of course, they would've eventually found out, but I still would've had the time to explain everything in a much better way.

"Listen, guys," I raised my hands defensively, "I know you're upset, but these people were not very kind."

"How do you know? Because they were *very* kind to me," Juanita said. The way *very* rolled off her tongue sounded like it was tethered to something that just went out the window with this sponsorship.

"I didn't want to tell you guys this, but Mr. Hudson Blue said some things to me privately. Things that were rude and... very close to being racist. He degraded our company. And then he did it again tonight, so I just—"

"You saw him tonight?" Carlos raised a brow. "I thought you were working late."

"I was." I nodded. "And then Mr. Blue pulled up in his fancy car and gave me a ride home. But halfway there, we got into an argument, and I ended up walking home. He left me there in the middle of the street. I took a bus the rest of the way."

Neither of them spoke. I thought this explanation would cool them down and help them understand why I did what I did, but the tension in the air only thickened as Juanita passed

139

Carlos a look. Suddenly, I understood the situation a little better. They didn't believe me.

"Guys," I opened my hands, "they were disrespectful. I just saved us from doing business with bad people."

"You never liked them in the first place." Juanita's voice was like fire. Every word burned with her fury, but it was Carlos' silence that worried me. He avoided eye contact with me, staring at his folded hands and nodding along with Juanita. They'd clearly had some kind of discussion before I got here.

"You're right. I didn't trust them before, and this is why." I glanced between them. "You both know I love this company and would never do anything to threaten us."

"You just did, Jonah! Making your own decisions without anyone's consent is threatening us!"

"Juanita, Hudson said we were *begging* for his money. He accused us of wanting a handout. Come on, we can't work with people like that."

"No, *you* can't." Juanita stood. "*I* was fine working with them. *Carlos* was fine working with them."

I took an involuntary step back. My face burned liked she'd just slapped me, like both of them had just slapped me. Juanita was leaning over the table, her teeth bared, her brows flattened in a straight line of anger, inching up on hate. Meanwhile, Carlos stared at his clenched hands, refusing to take part in any of this. His silence was just as insufferable. They blamed me for this. They were taking Hudson's side; despite all the things he'd said about us. Despite how he'd treated me.

"You have to believe me," I said, but my voice was so weak

140

the words were little more than a whisper.

Juanita shook her head. "You keep saying Mr. Blue said things to you, but you never told us about any of this. When did he say this stuff, huh?"

"Today, and a few weeks back when we had that presentation."

She rolled her eyes. "Incredible. You had a lie prepared for this. Well, thanks for ruining things for us. We'll be busy all weekend contacting sponsorships even though the dates are closed." She moved from the table, but I jerked forward, arms outstretched, like I could stop her.

"Juanita, you can't possibly think I'm *lying*!"

She backed up so fast, she almost tripped, like touching me was the last thing she wanted.

"Nita … Why would I lie?"

"You said he's *almost* racist. What does that even mean?"

"It means he's almost racist!" I yelled.

She folded her arms. "But did he call you a slur? Did he curse you and God? No. He said we wanted his money and, guess what, Jonah—we *do*. We applied for *his* money. We accepted *his* money." She stepped toward me, getting right into my face. "You don't want to hear it, but he's right. We *begged* for his money. And now we're going to suffer because of your pride."

"Juanita—"

"Please," she held up a hand and walked to the door, "I'm crashing at Carlos's place, since we're obviously not a team anymore. It's you and then it's us." She looked over at Carlos

141

who was still sitting at the table. "Are you coming or what?"

He raised his head, face full of anger and defeat. "Yeah, I'm right behind you."

I hugged myself as he brushed by me. I wanted to reach out, grab him, and beg him not to go. But I couldn't get myself to do anything but let him walk away. He left without a word or a glance, closing the door quietly behind himself.

It wasn't until I was completely alone that I sank to my knees. "God," I cried, "where are You in all of this? I need to hear You!"

But there was no answer, just the sound of my sobbing as I gripped the edge of our wooden table and dragged myself to my feet. The tears stung my eyes as they slipped down my cheeks. I was bitter and angry and hurt. I'd been offended by a business partner, then betrayed by my friends, and God had nothing to say about it.

I let go of an awful sob that wracked my entire body. There were no other words I could formulate, nothing I could say to God that would make Him answer. All I could do was suffer in silence. I was angry at myself for cancelling, but also angry at my friends for not believing me. Why else would I cancel a million-dollar sponsor? I'd been wary of them in the beginning, but even after that argument with Hudson, I chose to keep going with the sponsors.

So, why wouldn't my friends believe me? Should I have told them about that conversation with Hudson earlier? I groaned, shoving a palm to my forehead before wiping my tears. The damage was done now, there was no point in crying about it. But I still wanted to. Juanita was angry enough to move out! She's gone. And Carlos is gone too. He barely looked at me through it all.

I clutched my chest as his face reappeared in my mind. It was so easy to recall the way his eyes avoided mine, not because this happened only a few minutes ago, but because Carlos has never done that before. Juanita and I have argued, but he's always been our middleman, siding with me most times, if I'm honest. But this time he didn't. I hadn't realized how much I was depending on that until he left with Juanita. I don't know if he was picking a side, but I knew I'd pushed him further away than ever before. This was new. This was foreign. Would we ever recover?

With a sigh, I stood and moved to my bedroom. I didn't have an appetite anymore, I just wanted to sleep. But I couldn't. The moment my head hit the pillow, I became restless. I wanted to march across the way and make them believe me.

I sat up at the idea.

What if they were waiting for me to do just that?

Throwing my legs over the side of the bed, I slipped into my tan slippers, one sporting a hold in the bottom, and stumbled out the bedroom to my front door. I took three quick steps across the hall and raised a fist, but then I froze. Negative thoughts swirled in my head, reminding me of the anger on Juanita's face, the dismay on Carlos's.

With a defeated sigh, I retracted my fist and backed away from the door. They didn't want anything to do with me. That much was obvious. It's why they both left me there in the apartment alone. To sit with my own selfishness and wonder if they'd ever come back.

They *had* to come back. We had church on Sunday and work the next day. We'd be fine by then.

With a nod, I went back to my apartment with the sound hope that things would work themselves out.

Nothing worked out. In fact, three weeks of silence passed between me and them. It's literally me. And. Them. They eat lunch together offsite, leaving early so they're already gone and back by the time I return from the cafeteria with my lunch tray. They've squeezed me out. Coming home together. Going out together. I've heard them leave their apartment multiple times together. They even sit together at church while I sit on a different pew. Everyone's noticed that I've been ousted but no one at work blames them.

When the news hit the entire company, nasty looks were passed my way. Everyone has been working overtime because we need sponsors and ways to keep the lights on. And while everyone has each other to lean on, I've been left alone, praying for God to say something, hoping that things will work out.

"Maybe I should just go home," I said as I sat on the edge of my bed. Things weren't working out. Carlos and Juanita were taking meetings without me, which was normal, but before the fight, they always told me about the meetings afterward and kept me on speed dial in case they needed me.

"They don't need me anymore." Tears blurred my eyes,

144

and I tried my best to choke them back. Pulling my phone out, I decided that a trip home to Texarkana wouldn't be so bad. I needed to see all the things I'd left behind to chase a failed dream. A *stolen* dream. I wasn't needed here, so what was the point of being here?

∧ ∧ ∧

It didn't take long for me to book a flight and get across the country on a leave with no return date. It was approved within the same thirty minutes I'd sent it out to our scheduling guy. I was shocked, I thought John would at least ask the reason, but he said nothing in the email. It was just an automated approval letter.

While it didn't take long for me to go back home, it took me two full days before gathering the courage to see my mother. I knew she would chew me out, but she'd at least be happy to see me if just to make fun of me. Mom was right all along, I should've stayed home and learned the business from her. It was a sure-fire future, as opposed to my life that's been flipped upside down now.

I stood outside the boutique in confusion. For some reason, there was only one car outside the shop. It was Mom's car. Even before opening, there were always a few cars outside the store; employees *and* customers waiting for the boutique to open.

Crossing the parking lot, I took a breath as I pulled open the door.

145

"We're not—" My mother froze. Her normally soft brown skin looked leathery now. Like the last six years had drained her.

"Well, well, look who's returned," she sassed as she dropped her eyes back to the cash in her hands.

"Hi, Mom." I tried to sound enthusiastic to see her. I knew she'd be rough around the edges, but I didn't think she'd treat me like an old customer who's coming back around after shopping at the other boutiques.

"Why are you back? You know my doors don't revolve, and there isn't any room for you here." Her eyes reached mine as I came down the aisle. There were only a few clothes racks set out. I couldn't help but notice the chipped paint on the floors, and the lack of flare my mother always had. This store looked no better than a Goodwill, and even those have better used clothes than what my mother's boutique offered now.

"What are you gawking at?" she hissed.

I froze in my tracks, and that's when I noticed how thin she was. Her clothes looked grey, like she'd been washing them over and over.

"Mom, what's going on?"

"You come back six years later and expect me to scream and shout? I've got a store to run, not that my store has ever meant anything to you."

"You know that's not true."

"Then why didn't you call!" she blew up, tossing the money out her hand so it burst into a green cloud around her. "When I needed help, you were nowhere to be found. Now you come

146

strolling back after years to help me close up shop? Why? So you can hang it in my face?" She shook head. "No. I want you to go. Keep that same distance we've had all this time."

"Mom, that's not why I came back. I came—"

"I don't care!" she screamed.

I took a step back, but I wasn't going to leave so easily. Clutching my purse under my arm, I swallowed and tried again, "Mom, I just—"

"Get out! Get *out*!" She ripped the cash register from its spot on the counter and threw it. Shockingly, it was empty enough for her to heave it across the walkway, but I managed to dodge it, tripping into an empty clothing rack. The register exploded, releasing a handful of coins to roll across the floor. The little bell inside dinged loudly and the receipt paper tumbled across the floor.

Slowly, I took a stilling breath and stepped over the mess to head to the door. "I'm sorry I never called," I said stiffly.

Without another word, I turned and left my mother's shop and found my way to a bus stop. I hunched over the bench, swiping at my eyes. My mother was in no better condition than I was. I wanted to go back and help her, but in her state, she was inconsolable.

I had no idea what'd happened over the last six years, but I knew it'd broken her down to the feeble woman I saw counting the little money she had left. There was nothing I could offer her but another mouth to feed. We were about to take pay cuts at the program, and I was barely making ends meet already. My plane ticket took a bite out of my savings, and I was hoping to start making that back at the boutique. But now, I've got nothing left. Mom was broke. I was broke. *God? What do I do?*

Trust me.

I sniffled, looking up and around. "Trust You? After everything!?"

If you trust Me enough to question Me, then trust My answer.

I deflated, immediately letting go of the anger I *wanted* to feel because I hadn't heard from God. That anger had bubbled inside of me, fighting for a way out. God had just now answered, after *weeks* of silence, and the only thing He offered were two little words.

But … He was right. If I was going to question Him, if I dared to petition Him, then I also had to be bold enough to trust the answer He gave me. Even if I didn't like it.

Suppressing my anger with a heavy sigh, I stood upright and wiped my tears as the bus pulled up. There was only one other place I could go to find help. The only place that's ever been my refuge.

Pastor Izzy kept his church open twenty-four hours a day. The cozy cream and red sanctuary felt like home as I walked inside. I found a bench and sat, staring ahead at the raised cross. Pastor Israel was specific when he had the cross mounted. I was still new to the church when he had their old cross replaced with this new one. Pastor didn't want it touching the floor. He said Jesus was hung high as a banner for all of us to always look up to, so the cross needed to be high.

"Hello? Is someone there?" Israel stepped out the back. He was wearing a green polo and black pants, squinting into the sanctuary.

"Hi, Pastor Izzy," I said softly.

He stiffened, but just for a second. Wearing a grand smile, Pastor Izzy moved down the pulpit and through the pews to me, quickly pulling me into his embrace. "My little Jo-Jo is home! When did you get here?"

I wanted this reunion to be a happy one, but all I managed to do was crumble in his arms and weep. "They hate me, Pastor Izzy! Everyone hates me!"

"Slow down." He began to rub circles in my back. The fresh smell of cypress trees filled my nose as I clung to him.

"Pastor Israel," I sniffled, "I messed up. I screwed up with everyone in my entire life."

"Not me. Not God."

"God barely even answered me." I pushed away from him to scowl. "It's not fair."

"But He answered, didn't He?"

"Really late." I threw my hand up and flopped down on the bench. "Three weeks ago, I needed Him to answer me."

"So you don't need Him to answer ever again?"

I sucked my teeth, dragging my eyes over to him. Pastor Izzy smiled as he sat beside me on the bench. "You know, every time you ask God for an answer, you're exhibiting faith. You believe He'll answer and that moves Him."

"He moves too slow."

Izzy laughed, his cheeks dusting with a pink blush. "God

149

doesn't move in time the way we do. He exists *outside* of it. Have you ever noticed, time is the only thing God doesn't bind Himself to? He's never given us a promise with a time stamp. So even if we call right now, there's no guarantee that He'll come *right now*. But there is a guarantee that He's coming."

I wanted to tear my hair out as the frustration mounted. "How is that any better? How does that help me? Why even create time if He's just going to ignore it?"

"Time was created as a tool of measurement. But no one ever says what is measured." Pastor Izzy had a proud look on his face now, like he'd been waiting for the perfect opportunity to explain this to someone. "Time measures patience. We know exactly how long Abraham and Sarah waited for a son. We know exactly how long Joseph's journey was from the pit to the palace. We know exactly how long Jesus was dead for. All of those specifics were measurements of patience."

I blinked away at the cross. Jesus hadn't been on that specific cross, but I couldn't stop myself from staring at it now that I began to understand what Pastor Izzy was saying. "I thought we weren't supposed to count how many years we wait?"

"We don't have to." Izzy shrugged. "But time is measured for sake of testimonies. Why do you think Jesus waited four days to raise Lazarus? It was not just a show of power, it was a testimony to us that even after someone's been dead for a long time, Jesus can resurrect them. But only if you believe. Patience is tied to faith. It increases it, not decreases it."

"But don't you get tired of waiting for promises never

fulfilled?"

He slowly nodded. "Sometimes. But we must remember, patience brings character, and when you have character, you have hope. And when you have hope, you have faith, because faith is the substance, the tangible piece of the puzzle, of the things we're hoping for."

I bit my lip. "Faith is the substance of things hoped for, the evidence of things unseen. I don't get it."

"In the midst of trouble," Izzy began as he grabbed my hand, "we sometimes aren't rescued right away so that we have the chance to produce patience, which is synonymous with endurance. Enduring your trials and tribulations brings experience to you, or character." He nodded. "When you have experience, it's like those smooth stones David picked up to sling at Goliath. They were smooth as evidence of God's faithfulness."

I could feel myself squinting, and it made Izzy laugh.

"I'll explain," he said. "Stones are smooth after abrasions. Constant rubbing over and over, sanding the stone until every edge is smooth to the touch. That takes some friction and some time. That's why patience produces character, because your character is developed through everything you've experienced that has smoothed your edges. And when your edges are smooth, you can be used by God. Because your experiences are your testimonies."

"My experiences are my testimonies?"

He nodded with a smile. "Every sanding session, every abrasion, is a storm you made it through that produced

151

character in you. And now, with this character, you've learned through these experiences that God is not man that He should lie. He will be there in the time of trouble. He will be there when you least expect Him. He will be there, no matter how long it takes or what it looks like. God will be right there when you call." He held up a finger. "But it depends on your level of faith that gets Him to move quickly. That's why some people who have been through so much, their prayers are sometimes answered very quickly. They've seen God's miracles. They've seen His faithfulness, they know they can trust Him, so they never falter."

"Well, what about me? God took three weeks to answer me."

"Did you truthfully want an answer, or did you just scream at Him and want Him to pull out a hat trick to make you feel better?"

I cleared my throat in shame as Izzy chuckled and went on.

"So," he said, "now that you're trusting God, you've developed some character. Now you have hope. Hope is the first step to faith. You have to have hope before you have faith. Which is why you have to experience things because hope is birthed where there is lack."

"What do you mean? Like, when we need something?"

"Yes. We hope we can make it. We hope we've got enough money. We hope we can be there on time. We hope first, and then we have faith. We hope we've got enough money, and then the faith is activated as we cast our cares to God." He tossed his hands up as if to give his cares to God. "When you give something to God, you prove that He is real. And if you're proving God is real, that means you are providing evidence for things unseen, which is faith."

Pastor Izzy poked my shoulder playfully and I chuckled. "When you have faith, you are literally proving that God is alive, and He can make a way out of no way. You provide the substance, the tangible piece of evidence for onlookers to see. Your faith is tangible to the eye of the beholder. Because," he paused and made a fist right in front of me. Veins pushed to the surface of his skin through his strong forearms as he looked over at me with his deceptively gentle face. "They are watching you hold on, even when things look bleak, when there's no way out. Your faith provides proof that the dreams you've been hoping for all these years are attainable."

"So that's why our faith is evidence, and it is substance. It's not something physically here in my hand." I looked down at my hand, closing it tightly. "It is the proof you place in the hands of those who are watching. It's substance and evidence for *them*."

Pastor Israel was beaming now as he leaned over and bumped his shoulder with mine. "There you go."

"But I'm still lost about what to do for our company." I dropped my head with a sigh. "I ended our deal with a sponsorship without consulting Carlos and Juanita first. Now they think I'm a liar and that I'm trying to sabotage the company."

"I'm sure they—"

"They hate me," I said over him. "They hate me even

though I'm telling the truth. Mr. Blue was awful towards me. I just didn't want to deal with him anymore."

"Did you get into another fight?"

I stammered, pulling my hand from Pastor Izzy's secure one. I always felt so safe with him, like the world couldn't harm me as long as Israel was there. Even my mom seemed like a fire that could be tamed if Izzy was near or had given me advice.

"We did."

"Did you do what I said? Turn the other cheek?"

I avoided his eyes, but I didn't need to. Izzy's bright blue eyes pierced straight through me, letting me experience a horrifying and stiff chill. "I tried, but I didn't do it," I confessed. "I was still so angry at Hudson. I tried to get him to apologize, and it blew up in my face."

"Jonah…" Izzy sighed. "Have you repented? Did you apologize to God for disobeying the words He gave me to give to you? There's a reason why you needed to show Mr. Blue kindness."

"I'm sorry!" I cried as I hunched forward. "I know I screwed up."

"A simple apology will make it all better," Izzy said as he patted my back.

"An apology? To Mr. Blue?" I peeked between my fingers at Izzy. His chin was raised and his eyes met mine slowly. Israel was too nice to ever scold me, but his quiet and disapproving look always shook me to the core. With a sigh, I dropped my hands and sat forward. "I have to apologize to God, and Mr.

Blue. And to you, Pastor Izzy. I'm sorry I didn't listen."

"It's alright." He pulled me in for a hug. "Withdrawing from a company like that and defending yourself wasn't wrong. I want you to know that I'm proud of you for making such a tough decision." He patted my arm as he still held me. "But it's because God wants the glory in this, He wants to change Mr. Blue, and your apology will open the door for that. Just this one apology, Jonah, and it'll all be well."

God changing Mr. Blue through an apology seemed impossible. But how could I fight God? I had to do this, despite the way my heart cringed at the thought of an apology. I'd already messed up by disobeying God, now I had to make things right. I had to do this.

I sat up with a sigh and Pastor Izzy rested a hand on my shoulder. "Something else is still bothering you."

"What if he doesn't accept my apology? What will God do then?"

"No one said he would accept it. Just leave that to God. You just do your part and open the door."

I groaned. "Ok, but what if everything goes right and my friends are still mad at me? What if Carlos is still…" I stopped, letting my shoulders sag.

"What are you more worried about; your friendships, your company, or Carlos?"

My ears burned, and I looked to my hands. "Honestly, I don't know. I love my friends and the organization so much."

"And is Carlos included in those friends you love?"

"Of course."

155

Pastor Izzy looked sympathetic, taking one of my hands from my lap like he was about to deliver some very bad news. "You're still worried. It's easy to trust that God will fix things with your business and even bring your friends back around. But you're worried that things with Carlos won't go back to the way they were before."

I nodded. "Juanita moved in with him. She left after we argued and hasn't been back at all. Not to grab clothes, not even to get food. We always share supplies. I guess she moved everything over there while I was still at work."

Pastor Izzy nodded, looking off at the cross ahead. "I want you to go back to New York tonight, and I want you to go back with your head high."

"Why can't I stay here with you a little longer?"

A gentle smile claimed his youthful face. "Because you're needed there. Things may not be the same between you and your friends, but you will remain a light for them. Each of you is about to enter a storm in your lives, but you'll be the only leader with a torch in your hand. *You* have to light the way for them."

"No, Pastor Izzy, I can't do that. I'm not equipped for that. And what about my mom?" Her screams filled my head as I whispered, "She's so lonely and broken. I can't leave her now."

"Jonah, you are more than ready. Pray for your mother. Prayer can reach God from anywhere, even from New York." He placed a hand on my shoulder and squeezed it. "Go home, kid. Your friends need you. I'll keep an eye on your mom."

I slouched back against the pew. I would be the torch for

156

my friends. What kind of storm was going to hit all of us? All I knew for certain was that the torch I'd be holding at the end of it all would be burning with the flame of fire from heaven above. God would crown me victorious through Christ, and that would be the only thing I'd keep my focus on.

15

Hudson Blue

Three Months Later

Lolita's anger matched my father's. She was outraged that we dropped the My Fellow American Project, though they had withdrawn willingly. She got the email three months back and came storming into my office wanting an explanation. I'm certain she would've demanded one even if I wasn't her boss. I knew that no matter what explanation I gave her, Lolita would blame me for losing that organization, so I told her I didn't know what happened. Which was true on some level. She didn't push any further, just nodded and began necessary preparations to take on another charity.

"That drama was three months ago, Lolita, and you're still giving me the same excuse." I slammed the folder down on my desk and looked up at her as she stood across from me. Her hands were folded, and she avoided eye contact. "You're dragging your feet on purpose."

"I'm not," she said softly, despite how red she was. She was redder than the rouge frilly top she had on.

"You are," I said firmly. "Now stop making excuses and get me another charity. It shouldn't be this hard to give people my money."

"Yes, sir."

"You're calling me *sir* now?" I called as she moved toward the door.

She looked back, holding in all her emotions. As my secretary, and my father's, I know Lolita has had to look the other way on a lot of things. She's had to pretend she was okay with the way we've treated her. I'm undeserving of such a woman, but she's here now and I won't give her up. But I hate the way she's looking right now. Holding back her anger because I'm her boss. If she knew I wanted this for her then maybe her anger wouldn't be so strong. If she knew I hadn't thought about that when I'd pulled Jonah aside, and when I'd snapped at her in the car, when I was too prideful to just apologize, I'm sure her anger would be relentless. The My Fellow American Project was personal for Lolita, and I took that from her.

"What would you like me to call you?" she asked.

"Hudson," I said dramatically. "You're the only one in this office who never has to refer to me as *sir* or *Mr. Blue*, and now you *want* to? Is that what this has come down to? Formalities?"

Lolita glanced off, shaking her head just enough for me to catch it. She looked so disappointed. Now, I regretted all the things I'd said to Jonah. If I'd remembered Lolita in my fit of anger, things might've been different.

I can't even explain why I pulled Jonah aside. I challenged her on her knowledge of her company. She knew the program and explained it well. But that wasn't what bothered me. She showed me up right in front of my father and he'd applauded her. Still … I don't think that's the root either. Jonah just bothers me.

When I see her, or think about her, I'm immediately annoyed. She's such an annoying person. But I don't know *why* she annoys me. The best way I can explain it is that whenever I see Jonah, she brings out this reaction from me. It's like she rips the covers back and exposes me for who I really am. She brings out the worst in me *because* she annoys me. Smiling all the time, always polite, always knowledgeable. She's everything my father said *they* weren't. And that infuriates me. She's proved him wrong. She's proved that I've been brainwashed all my life.

Jonah is everything a great woman should be. Somehow, she's even better than that. Better than *Macey*. I'm at a lost for why. What makes her so great?

"Mr. Blue," Lolita's voice pulled me back and I realized she still refused to call me by my first name. "I made the mistake of dropping the formalities and forgetting that first name basis doesn't make me any more important in your eyes. I'm still just your secretary, and what I care about will not be taken into account."

"Lolita—"

"You've made yourself very clear, Mr. Blue." Twisting the handle, she opened the door and stepped out.

"Lolita!" I yelled.

She looked back, eyes brimming. I bit my tongue, still finding the pride in my heart as my own enemy. Memories of my father flooded my mind; him telling me never to forget who I am. Never forget who everyone else is. I never owe an apology for being a man, especially not for being the man in authority. If my father ever knew how badly I wanted to apologize to Lolita, he'd curse me for my weakness.

Swallowing, I stood and said, "Can you close the door when you go?" I wouldn't look up at her because I knew she was waiting for me to apologize, just like Jonah, but I just couldn't do it. When the door shut, I grabbed the bottle of champagne on my desk to throw when I saw a little pink card attached to it. Lowering the bottle, I stared at the card for a second before reaching up and opening.

These dates have been fun! Cheers to more. — *Ms. Lion.*

"Kressa," I whispered. Dad had been getting on my nerves about her, pushing me to make things official or at least take the next step with her. That was his very delicate way of saying he wanted me to sleep with her. I understood why. It's much easier to do business with a woman who's smitten than a woman who isn't, but still. I wasn't into Kressa. She was beautiful and charming and went through the trouble of sending me champagne, but that didn't mean I had to take her to bed.

I grunted, shoving the champagne across my desk. I didn't

like Kressa very much, but I needed an outlet. Quickly, I grabbed my phone and shot her a text before I changed my mind. I asked her to meet me at the Fortune's Home Away From Home. It was a five-star hotel in the center of Manhattan. People seeing us there would gather enough positive attention to push her father over. He's been dangling his money over our heads for long enough, mentioning to my father that I'm respectful to his daughter. I don't know why that bothered him or Kressa, but I'd been choosing not to deal with it. I preferred to keep things basic with enough interest to satisfy Kressa. However, if there was any time to give her what she wanted, it was now, while I was trying to feel something besides regret.

I grabbed my coat from the chair beside my desk and stepped out of my office. Lolita was there, hammering at the keyboard like she was beating it. As plainly and unemotionally as possible, I threw my coat on and walked by.

"Clear my schedule for the rest of the day."

"Yes, sir," she said over my shoulder.

I almost turned around and apologized, but instead, I rolled my eyes at her stubbornness and made my way out the building

∧ ∧ ∧

Kressa took whatever I gave her and asked for more. I didn't mind. I'd arrived at that hotel with one thing on my mind, the fact that she enjoyed it made up for how much I hated it. I

162

could hardly concentrate while we were together. My body worked like muscle memory while I thought about Jonah the entire time.

Calm down. I wasn't fantasizing about her; I was wondering if there was a way I could speak to her. Not just to make things right for Lolita but maybe issuing her a real apology would get her company to work with us again. From what I've heard, they're struggling to find new sponsorship. Jeremy said his father's company received a query from them, but they had to turn them down because they already had a company to sponsor.

Getting them back would do a one-eighty for Blue Barn. We've been able to mitigate some of the damage from their withdrawal, but public opinion went down once the news hit the papers. My father was not surprised. The smaller columns immediately played the race card which, of course, got other newspapers going. Despite all that, our official statement was clear:

The My Fellow American Project willfully withdrew their contract due to internal issues.

Whether or not that was the truth didn't matter, since by the time any reporters caught up with the charity, the building was divided. Their division only backed our statement and helped clean up some of the spilt tears from the public.

Big questions still hung in the air. Would Blue Barn accept the My Fellow American Project back if they asked? Would

Blue Barn try to reach out to them? Would that be okay?

"Earth to Hudson," Kressa snapped her fingers as she lay beside me. "Do you want to go another round? We've rested enough, and there's still a little time before you need to be at the office." She turned onto her side and placed a hand on my bare shoulder. The morning sun rolled in on its high horse, glaring into our hotel room.

"Sorry." I looked at my watch, though I had nothing to do. "I better shower and head out."

"Want me to meet you in the shower?" She moved to kiss my neck, but I slipped away before she could touch me.

"I think I'd better do it alone."

She sat back, looking me over. There was a bit of liner smudged in the corner of her eye, left over from the previous night. Her lashes were crinkled with mascara. I don't even remember eating last night, but there was takeout piled around us as I got out of the bed. Maybe Kressa ordered it. I had no idea.

Kressa fell asleep during my shower. When I got out and found her in bed, I wrote a note on the pad left on the desk and told her to return the key to the front desk whenever she went home. I didn't mention that we should do this again, because we shouldn't. Our night wasn't memorable, considering I had too much on my mind to really pay attention to her.

As my driver cruised down the street, my cell phone rang. With a sigh, I grabbed my phone. It was my father, and not Kressa—thankfully.

"Hello?"

"Hudson."

"Yeah?" I ran a hand through my hair as my father spoke in a panicked voice.

"Did you sleep with Kressa?"

"Why?"

"Because I got word from a friend who goes to the same country club as Mr. Lion, Kressa's dad."

"I know who he is."

My father was likely being over dramatic, but I listened anyway since I had nothing better to do.

"There is gossip going around the country club."

"Of course there is," I deadpanned. The country club is just high school for old people. I'd be surprised if there *wasn't* gossip swimming in the jacuzzi hot tubs.

Dad said, "I got word from the friend at the country club that Kressa wants to start a family."

"Good for her."

He made an ugly noise. "She wants to get into Blue Barn, you idiot. A baby is the ticket, and you might have just handed it to her!"

"I thought you wanted us to get on nicely. I could just as easily marry her if she wound up pregnant. Our companies would be united. That's a good thing."

He cursed. Hard. "The Lion's company accountant just filed for *bankruptcy*. They're flat broke."

My mouth went dry. "She's been using me."

"Yes. Did you use protection?"

165

"Of course I did."

"Oh." He sounded surprised. "How responsible of you."

I'm not all that responsible. I started using protection with Macey because I couldn't afford an accident. If she ended up pregnant, I would never be able to tell my father.

"You really don't want kids," Dad said.

"Yeah, something like that."

"Good. Keep it that way until you've found the right girl to give us an heir. Got it?"

I picked lint from my suit jacket. "Got it."

"I've got to go." My father huffed like he was walking around his bedroom. Before he hung up, I heard a door open and a feminine voice call out, "I'll be back this evening—"

"You've got company?" I teased.

The comment was genuinely a joke, but my father's sharp answer made my ears burn. "My company is none of your business."

"I was just—"

The phone clicked. My father has always had an array of women, I don't know why he would hide it now, and normally I wouldn't care. But this time I felt an unfamiliar prick of anger swell inside of me. That woman's voice... I recognized it. I couldn't place it, but I know I've heard it before. Maybe that's why my father was so short with me. Does he know that I know the woman he's with? Does he have a secret?

I shook my head, denying the very thought. My father wasn't a very committed man, but he respected what he called *territory*. As if women were land to be claimed and conquered.

166

When I made it into the office, Lolita was there, flagging me down. I jogged over to her desk and grabbed a mint from the mug I'd bought her two years ago. She was on the phone, whispering fiercely.

"What's going on?"

She covered the receiver. "It's Jonah King, from the charity. She's asking to speak with you."

I frowned. "Why?"

Her shoulders lifted. "She left a voicemail yesterday and then called again today."

My eyes rolled on their own, like a gut reaction. I headed for my office. "Put her through." This was not on my list of things I wanted to deal with today, but I supposed it wasn't going to simply disappear.

Tossing my coat aside, I picked up the phone on my desk and stared at the blinking red light before I tapped line two and took a seat. "This is Hudson Blue speaking."

"Mr. Blue, sorry to call you so suddenly."

Her voice was soft, a melody to listen to. "No problem. What can I do for you, Ms. King?"

"Can we meet somewhere?"

It took everything in me not to scowl at the award shelf I had across from my desk. The shelf was full of achievements I'd made over the last six years. When this was my father's office, the shelf got so full that every few months he changed out the awards to make sure they were all displayed at some time.

"Why do you want to meet?"

167

"I thought it'd be better if I spoke to you in person."

I checked my watch. "Are you busy now?"

"No."

"Do you know where Sessa's Diner is?"

"Yes, I can meet you there in ten minutes."

"Alright."

"Thank you," she said.

I sat back in my seat and looked out the door. Lolita was peeking in. I gave her a little wave as I said, "Sure thing, Ms. King."

16

Hudson Blue

I sat in the diner, tapping my finger against the checkered table. I loved this little place; it was a tight spot, not a place for billionaire business owners to eat. Erma used to bring me here when she picked me up from school. She'd let me get all the pancakes I wanted and paid for them with her own wages. She always wore a bright and tired smile, teaching me things and reminding me of the things my father expected of me, and pretending he didn't expect me to treat her differently.

Erma never tried to change my mind about my father's lessons. If she had any opinion on them, she didn't let me know. She did her job and took care of me and made it a point to keep her nose down, even as I got older. Late nights with my friends earned me a scolding from her, but Erma always covered for me against my father. She'd bring me to this diner after a night I stayed out too late, or even when she caught me sneaking out. We'd sit across from each other in one of the red and white booths and Erma would give me an earful before huffing out her last sentence and letting me order whatever I wanted.

I felt a small smile tugging on my lips as I sat there in the same red and white booth Erma and I had always eaten in. It was in the back corner of the diner, the checkered table with a red seat and white leather cushions. They served breakfast all day, Greek food, and the best pot roast I'd ever had—right after Erma's. My fondest memories usually involved Erma, and the most stressful ones involved my father.

I sighed as I glanced away from the table, looking outside through the big windows. I used to sit here and complain to Erma about my father, and she'd flip it around and make him sound like the best man in the world. Now, I'm here not to complain but to make amends, though I don't know what Jonah could want. Maybe she'll actually beg for my money, like I'd accused her of in the past. Shamefully, I already decided to accept her begging.

A deep chuckle slipped between my lips at the thought of Jonah. I suddenly felt a knot in my stomach as she appeared in the crowd. She was rushing toward the diner, wearing a nude pencil skirt with a split up the side. Her eyes were wide as she checked the traffic, weaving through cars to cross the street, and her curls bounced around her shoulders. They weren't completely loose, the sides were pinned away as the rest of the kinky coils sprang loose as she moved through the crowd. I watched her grip her purse strap as she came to a stop right outside the door. I had to lean close to the window; I could feel the coolness from outside beating against it as I watched Jonah. She closed her eyes and took a deep breath, just like she'd done when she faced my father and covered for me. My father was certainly a monster to prepare for, but *me*? I never once thought of myself as a monster. Not until today.

She pulled open the door and stepped inside. I watched the server greet her and they spoke a few words before the woman turned to me with an open hand and a question on her face. Jonah paled, her jaw tightened, and she looked so nervous it left a sour taste in my mouth. I felt awful.

Jonah forced a smile before coming to the table. My eyes stroked her frame, watching her hips and the frilly white shirt she wore beneath her beige jacket that matched her skirt and nude shoes. She looked good. Really good.

"Hi," she said as she came to the table.

"Hi."

She sat across from me, eyes glued to her menu. She didn't even remove her purse or jacket.

"Do you want something?" I asked.

"Just a coffee."

I nodded and waved to a server. A lanky boy came over and I told him, "Two coffees."

"Any creams? Sugar is on the table."

I shrugged, sliding my eyes to Jonah. She shook her head, looking up at the server. "No, I prefer black."

"I'll be right back."

The server walked away, and Jonah sighed. I felt myself getting angrier by the second just from looking at her. She was

171

beautiful and she didn't even know it. She was classy and elegant, smart and intelligent, but I couldn't say any of that to her. I couldn't tell her that I was angry at her because she's nothing like what I had expected. Or that I was angry because, truthfully, Jonah had me wrapped around her little finger since the day I laid eyes on her. I was smitten by her. Not just because she reminded me of Macey, but Jonah was the complete package. She's who I would've wanted Macey to become. But I'm not foolish enough to indulge in those thoughts. So instead, I've become angry and annoyed with her. Wishing that I could freely enjoy her if she would have me. But I knew she wouldn't. I ruined those chances the day I told her she'd begged for my money.

"So, Mr. Blue," her voice was soft, like she feared making me angry by speaking too loudly. "I know it's—"

"Two black coffees," the server said as he set down two mugs and filled them with coffee. "I'll come back in a minute for orders."

"Thanks," I said.

He nodded and his eyes slid over to Jonah, lingering on her before walking away. She didn't notice. I've never seen a woman so pretty and so clueless about it.

"Sorry." I opened a hand to her. "Go on."

"Right. I was just going to say that I know it's been a while since you've heard from us. You shouldn't really be hearing from us since we're not working together."

"It's been almost four months, so spit out whatever you want to say so I can go back to work."

She nodded. "I'm sorry, Mr. Blue."

I was mid slurp when she said that and it surprised me so much, I held the searing black liquid in my mouth. After a second I gulped it down and cleared my throat. "I'm sorry? Why are you apologizing?"

"Because I shouldn't have tried to force you to apologize to me in the car. I talked to my pastor, and he told me that in our interactions, I needed to turn the other cheek. I needed to grant you kindness so that you could see the Light of Christ in me." Her eyes found mine, and she looked a little relieved. "I'm sorry, Mr. Blue. I was wrong for snapping at you, and getting out of your car, making a scene. Withdrawing the application was a little dramatic. I should've talked things over with my team, and with you, for that matter." She shrugged. "I didn't know how much backlash your company would receive, and how much heartbreak I would end up putting my organization through."

I was shocked, still clutching my mug to make sure this was all real. She'd read the papers about us and didn't cheer for the angry mob. She felt *responsible* for it. And she was sorry for causing us problems.

I felt the heat from the mug rush through my hand to burst in my chest as I said, "You think a little apology is going to make me give you money again?"

She tilted her head to the side. "Mr. Blue, I didn't come here to ask you to reinstate your sponsorship. I came here to apologize. Nothing more."

I sat back against the booth, blinking at her. She lifted her mug to her lips and sipped her coffee, leaving a baby pink lipstick stain on the rim.

"Well, I don't accept your apology."

She nodded. "God never said you would, but I had to do my part." She lowered her mug. "Coming here wasn't easy. It took me three months to get over myself, to swallow my pride and stop wrestling with God over this. But I knew that your door was hanging on the hinges of my apology. I couldn't keep holding you back."

"So what, you're saying you're doing all this for *me?*"

Jonah smiled, her dazzling white teeth and raised cheeks formed into a picturesque grin. "Yes. I'm doing this for you, not me, Mr. Blue. God wants you for something, and all I can do is my part. That's all any one of us can do."

I ground my teeth together as I looked away from her. "You're mistaken and you need to leave. Coming here and spewing—"

"The truth will set you free," she cut me off. "Jesus is the Truth; that's why the Truth will always set you free. Because Jesus died for your freedom. So, the sooner you face the truth, the sooner you'll be free." She dug through her purse and set a ten-dollar bill onto the table. "God told me to tell you that today."

I watched in silence as she stood. In my heart, I was begging her to come back. I'd never told anyone I was struggling with the things my father had raised me to believe, but here was Jonah telling me that *God* wanted me to face the truth. How could I face the truth if I didn't know the truth?

174

Well, that's a dumb question.

You're never asked to face the truth because you don't know it, you're told to face the truth because you *do* know it and have chosen to turn your back on it.

Watching Jonah leave, I scrambled from the table to catch up with her, shoving my way through the crowd outside. "Jonah!" I shouted. "Jonah!"

She stopped and turned back. She was already at the crosswalk; people brushed by her as she searched for the voice who'd called her name. I stood there, wondering what I would even say to her. Wondering how to even begin to tell her the truth.

Why should I tell? I asked myself. But I wanted to tell someone. I couldn't keep this frustration inside any longer.

Tell Me.

I gulped, backing into the crowd. "Who said that?"

People walked by me, annoyed and rolling their eyes. It felt like the entire world was spinning. I broke into a sweat, glancing around like a madman. I knew if I moved too fast, I'd fall over—I *did* fall over. Out of nowhere, I sank to my knees and hit the cold concrete, seeing stars fade into night.

∧ ∧ ∧

I sat up out of bed, panting hard. Pain bloomed in the back of my head, and I winced, reaching up to touch a wad of bandages.

"If that hurts, I can heal it."

175

I looked and saw a man standing at the end of my bed. I recognized Him right away. Who wouldn't? *Jesus* was at the foot of my bed. He was holding one of my freshly polished shoes.

"What are You doing here?" my voice cracked.

"Calm down." Jesus casually glanced at me before looking back at my shoes. "I wanted to come see you, Hudson Blue."

"Why?"

He lowered the shoe. "So, you can face the Truth."

Jonah's words rang through me. It was the only thing I could remember while I sat in bed with Jesus standing at the foot of it. He came around to the side, and slowly I felt myself sinking into the bed from the sheer power He emitted.

"Can you face the Truth?"

I shook my head. "No. I can't."

"Have I not enabled you to face the Truth, Hudson? Have I not given you example after example of people in your life who are the very opposite of what you have been told?"

I swallowed, unable to give Him an answer.

"We created man in Our image, male and female, black and white, Asian and Hispanic. We love them all. Equally. There is no race better than any other."

"The Hebrews," I tried to counter, but it was like a rage rushed off Him and shoved me further into the bed.

"The Hebrews were chosen for their stubborn spirit. Not because of the color of their skin. But you have decided to play God and sit on your own throne and choose who is worthy and who is not. Will you then tell Me that I am not worthy?"

"No…" I shook my head.

"Will you tell God, the One who breathed life into all of humanity, that He is not worthy?"

"No…"

"Then why do you tell those who bear *My* image that they are not worthy just because they look different from you?"

"Because I have to!" I screamed and it was like something shattered within me. The weight of the power from Jesus was suddenly lighter.

"My son," His voice was cooling, like a breeze swept through the room and calmed me. "You were chosen long ago to be the change in Blue Barn, and in this industry. For too long, My own brothers and sisters have been disregarded by your forefathers. God is tired of it."

I panted, chest rising and falling in short quick breaths as I tried to speak. "I-I'm sorry. I d-don't know what to do. I'll lose everything if I speak up. If I change."

"Because you count the world as your possessions, and not the glory from on high."

"How can I count something I don't have?"

"Because you have Me, you have everything in this world and in heaven. There is nothing I won't give you if you give up the world for Me."

I shook my head, trying to catch my breath. "I'm scared. I'm scared to walk away, to believe and tell everyone that I … I like *all* people."

Jesus smiled as He rested a hand on my head. "Hudson, you will do the right thing, even after the mistakes you make

177

and have made. You will make the righteous choices. It will not feel good, but I promise you, Hudson, I will be right there with you."

"What do I do?"

"You start to change," He said as He leaned forward and kissed my forehead. I felt dizzy from His touch, and my heart wept harder than my eyes with joy and relief. It was unspeakable joy, senseless peace, that enveloped me. "I am with you, Hudson."

When I opened my eyes, Jesus was gone. I was alone again in my bedroom, staring ahead at my feet beneath the blankets. "God, I'm sorry for ignoring the truth for so long. I lost so many good things." I could feel the lump in the back of my throat forming as I went on. "I lost Macey, the one good woman You brought into my life. We did things we shouldn't have, and I'm sorry. And I pushed her away because I wasn't able to do the right thing." I balled up the blankets in my hands as I huffed through the tears that began to fall. "But I have to move on. I have to do the right thing this time. I can't make another mistake like that."

Ripping the blankets back, I swung my feet over the edge of the bed and shoved my face into my hands. "God? Please forgive me of all my sins, in Jesus's name, amen. I accept Jesus as my Lord and Savior. In His name, amen."

Those were words Erma taught me long ago as a kid. She said she believed in Jesus, but she didn't follow Him like she should. Her work here forced her to sometimes turn her back on God, but whenever she'd been through the ringer, she

178

found herself turning back to her Savior, and He was always there for her. Erma said one day she'd get better and never disappoint God again, and she wanted that for me too.

Erma was the other example God had placed in my life, another woman who was nothing like what my father said she should be. Erma wasn't beautiful, and she didn't have any education, but she took care of me, raised me, and taught me how to respect myself and others. Things my father never did. So, I couldn't judge her or criticize her. Erma was only a maid because she had to be. If she had a choice, if things had been better for her, I'm sure Erma would've chosen something else for her life. There will always be people who want handouts, I know that, but Erma wasn't one of them. She was hard working, just like Jonah.

Her named summoned memories of the diner. She was the one who shared her faith with me. And she's the second chance I can't let get away from me. Not because I like her, but because she really opened a door for me to change. I won't walk away from God or this chance to make things right. I have to do this. Though, this was all much easier said than done, here in the confines of my head and bedroom.

"Alright, God, I'm going to try to do the right thing."

Snatching my phone from the desk, I sent Lolita an email:

The My Fellow American Project has been reinstated. They are our charity of the year.

179

17

Jonah King

An email came directly to me from Lolita. She said that Mr. Blue wanted to sponsor us again. I was at a loss for words, but I sent her an email back right away to tell her we accepted the offer since we really didn't have any kind of sponsors barking up our tree. I was getting ready to call Carlos and Juanita when a knock came to my apartment door. I wasn't planning on having any visitors, so I took cautious steps to the door and peeked through the hole. It was Carlos.

I couldn't help myself, I was smiling ear to ear, excited to see him. Ripping open the door, my smile dropped immediately. He was sniffling, tears rolling down his cheeks.

"Carlos? What happened?"

He shook his head. "I'm sorry, Jonah."

"You're scaring me," I said, placing a hand to my chest.

He gave up, letting himself crash to the floor right at my feet, sobbing away.

"Carlos, say something." I knelt across from him, and tried to lift him, but he wouldn't move. He fought against me, locking his arms to his body and forcing himself to stay buried to the floor as he cried aloud, "I'm sorry, Jonah!"

"For what?"

He hiccuped and raised his head. His brown orbs were overflowing with tears as he said quietly, "We had sex."

I blinked. "What?" I could feel my head spinning. But it was spinning because I was shaking it and trying to back away from Carlos. I knew exactly what he'd just said. I knew exactly what he meant. He'd slept with Juanita. My crush went to bed with my best friend. Two Christian people I'd trusted with my friendship, my business, my heart. They betrayed me, even worse, they betrayed God.

"We were so close. We were *living* together, and I got weak," Carlos blubbered. "And she just wouldn't stop. It was only supposed to be one time, but we've been," he stopped, "we've been having sex for two months now. I don't know *how* to stop."

"I can't help you," I whispered. My eyes blurred with tears. How could he do this to me and then come back to me for help? *God*, I prayed inside, but there was no strength to say anymore. I didn't know what to say, not to God or Carlos. So I got to my feet, hands trembling as I clutched the wall, and I grabbed my doorknob.

"Jonah, please," Carlos sobbed. "I'm sorry! I never wanted Juanita. I always wanted you."

I backed into the apartment and closed the door with him

181

still out there. I couldn't even speak, couldn't begin to wrap my mind around what Carlos had just said. He and Juanita had been sleeping together. For *months* they'd been sleeping together. They went behind my back. Was I to blame for this? Did I push them to do this?

"God, please," I whispered as I leaned against the door. "I'm so confused. My heart is so heavy. What do I do?"

Cast your cares upon Me because I care.

I bit my lip. "The pain will still be there. I'll still know that they're sleeping together."

But you will begin to heal. I can take away the pain. I can make you forget the pain if you will allow Me.

"How can You take this away? Why did this have to happen!"

My strength is made perfect in your weakness.

I fell to the floor, letting an aching sob tear from my lips. Carlos, the boy of my dreams, was sleeping with my very best friend. Juanita was like a sister to me. How could they do this to me? I stayed there on the floor, sobbing like a child. I was in pain. I was heartbroken. Not just because Carlos was gone, and Juanita too. Not because everything Pastor Izzy said was manifesting, but because I was truly all alone. All I was left with was God. He was more than enough, but it didn't feel like it. Not when my heart was aching. But I knew I had to choose Him if I ever wanted to get better.

"God?" I whispered as tears rolled across my face and to the floor. "How can I light a torch for someone I don't want to forgive."

182

His words were simple yet soothing, and I trapped them in my heart like a box of hope I couldn't let go. **Jonah, you will get through this.**

∧ ∧ ∧

All of that drama happened Wednesday, so I had to get through Thursday and Friday before I could fall apart again for the weekend.

I stood in my office. It was a wide and spacious room, the only one that didn't connect to another, so I didn't have to share it with anyone. Thank God. I felt bad about it since Juanita and Carlos were kind enough to let me have the only single office. So, when we first moved here, I had part of the wall knocked out and replaced with a glass window. There was a curtain in place if I ever wanted privacy, but I never used it. I always wanted to be able to see Juanita and Carlos. Not because I didn't trust them, but because I didn't want to be different from them. I didn't want to fall behind. When they laughed, I wanted to laugh too. And when they were angry, I wanted to be fueled with fire right alongside them.

We were a team. That's all I ever wanted. I was willing to never have Carlos if it meant keeping things perfect within our trio. But now, I wasn't willing to have Carlos ever again and I didn't care what that meant for our trio. I was angry, so angry, but there was nothing I could do. There was a part of me that was still willing to overlook this and just make amends. But if I just swallowed the pill without reading the label, there was no telling the side effects. There was no telling what would happen later if I never dealt with the problem now. I couldn't let myself be that desperate. So today, I used the black curtain.

I got to work early and pulled it shut. I had Momo, my secretary, put a memo together to be sent out later that Blue Barn was sponsoring us again. I didn't want to give them the good news myself, like I'd planned. I didn't want to be around anyone. I just wanted to sit in my office and force myself to work. Working was the only distraction I had. It was a good distraction because I hadn't even realized it was lunchtime when I heard frantic knocking on my door.

I sighed as I moved from my desk. "Momo? I told you to email me everything."

"It's not Momo." Juanita's voice stung today, like one of those fiery darts the Bible talks about.

"Can it wait?' I asked as I pressed my head against the door.

"Come on, Jonah, you know I got that memo."

"I know."

"Aren't you going to open up?"

It took everything in me not to make a snarky comment back. Instead, I took a breath and pulled the door open. Juanita stood there, a shy look on her face as her yellow floral dress flared around her.

"Are you going to tell me how you swung this?"

"No," I said plainly.

She huffed, placing a hand on her hip. "Come on, Jonah. I'm trying to talk about this and you're completely shutting me out."

"Just like you and Carlos shut me out?"

Juanita scoffed. "You lost our sponsor."

"So, now that we've got it again you've found it in you to speak to me? Now you want to talk? Well, four months ago I wanted to talk. Guess time keeps getting away."

I backed up to close the door when she sneered, "What happened to forgiveness? Doesn't that matter to you?"

I was suddenly dizzy. I felt my legs turn to jelly. She had the audacity to throw forgiveness at me when she hadn't forgiven me in *four* months. And if God Himself hadn't intervened and gotten this sponsorship back, I'd still be *un*forgiven.

"I forgave you a long time ago," I said. "But you never once forgave me." The phone began to ring in my office, and I shrugged, "I've got to answer that."

She was pouting as she nodded. Slowly, I pushed the door shut, and I couldn't help but feel like I'd just closed the door on a lot of other things.

Stumbling over to my desk, I picked up the phone. "Hello, this is Jonah King speaking."

"Hi, Ms. King, it's Hudson Blue from Blue Barn."

His voice was like silk through the phone. Washing over me in an uncomfortable way. I cleared my throat and said, "Sorry, I meant to call earlier to thank you for sponsoring us again. Time got away from me this morning and I just hadn't gotten the chance to call."

"It's alright, I just thought I'd give you a call."

"Yes, well, my colleagues and I are very," my voice began

to shake, and I took a breath.

"Is everything all right?"

"Sorry. Just a rough day." I tried to play it off as the tears sprang from my eyes and my voice was struck with emotion.

"Ms. King?" Hudson said, the kindest I've ever heard him. He sounded different somehow, but I couldn't tell why.

I sniffled to cover my emotions, but it was too loud. I know Hudson heard it, I could only hope he took it as desperate gratitude. Tears of joy for his sponsorship again. "Everything's fine," I said. "I should go. Thank you very much, Mr. Blue."

"Hold on," he said quickly. "I was calling for something else, too."

I nodded, but after a moment of silence I realized he couldn't see me nodding and I murmured a measly, "Okay."

"About your apology yesterday, I'm sorry I said I didn't accept it. I do, and I want you to accept my apology. The things I've said to you haven't been very good. And it hasn't depicted Blue Barn as the company it is."

"Oh…" I struggled, forgetting my own tears as I leaned over the desk. "Mr. Blue, you don't have to apologize. I didn't say those things to get you to finally say sorry to me, I was just—"

"I know, and that makes me an even bigger jerk, doesn't it?"

I snorted. "I don't know if I should answer that."

He chuckled too, it was throaty, like it was vibrating the phone. "That's alright. Well, I should be going. But I hope you feel better, Ms. King."

186

Suddenly the dark cloud that'd been raining over me all day reappeared, and I sighed. "Why did you remind me?"

"Sorry."

I fanned a hand. "It's alright. Thank you, Mr. Blue, for taking the time to give me a call. I really appreciate it."

"Of course, Ms. King."

The airwaves were quiet as we hung in an awkward silence. "Uh, well, goodbye then."

"Yes, goodbye," he said as he hung up.

I pulled the phone from my ear and blinked at it. The world must've been spinning off its axis for the craziness that just bombarded my life to happen in a matter of twenty-four hours.

18

Hudson Blue

Thanksgiving, Christmas, and New Years passed. We were heading into March now, and I still hadn't gotten it together. Like I said, it was easy in my bedroom to swear I'd be a better man, and I think in some ways I have been one. But the alcohol hasn't stopped. The sex is still on and off, and I've still got no way to tell my father that he's wrong and God is right. I haven't even found a church yet. I was having a difficult time on top of work and on top of the charity.

Since we took the My Fellow American Project back in, we had to begin preparation for the banquet just after finishing a banquet for another charity. We do one every year, so Jonah's charity was for this year, and Lolita was beginning to scout a charity for next year. I honestly hated charity work, and with only a few months until we passed them a check, our company was expected to participate in one of their annual events. The last charity we had was an animal shelter. They held a school's petting zoo, and I had to be there with all the smelly animals. Animals were my least favorite and I did everything in my power to give the charity half of the promised million dollar pay off, but Lolita forced me to uphold my word and give them the full amount.

I sighed as I sat in the conference room of the My Fellow American Project's building. Juanita was there and so was Carlos, but Jonah hadn't showed up yet.

"Well, we can begin without her. I'm not sure where she is," Juanita sounded apologetic, but my father beside me waved.

"Don't look so tense sweetheart, we can wait."

Juanita gave my father a shy smile as she turned away to whisper to Carlos. He nodded, his eyes locked with hers like they were closer than any of us knew. Even my father noticed it. He elbowed me and whispered, "Don't those two look like lovers?"

I leaned forward. "You sound jealous, old man."

My father snorted, turning in his seat to stick his tongue out like he was sick. "I'm only wondering because this is a Christian organization, isn't it? Shouldn't they be waiting for sex and all that?"

I forced a laugh. There were knots in my stomach. Even my father, corrupt as he was, knew that sex was for married people, but here I was, a self-proclaimed Christian still sleeping my way through women when I couldn't turn Jeremy down for drinks, or say no to my father's blind dates.

The door opened, and Jonah stepped inside, distracting

me from my troubling thoughts. This was the first time I'd seen her since we met at the diner, and I was gawking at her. She'd gained a little weight, but only in the right places. Rounded hips swayed in the green and white dress that hugged her body. I was staring at her lower body (ahem) as she glided through the room in white heels to lay her jacket on a seat. Juanita and Carlos were staring at her, too. Her swooped hair and lightly lined eyes, Jonah looked like a woman I'd take to bed this instance.

"Sorry I'm late," she apologized in her sweet voice.

I shifted in my seat, catching her attention. She smiled at me and nodded, and I thought my soul escaped me for a second when I got to look at her dead on. Puffy lips that looked as kissable as ever, cat eyes, and fluffy lashes that caught your attention made me want to gasp.

"Well, I see why you were late," my father joked. "What an entrance. You look dazzling, my dear."

Jonah blushed. "Thank you, Mr. Olan. I was caught in traffic today because I left my shoes at home, so I had to turn around and go back." She tossed her hands up, gold bangles shimmying down her arms. "So, I deeply apologize. Are we ready to begin?"

"Yes." My father nodded.

Jonah turned to Juanita and Carlos, who were both staring at her. Juanita looked like she would explode from anger, and Carlos looked as smitten as every other man in the room.

"So, the meeting today is for our Young Americans Night. It's a day we dedicate once a year to the youth since we spend every other day dedicated to adults."

"Why do something for youth if your program is for adults?" Olan asked.

"Great question." Jonah opened a folder identical to the ones we had in front of us. I watched her eyes jump across a page until she spoke. "If you look on page four in the folder, we actually mention that one of our expansions to the program is a youth addition. After school programs, tutoring, etcetera, to help young people get a head start so they won't need us in the future. Plus," she closed her folder and looked out at all of us, "we want to bring awareness to young people that a program like this exists. We want them to know that someone has their back if they fall down, so they can run freely at opportunities. That's not to say we want them to be careless. Our youth night will be equipping them with tools to face the real world, but we do want to encourage them to run and not walk towards their destinies." She shrugged. "Just run responsibly."

"You always speak so beautifully," my father complimented.

I cleared my throat and raised a hand. Jonah gave me her attention, but she didn't look combative, just nervous. "What kind of preparations do you need for this event? I'd like to help, if that's alright."

My father and everyone from Blue Barn turned in their seats to stare at me while Jonah and her colleagues just blinked. Her *colleagues*... the word hit me like a storm. The last time I spoke to Jonah was on the phone the day after we visited the

191

diner. She was upset, nearly in tears, and she said something about her colleagues. I wondered briefly if she meant Juanita and Carlos, but there was no time to dwell on it. Jonah was answering me now.

"Well, there are certainly things we could use some extra hands with," she admitted. "We've got to do some supply shopping and set building. We could really use more hands than funding."

I nodded. "Send Lolita what you need, and she'll get it done."

Jonah looked shocked; her eyes dropped to the floor as she nodded. I could see the small smile winning the silent battle within herself. When she looked up at me, there was a half-smile there as she said, "Thank you, Mr. Blue."

When the meeting ended, I took my time gathering my things. I spotted Juanita leaving the room quickly. She seemed especially restless today. Carlos escorted the rest of the group to the cafeteria with my father trailing. He looked back at me, and I gave him a firm nod before he went on with the group.

"Hey," I said as Jonah collected the leftover materials.

"Hi." She slowed, placing the folders down on the table. "Um, listen, I really appreciate the help you're offering."

I slipped my hands into my pockets as I bunched my shoulders. "You're our charity, we'll be helping in whatever way we can."

"Thank you."

"You were uh," I swallowed, "you were really great today."

"Oh," her eyes looked away, and I stared at her face, letting

192

my eyes trace down to her neck until her collar began. Her eyes came back to mine and I was hoping the lust in mine had left as she said, "You're making me so nervous."

"Sorry."

"It's okay."

I shrugged towards the door. "I guess I better get down there."

"I'll walk you," she said. "Do you mind stopping by my office? I just want to put my jacket inside."

"Of course not."

She marched across the room and retrieved her jacket, waving for me to follow her. We walked in silence, her leading the way, my eyes glued to her figure. My hands were burning in my pockets. It was killing me not to touch her. I was such a pervert, and I hadn't realized that until now.

We stopped at a grey door, where she unlocked it and walked inside. Clicking on the lights, she walked around her grey desk and laid her jacket over her black leather chair. The room lacked color of any sort. A desk covered in folders and papers with two monitors. Of course, the leather chair, two more chairs on the opposite side of her desk, and two big silver filing cabinets. The rest of the room was just empty space.

"No pictures," I commented as I stepped inside. There was a big black curtain pulled across the wall. "What's this?"

"Divider," she said over her shoulder. She was leaning over the desk, and I had to look away to keep myself under control. I went over to the curtain, and pulled it back a little, surprised to find a window that displayed two other desks.

"Is that your colleagues' room?"

"Yes. Sorry." She came over to me. "I needed to write something down before I forgot."

My mouth was dry with her so close. I was standing over her, even in her heels, she was blinking up at me.

"Are you ready?"

"Yeah." I nodded.

She turned and I asked, "That day when I called you. You mentioned something about your colleagues. Is everything alright now?"

Jonah clutched the door, and I realized I was prying too much. But she was a sucker, like she'd always been. She gave in and said, "I just hope it wasn't obvious during the meeting."

"Your secret's safe with me."

She laughed gently, a smile crossing her lips. "Thank you, Mr. Blue."

I extended a hand to her. "Hudson."

This time, her smile widened as she took my hand. "Jonah."

"The pleasure has been all mine." I lifted her hand to my lips and kissed it. She didn't pull her hand away, instead, she blinked in silence. Another moment ticked by with her hand in mine and she finally retracted, looking at the place I'd kissed.

"We should go," I said.

Her words were gone as she nodded and headed out the door. This was a new door between us now, an *opened* door of opportunities. Things were starting over for Blue Barn and My Fellow American, and it started with Jonah and me.

19

Jonah King

God made it possible for me to go to work everyday, even after I found out about Carlos and Juanita. I chose to forgive them, but I didn't choose to continue associating with them. I spent my days off at evening church services, alone at home, or working in the office. I was getting used to the quietness of the apartment.

It took some adjusting, especially on weekends when I'd go grocery shopping and hear the two of them laughing so loudly across the hall. Some days were unbearable, and I felt like my world had become ashen and grey. Like the colors Juanita brought into my life had been snatched away, and the delight Carlos gave me died with a cry. I was in limbo for a while, until I realized that I'd become dependent on my friends for happiness, instead of letting God give me joy. So I had to change.

Living a life dependent on God and realizing who you are

in Him changes you completely. I stopped wearing my homey clothes and went out shopping. I stopped trying to stay in the safe zone with my outfits and even my makeup. *Modesty* was a word that'd been hammered into my head since childhood, but I stopped letting it shackle me when God reminded me that He looks at our hearts. That modesty is a *lifestyle*, not a fashion statement. You can be immodest in a long dress just as much as a short one. So, I bought new clothes, bright clothes, spunky clothes. And I bought some daring lashes, just to try them.

I stopped comparing myself to everyone around me and even got a gym membership. Now my body is starting to look the way I've always wanted it to look. At first, I tried to drown myself with work, but when I took my troubles to God, He came in, pouring His love out and comforting me. He brought me a resounding peace that never leaves me.

I really found out who God was in those dark days, and I've come to understand exactly what Romans chapter five and verse five meant that Pastor Izzy explained. Those tribulations bring you patience and endurance, and from there, experience and character, which bleeds into hope. The smoothing process was not easy, the storm was uncomfortable, and I know there's still so much for me to experience, but I've made it out of this storm and I'm moving forward. I don't think I could be who I am right now if I hadn't lost everything I once had.

Seeing Juanita and Carlos together doesn't bother me anymore. I only notice them when Carlos looks distant. His eyes sometimes won't reach Juanita's though she's blabbing and smiling at him. Other days, I catch him glancing off at

197

nothing, wondering about things he doesn't have the answer to. Sometimes, I want to say something, to tap on the glass and catch his attention, but I don't. The distance I've created between us is good. We're able to work together as a team without infiltrating each other's business and personal space. Though, it's been harder to work with Juanita since I've stopped living in her shadows.

Juanita has always been beautiful. Skin like the night's sky, and a face that glowed like the stars were locked inside of her. She was always a wonder to admire, and I loved being her friend. I loved seeing her smile and the confidence she wore despite the kickback she received for wearing bright colors against her dark skin. Juanita was a great girl, but she was a jealous girl. She was cold and selfish on the inside, you just didn't know it because of her betrayingly kind smile. But now I know the true Juanita, and I know the true Carlos, too. Because Juanita wasn't in bed with herself. Carlos played a role in their sin. In their immodesty. All his life, he always played background to Juanita and me, but I have not overlooked him. I haven't forgotten the part he played in all of this.

People who are quiet and meek tend to drift to the back of the crowd. That was Carlos. He was handsome but quiet, never brandished his good looks, always choosing to let Juanita and me shine. He used his kindness to reel me and over time he showed me how kind he really was.

Through it all, I don't think Carlos was the sort of person Juanita turned out to be. She was jealous, but he was dangerous. Dangerous because it's impossible to know what

198

he is truly capable of. He was dangerous because Carlos is the guy who brings his own cards to play. He shuffles them, and deals them, knowing ahead of time how the game will go because he doesn't play fair. Carlos knew that I liked him. He liked me too. But he chose to sleep with Juanita. Not just once, but for two months straight, and however long it's been since then. Maybe it started as an accident, but whatever it is now is not so accidental.

Shaking my thoughts away, I gathered my things from my office and stepped out. Momo, my secretary, was there with a mask on. "Momo? You alright?" I asked as I pulled my door shut and locked it.

"Feeling a little under the weather, but I'm fine." She waved. "I came to ask for the shopping limit for our youth event. I was going to start putting in some orders for the prizes."

Momo looked tired. She had dark circles around her eyes that were half lidded from exhaustion. Her voice sounded like it too. She sniffled, waiting for my answer and I sighed.

"I'm not doing much today, so I'll go shopping for you."

"Oh no, Ms. King, you have plenty to do. Please don't worry about me. I'll be fine."

"I am worried about you, Momo. Go home." I patted her shoulder. "And take some days off. I'll be able to handle myself for the rest of the week. We don't have too much going on."

Momo looked crossed, just her brows coming together above her mask.

"I'll be fine. You go."

"I'm sorry, Ms. King."

"Don't be." I fanned. "I'll see you Monday."

She nodded. "Thank you."

I waited for her to leave before going back into my office and printing the email she sent for me to approve of the prizes. It wasn't going to be too difficult. A gaming system, a snowboard, bicycles, and other small prizes for the gaming part of the night.

I studied the list as I made my way through Brooklyn. I felt kind of bad for Momo. She had to get all these things herself. Not that she minded. Monique Willis was a hard worker. She joined our team three years ago when I was seriously overwhelmed, and she's been the glove to my hand ever since. She takes care of everything I can't, and when we need small jobs done, she's always willing to do it. I'm not surprised she got sick since we've been working overtime after we lost the sponsorship and then gained it back. Planning events and keeping the charity running was always a full day's work and more.

I stepped into the first store and found some knickknacks that were perfect for kids. Small toys, retro things, anything small enough to put in a kid's hand and keep them occupied. For the older kids, we were thinking about gift cards. Thankfully, Momo had already put the gift card orders in as well as the Bible orders. We'd be giving them out for free at our event. Once I found a snowboard and gaming system (I knew where to go to get bikes), all I'd need to do was visit the printing store to put in our order for flyers.

200

I checked my watch as I stepped out onto the curb, it was already six and I hadn't eaten yet. Lunch was at noon, so I was feeling atrociously hungry. But I was close to the printing shop, so instead of hitting that place last, it was best to go now.

Strolling along, I pushed open the door to the printing shop and stepped inside. The place was quiet, a few people standing at kiosks, a few workers in red shirts walking by and nodding at me. I smiled back, reading each sign to find where I could put in an order. Clutching my strap, I shuffled forward, crashing right into a very firm chest.

I stumbled back. "Sorry, I didn't…" I stopped as tall man leaned down and retrieved his phone. When he stood, I was met with the eyes of my sponsor. "Mr. Blue?"

He raised a dark brow before submitting to a nod of recognition. "Ms. King, I didn't see you there."

"Sorry," I muttered. "I was reading all the signs, and I wasn't paying attention." The smell of his cologne invaded my nostrils in a dizzying sensation. I was breathing in a woody and earthy smell. But it was so expensive, it smelled like what I believed the earth probably smelled like when God first created it. Fresh pine and wood, as if someone dug deep to find the roots of the biggest pine tree ever and dusted it on his shoulders. When the ground was still healthy, and corruption had not reached the earth, that's what Mr. Blue smelled like.

"It was my fault, actually." He pressed a hand to his chest, a vein ran from his finger across his hand to hide beneath a silver watch against his navy suit. It looked expensive, like they threaded the material around his broad shoulders and tight

201

frame. Looking at his hand on his chest, I hadn't forgotten how firm the guy was, or that his hand had held mine and kissed it. Hudson Blue was something to wonder about. Not that I was wondering. I can admit that after the kiss to my hand, he'd been a thought in passing, but it's been a while, and that memory was suddenly replaying in my head. Forced out of the grave I'd buried it in.

His voice snapped my attention back to him as he continued. "I was staring at my phone, something about a pickup order." He shook his head. "I don't know why Lolita couldn't get this today."

"Maybe she's sick," I offered. When he looked up with a question on his face, I shrugged. "My secretary's sick."

"Oh. I'm sorry."

"She'll be fine, she's just overworked."

He nodded. "Lolita sent a detailed email, but it was too long. I just saw the note she had in bold at the end, for me to grab the paperwork because I had to sign it myself."

"What's the point in being a billionaire if you've still got to do your own work?"

Mr. Blue's stiff expression warmed slowly as he let out a little laugh. "I absolutely agree."

I chuckled, shifting my weight from one foot to the other. "Well, Mr. Blue, I've got to figure out how to place a printing order fast or I'll die of starvation."

He laughed again. "Are you…" his voice trailed into a whisper, and I watched as he raised his fist to his mouth, clearing his throat. "Are you hungry?"

"Oh ... Yeah." I glanced away. "I wasn't trying to coerce you into dinner or anything, I was just saying that because I ... am hungry."

We blinked at each other until we both began to laugh.

"I think I just made things worse. You only asked if I was hungry, and I assumed you were asking me on a date." The laughter turned to embarrassment in a heartbeat, and I was covering my face now. "Oh goodness, I am so embarrassed."

"Don't be." Hudson rubbed the back of his head, mussing his wavy hair. "I *was* asking you out." He gave me a grand smile and a bob of his head. He hardly ever did that from the few times we'd met. Mr. Blue scowled a lot, but as he looked at me now, I only saw joy on his face. And confidence. His face was smooth, skin as pure and creamy as milk, not quite as pale though. Hudson had an olive tone that went well with his green eyes and dark hair.

"I was asking you to dinner," he said again, just to clarify.

Now my hand was on my chest. "Really? Why?"

His brows slanted downward, like he didn't really know why he'd asked me either. But he gave a good excuse. "I think I owe you for the hard time I put you through before."

An awkward silence wrestled between us as I shifted again, and he slipped a hand into his pocket. I couldn't leave him there in silence, so I nodded.

"Ok, but you don't owe me."

"I won't owe you after this."

A half smile took over as I clutched the straps to my purse. "Ok."

"I'll wait in the car for you."

I watched him leave, enjoying the way his shoulders moved in a rhythmic dance, wavering from left to right.

After placing my order, I stepped out of the printing shop to find Hudson's shiny black car out front. I knew it was a sports car but to me it only looked like a bug with red lights along the bottom.

Mr. Blue stepped from the car, coming around to open my door for me.

"I could've gotten that," I said.

He waved me off. "It's fine."

"Where do you want to go?" he asked once I slid into my seat.

"It doesn't matter."

"Where were you going to go if we hadn't bumped into each other?"

"Well, I was going to this small place for some Greek food, but I knew by the time the bus came I'd have a change heart." I didn't tell him why my heart changed. He didn't need to know that my wallet was empty so a mustard cabbage wrap with day old rice in the back of my fridge would've been for dinner until I got paid.

"Greek food?" Hudson repeated. "I know a place."

"Ok." I sneaked a glance at him. He looked calm, like he was totally in control of this situation, and I was just a girl in his car. I didn't really need to look at the situation that way, but this was a new side of Mr. Blue I'd never seen before. I didn't know what to make of any of this. Maybe he was always a gentleman, or maybe not. Maybe he'd changed too.

"Mr. Blue?"

He looked over at me as we slowed to a light. "You can call me Hudson."

"Right, sorry. Hudson," I said slowly, "why do you drive your own car?"

He snorted and leaned his head back to laugh. My eyes traced down his square jaw that was stubbled with a little facial hair, to his neck, where a thick apple bobbed as he swallowed. "My arms didn't fall off once I became a billionaire, you know."

I laughed, covering my mouth and exhaling my nerves.

"I like driving," he said. "So I do it as often as I can."

"I haven't driven anywhere in six years."

"Really?"

"I take the bus everywhere I go."

He looked at me in horror, glancing down my frame to see my feet. "You take the bus in those heels?"

"I march all across New York City in my heels."

He seemed impressed, a grin—not a smile—etched onto his face as his eyes slowly dragged up my frame. I felt naked, like he was looking at parts of me he shouldn't. When his eyes finally met mine, I blinked away at the building in front of us. It was a swanky little blue place that didn't look too fancy, which was good for me.

"Is this the place?"

He looked ahead and then back at me. "No," he pointed over my shoulder, "that's the place."

205

A huge black building, shining and glistening in the evening city lights that had big white letters that read, *Greekings!* waited for us. Suddenly, I felt out of place, and I couldn't help but squirm in my seat.

"We're going there?"

"Yeah. Best Greek in the city."

I gulped.

"Come on, let's go," he said, and I listened without hesitation.

What else was I supposed to do?

20

Hudson Blue

Truthfully, I have no idea why I asked Jonah to dinner with me. She was smiling and laughing and just like that, we shared a perfect moment together. A moment free of judgement or demand. I wanted to preserve that moment because that was only the second time I'd seen Jonah and didn't feel agitated.

Since we agreed to start over, whenever Jonah or her charity was brought up around the office, I didn't feel angered or annoyed. Something's been rewired in me since I've started trying to be a better Christian. My faith was still a secret, but I could proudly say I felt the changes within me pouring into the rest of my life.

Jonah looked nervous as the servers rearranged tables for us to have private dining. She watched through her brown marbles, taking in everything in wide-eyed blinks. I was certain this wasn't the first time anyone's rearranged tables for her, but I was also certain she wasn't expecting to dine privately with me. There was no other way to dine. I wasn't purposely making it private or romantic. I couldn't afford word getting back to my father about this, though it wouldn't be terrible since she's the charity leader.

In fact, this might look really good for our company. The president of Blue Barn out to dinner with the founder of the My Fellow American Project; it would make things look like we were off to a better start than before. Even though this little dinner was strictly for me, I at least wouldn't receive any flack about it.

When the waiter finished, he offered us our seats and we sat across from each other at the dark table under soft lights that mimicked the glow of a fire. Jonah was radiant and nervous. She was a beautiful woman, and the fiery orange glow around her made her look stunning.

I passed her a menu, and she thanked me. We sat in silence for a few minutes, just reading over the menu, until a waiter came over.

"Can I get you guys started with anything?"

"I'm not ready yet. Jonah?"

She shook her head. "There's a lot to look at."

The waiter nodded and turned away.

"Have you looked at the drinks?" I asked.

"I have, but I can't decide what I want."

"Do you want wine?"

She peeked up from her menu, voice a soft whisper. "No, thank you."

"Oh, right. Me either." I lifted my menu. I forgot I'd

changed.

"I wasn't trying to stop you from ordering it."

I lowered my menu and sighed. "I'm trying to get away from alcohol, too."

"Diet?"

"Lifestyle change."

She smiled like she was proud of me. I could mention that the lifestyle change was not the one she was thinking, but I didn't think the conversation called for that. And I wasn't sure if I could say that out loud. Dad had never mentioned anything about religion during my childhood, but he also never seemed offended by it, either. Despite that, I knew we certainly were not Christians or anything else. My father attended church services for the papers. He's been photographed at Easter and Christmas services, but that's it. I don't think he would be upset if I told him I'd converted unless it somehow interfered with Blue Barn or made us look bad. Still ... I wasn't ready to share that part of me yet.

"Have you made any lifestyle changes?" I asked Jonah. The look on her face made me drop my gaze to my menu. "Sorry, that was weird to ask."

Jonah melted into laughter. She'd been wearing a very serious expression before, but now she seemed relaxed. Her smile was wide, and her eyes were glowing in the low light. Brown skin, even in color, smooth in texture. Jonah always knocked me off my feet whenever I saw her. Her curls were pinned up in a ponytail, and some hung loose around her shoulders and face. I noticed the gold bracelet that rolled down her thin wrist, sliding right into her folded white sleeve. There were charms on it, a cross, a dumbbell, and two flat circles, but I couldn't tell what they were.

"I think I've changed a lot," she said finally.

"It seems like it hasn't been a good change."

Her smile didn't return, in fact, her eyes grew more distant as she looked off. Memories swirled behind her vacant stare, and I wondered what she was thinking.

"The change was good." Her eyes cut to mine and I took a deep breath to cool myself. "But the circumstances that brought the change weren't good."

"I understand." I wanted to pry but Jonah was miles away from the dinner table, lost in her memories. I needed to bring her back somehow. "I think the Greek salad will make up for those circumstances."

Jonah blinked, and I thought she was going to tell me not to joke around about something serious because I was scolding myself internally. But she hunched forward, dropping her head to laugh. "Who knew Hudson Blue was funny?"

I shrugged, feeling relieved. "I'm not usually like this, so this is our secret." I winked at her, and her lips parted just a little bit in surprise.

"Well, as long as this secret stays ours, I'll keep it."

"My comedy is forever reserved for you, Ms. King."

She giggled and then nibbled her lower lip, gazing at me through the low lights. It wasn't sultry, it wasn't seductive. Jonah was simply looking at me, an air of confusion surrounding her.

"Who are you, really?" she asked. "Who is Hudson Blue?"

My eyes could no longer meet hers as I stared down at the onyx table where our menus sat discarded now. "I ... I don't know."

"I think that's a good answer for someone making a lifestyle change."

I looked up. "Really?"

"Of course. You've got to figure out who you are now, and how to be different from who you used to be. It takes practice. Trust me."

"I take it that you know who you are?"

"I'm learning who the new Jonah King is."

"Do you like her?"

Jonah raised her chin and straightened her back. "I love her. I think everyone will, too, once they get to know me."

"Even me?"

She hesitated. "I don't see why not. We may have started off on the wrong foot, but that's why God gave us two. So that when one foot trips, the other comes down to take a step in the right direction, stabilizing everything."

"He also gave us a path to follow."

Jonah's eyes widened. "I didn't know you believed."

Crap. I wasn't supposed to let that out. But I guess telling Jonah was fine. "Yeah, after the conversation at the diner, I started trying to be different."

She folded her arms. "No way."

"I don't know if I should feel offended by how shocked you are."

211

"I'm not shocked. I'm happy. I'm *really* happy for you, Hudson. God is the best way to make a real change. He's the *only* way."

"I'm learning that I can't do it on my own."

"Well, I'm always here, too," she offered herself to me without a thought, but if she knew that I was willing to forsake God to take her home and enjoy every inch of her, she'd shriek and curse me to hell. And then she'd recant that statement. But I'm changing. Slowly. I'm trying to enjoy other things and trying not to want *those* things. At least not all the time.

"I appreciate that," I said honestly.

The mood between us changed for the rest of the evening. Jonah was more open, laughing and telling me things about the charity, like the way it started. She told me how she'd lost her dad and basically lost her mom, too. I retold the tales of my mother, and how Erma had always been there for me in her stead. Literally. It was Erma who found me that day when I passed out in front of the diner. She was running errands and spotted me in the crowd. She was coming up to me when I dropped to the ground and didn't wake up until I got home.

Jonah loved the stories of Erma. She said Erma seemed like a wonderful woman. She really was. But recalling all of those stories brought back memories of Macey and brought back those thoughts my father had been planting in my head for so long. All the lies he'd told.

When I was with Macey, I was always myself. She remembered who I was for me and always pulled out the real Hudson Blue. Now, it seemed like Jonah King would be doing

212

the same. If not forever, then at least over these last few months we had together. She'll bring back the me I used to be, the me I've always been but has been buried beneath the gravel of Olan Blue and Blue Barn. I liked who I was when I was with Jonah, and I liked Jonah.

∧ ∧ ∧

"Well, Hudson, dinner was great," she said once it was over. I'd given her a ride home and walked her to the front doors of her apartment building. "I really appreciate you taking me out today."

"The pleasure was all mine."

She looked at me, wide eyed, undoubtedly remembering the first time I told her the pleasure of starting over was mine. I kissed her hand that day, and Ms. King was a nervous wreck until we reached the cafeteria with the others, then she was a charity leader all over again.

"I guess I should go now," she said softly, eyes dropping to her hands.

"Is something wrong?"

She shook her head. "Sometimes going into that building feels like a chore."

"Is it the stairs? They don't have an elevator?" I leaned back to take in the height of the building. It wasn't that tall, but it should've had an elevator since it wasn't too old.

"It's not the building; it's the people inside."

"Neighbors?"

"Something like that."

My eyes fell to her, and I reached out and took a chance, placing a hand on hers. "You sure you're okay?"

She bit her lip and shook her head. I watched as her shoulders began to tremble, and her small frame hunched over. But it was her hand moving in mine to take hold of it that made my heart race. She was clutching me as her tears fell.

"I'm supposed to be strong. But every day I walk into work, or I walk into my apartment building, and they're there. Smiling and happy. While I'm still putting myself together." Frantically, she wiped her tears. "I'm sorry. You don't need to be burdened with all this."

"No," I squeezed her hand, "you're not burdening me at all, Jonah."

When her red and glossy eyes finally looked over at me, I had to beg God to keep me from flinching away. Not because she was hideous when she cried—which she wasn't—but because Jonah looked just like Macey the day she realized she would never be more than a secret. Tears of betrayal while a raging storm of all kinds of emotions continued to brew.

"Jonah," I whispered, feeling my heart clench with a bitter grip, "I'm so sorry."

Her tears fell more rapidly after my apology. She tried to wipe them away, smudging black liner across her cheeks, but she couldn't fight what she'd been feeling, what she was *still* battling. There are always good days and bad days; days where you believe nothing can break your trust in God, and then there are days like this when everything is unclear and you're wondering if God still hears you. I've been struggling the same way Jonah has, yet I would've never known that if she hadn't broken down in front of me.

Despite her own problems, Jonah was eager to help me. Despite the pain that's rioting through her frame, the pain she's been covering up, Jonah cared about me. The same guy who was a jerk to her.

She took a stilling breath. "Sorry I broke down like that."

I looked at our hands, her fingers still interlaced with mine. I don't know why she held onto me tonight, but I was thankful. Maybe she felt like she'd float away, maybe my hand was just there at the right time. But I wouldn't ignore the way her hand felt, interlaced with mine in this intimate moment.

I lifted her hand to my lips and kissed it. "Thank you, Jonah, for caring for me even while you're hurting."

Her brows lowered as she sighed. "I wish I hadn't broken down, then you'd never know."

"I'm glad I do know. It makes it easier to believe. Knowing that your strength comes from God gives me hope that one day, even when I'm hurting, I can still help others."

Jonah finally smiled. "Until that day comes, no matter what, I'll still be there for you. Running eyeliner and all."

I snorted and she laughed, wiping at her eyes. I felt her hand tug in mine, like she wanted to break free. But I clutched onto her delicate hand just a second longer to ask, "Are you sure you'll be okay to go in?"

"I'm sure."

I nodded, finally releasing her hand. Her warmth resonated

in my palm, making me miss her nearness.

Jonah sighed. "Thanks again for today."

"No, Jonah, thank you."

She grinned and leaned toward me, her voice dropping to a whisper. "The pleasure was all mine."

I chuckled as I leaned forward too, my voice equally quiet. "No kiss to go along with it, then?"

Jonah's eyes dropped to my lips, and I felt my heart hammering so hard in my chest I had to hold in a cough in fear of ruining the moment. I didn't even mean to say that. I was supposed to say something funny, not something seductive... What was wrong with me?

She leaned forward, smudged eyeliner and all, but there was a calming look in her eyes. "Good night, Mr. Blue."

With that, she pressed her lips against my cheek, and I felt every hair on my body stand as my ears caught fire. I closed my eyes as the sweetest sensation tingled in my cheek, a warmth blooming from her gentle kiss. When she pulled away, I was lost for words. I was left with the scent of her perfume, subtle but lingering, as flowers and fruit intermingled in a dance for dominance. I blinked at her. She didn't suck my face off; she didn't get undressed, and she didn't do anything sensuous. Jonah King kissed my cheek with her runny makeup, and sweet perfume, and it made me feel like a ten-year-old boy getting his first kiss from a girl.

Jonah King was going to change me, even if I wasn't ready for it.

21

Jonah King

I don't know why I broke down in front of Hudson last week. The nerves I'd been fighting all night, paired with the reality of the night ending, made me feel overwhelmed. I'd had such a great time, and then it was over, and I'd realized the unexpected bubble of joy I'd been in had threatened to be pop once the date was through.

No matter how good I felt, there were days when seeing Juanita and Carlos together made my shoulders slump and my lips drag into a frown. Some days, I even cried about it. It was hard watching someone else be happy, and then when you are happy, you're in the oddest situation with the only person in the world who shouldn't make you happy. Life was so strange because God was mysterious.

He did things out of the ordinary because there was no such thing as ordinary with Him. God was always going to be God, just and fair and good. His ways were higher than our ways; He made the foolishness of the world the most practical and sensible thing to Him and in His Kingdom. Which was why Hudson asking me out to dinner and me kissing him goodnight after breaking down was only something God would've done. Because He wanted to show me something, He wanted me to see that tangible substance we call Faith.

Hudson said it, I thought as I swirled my finger around the rim of my glass of ice water. The morning sun just barely peeked over the clouds to break the blue hue that washed over the city. I smiled as I recalled Hudson telling me that knowing my strength came from God pushed him to go further. *Pastor Izzy will flip when I tell him.* The little thought of Israel made me giggle before throwing my head back to drink the rest of my water and get ready for work. The youth event was tonight, so we only had half a day, but none of that bothered me. I was so nervous to see Hudson again because our dinner has been seared into my mind. Playing repeatedly right before bed.

"I need to get out more," I complained as I used my fingers to detangle my curls. "One little dinner shouldn't have you up in arms, Jonah."

Today, I'd wear my curls partially braided, and partially loose in one of my favorite Ethiopian styles. I divided the front of my hair from the back of it. The back was going to be loose and curly, while the top of my hair would have different sized braids. Nine, to be exact. Two long braids that hung right in front of my ears, dragging down and over my chest. Then I divided the rest of the hair that was left into three chunky braids, one on either side of my head, and one down the

219

middle, with four microbraids in between each chunky one.

When I finally finished my hair, all thoughts of Hudson had been lost, and I was rushing down the streets of Brooklyn to the office. Shoving open the doors, Jess greeted me at the front desk, passing me a folder to check over everything for the event today.

"The event meeting will start in five minutes," she said.

"Take my coat to my office for me. I've got everything else on my phone." She nodded as she came around the desk to grab my things. "And Jess, tell Momo to bring me a black coffee. Dark roast, with two shots of espresso."

"Yes, ma'am."

I headed down the hall of the first floor to one of our meeting rooms. As I stepped inside, I spotted Juanita and Carlos in the corner of the room laughing together. I dragged my eyes from them and looked at the rest of the committee. Everyone looked angsty and eager to get going, which put a smile on my face.

"Good morning, everyone," I said over the murmuring. The group took their seats, Juanita and Carlos made their way to stand beside me. "Tonight is our youth event, and I'm really thankful for everyone's hard work. Just one more night and we get to relax."

The room cheered and clapped.

"So, let's go over some things for tonight."

"Excuse me, Ms. King?"

I looked over my shoulder to find Momo standing in the doorway with my black coffee. I could smell it from seven feet away. "Come on in." I waved her over.

"Um, I don't think Blue Barn got the memo to arrive at noon."

"What do you mean?"

In walked Hudson Blue, or should I say, in *glided* Hudson Blue. His feet never touched the floor as he stepped inside wearing a dark suit and a crisp white shirt.

I cleared my throat. "Oh, good morning."

He smiled. "Good morning, Ms. King." Then he turned to everyone else and nodded. I didn't have to look around the room to know that everyone just picked up on Hudson's point of addressing me and no one else.

"We were just getting ready to discuss things for tonight."

"I brought a crew with me, as promised."

"You're here to help, too?"

He shrugged. "I was just going to supervise."

I felt my cheeks burning as I smiled. Hudson returned one to me as his crew filed in behind him. He checked over his shoulder, stepping forward right into my personal space to get out of their way. With his eyes on me, I felt my mouth go dry.

"I didn't mean to interrupt," he said.

"It's okay. I'm glad you're here." I paused and corrected myself. "I mean, I'm glad Blue Barn as a whole is here. I'm not mad that you're here. I'm glad you came too, Hudson."

"I'm glad I came too." He winked, turning away to find a seat in the back of the room.

Swallowing thickly, I turned back to the crowd who were all chatting with the Blue Barn folks. Thankfully, they hadn't

221

paid Hudson and me any attention. Well, the crowd hadn't but when I looked over at Juanita and Carlos, both of them had eyes the size of the moon. One looked saddened, the other was fuming.

Peeling my vision from them, I cleared my throat and caught everyone's attention, including Hudson. He sat in the very back, casually resting against the back of his chair, his eyes only on me.

"We were about go over the event details, but I'd like to first say thank you to everyone at Blue Barn for joining us today. We really appreciate your contributions."

Juanita stepped forward. "Especially you, Mr. Blue. This wouldn't be possible without you and all your hard work."

My eyes were glued to the side of Juanita's head. Did she really just insert herself? Was I seeing things or was Juanita vying for Hudson's attention all of a sudden?

I took a look at Carlos who appeared as confused as I felt, and I knew we were on the same page. When he caught my eye, he gave me a small chuckle with a raised shoulder. It was the first communication we'd had in months, and it wasn't bad. I gave him a half smile, lifting my shoulder too.

"Actually, you should be thanking Ms. King," Hudson said my name and I glanced back out to find him. When our eyes locked, he said, "She's really passionate about this, which moved me and Blue Barn."

Juanita turned to me, a disgusted look hidden behind her plastered smile. "Of course, Ms. King is everyone's favorite."

Ouch.

"Now, now," I returned to the crowd, "we should really give *God* the glory. He brought us all together to do something impactful for the community. To do His will. So, let's do it."

The crowd burst into clapping and cheering, and I felt my heart stirring with joy. I ignored the rays of heat burning my left side as Juanita stared me down, and I let my eyes trail through the crowd to find Mr. Blue in the corner clapping.

Since Blue Barn came early, we were able to get set up ahead of schedule. Hudson and I spent most of our time supervising, chatting with each other and talking about the event. We kept it professional in a room full of people, and I was thankful. Because I caught Juanita more than three times glancing over at us, watching us carefully.

As the event rolled around, Hudson and I got separated. I was busy entertaining the youth and giving speeches while Hudson stayed at a table, talking to interested parties about Blue Barn. Most of the parties were single mothers who turned flush red whenever Hudson smiled. I did too, well as red as my brown skin could get.

As I chatted with a group, I recognized a woman in the crowd. She smiled when I spotted her and came right up to me.

"Pastor Anne Marie!" I embraced her. She was the pastor of my church here, Fire Baptized Ministries.

"I told you I'd try to make it." She beamed at me.

"I'm so glad you did!"

"You guys did a fine job." She looked around, brown eyes

223

sweeping the small gym with an approving nod. "I'm really proud of how far everyone has come."

"Thank you, Pastor, but it's all God and your prayers."

She laughed, her lovely voice was strong and womanly, something I wished I had. "We're all in this together. Which is why I brought along a few guests." She pointed over her shoulder to a short woman with a round belly, and a tall older man.

"Rashonda! Erik!" They were a couple who'd been taking classes at the Project for a while now. Both of them turned as I shouted and waved. Shon would've run over, but her pregnancy only allowed her to waddle quickly as Erik came behind her. "Thanks for coming," I said as I squeezed Shon. Her belly kept us pretty far apart, so I really only squeezed her shoulders.

"We were happy to come. Jeremiah won a bike at the raffle. We're more excited than he is!"

"I'm gonna teach him to ride it," Erik said. He was a tall man, laced with thick muscles and a rugged frame. His husky voice matched his salt and pepper hair and beard. Shon and Erik were years apart and worlds apart. He was a trucker, and she was a language specialist at a college. Jeremiah, Shon's eldest son, was her replica with brown skin and thick hair. She married Erik five years ago at the church, and Erik adopted Jeremiah since his father had passed on. I wonder what their child together will look like.

"Jeremiah will love the bike," I said.

We all laughed. Jeremiah was a rambunctious kid with tons

of energy. Bike riding would definitely give them a much-needed break.

"Excuse me?"

I looked over my shoulder to find Hudson. He looked apologetic as he said, "I don't mean to interrupt, Ms. King, but I think they're about to wrap things up."

"Oh." I nodded. "I'll be right there."

Hudson smiled, but Pastor Anne Marie said, "Excuse me, young man. You're Hudson Blue, correct?"

"I am." Hudson extended his hand, and Pastor Anne shook it.

"I see why God sent me here today. You need a church, but you're not sure where to find one."

Hudson was still holding her hand, frozen in place with wide eyes. "Uh…" He cleared his throat and finally let her hand go. "Yeah. That's absolutely true."

"Fire Baptized Ministries is on the outskirts of Brooklyn," Pastor told him. "You come on by this weekend, understand?"

"Yes, ma'am."

Pastor Anne smiled, and her eyes slid to me. "Ms. King will be there, too."

"You two should come together." Erik lifted his eyebrows and grinned.

I shot him a look, but he didn't see it because Shon was giving him a dirty look which he was busy sinking away from.

Thanks, Shon, I smiled inwardly.

"Well, let's all head to the stage so I can close the event." I turned to my pastor. "Pastor Anne, will you say a prayer to end

225

the night?"

"Of course. I'd be honored."

22

Hudson Blue

I checked my watch as I bit into my toast, although I wasn't hungry because my stomach was pumped full of nerves. Pastor Anne Marie issued me an invitation—more like a command—to come to her church today. In the moment, I'd been amazed that she knew I was looking for a church. She didn't mention *why* I was searching for a church, but I knew the only way she'd found out was because God told her. I hadn't even told *Jonah*.

In my stupor, I agreed to come to her church. I wasn't against it, I just hadn't expected the invite. I didn't want to be rude in front of everyone, especially Jonah, who was rooting for my conversion.

Dusting crumbs from my hands, I smoothed my tie against my lavender shirt. I didn't want to wear black and white again, and I figured everyone else would probably be dressed in colorful attire since spring had arrived. I just hoped I wasn't too flashy and gave off the wrong impression.

With a sigh, I raised my glass of cranberry juice when my father crossed the threshold into the dining room. He looked scruffy, his white beard needed a trim, and his short hair was getting long now. He was looking for a new barber since he fired his last one after finding out he was cutting hair for one of our rivals. Scratching his beard, my father came over to me, his long blue robe brushing the floor while his silk pajamas covered his leather, fur trimmed slippers.

"Morning," I said.

"Morning, Hudson," he grunted, looking me over.

"Everything alright?"

"I heard you went early to that charity event. Stayed all day. Missed a full day of work."

"Yeah, we promised to send extra help."

His cold expression didn't change. "Extra help doesn't mean you have to go there yourself."

"I'm just trying to make the company look good, Dad."

"Who are you trying to convince?"

I squinted and my father picked up my toast from my plate and bit into it. He munched in silence, keeping his eyes locked with mine until he swallowed. "You better make this company look good and nothing less than that." He didn't wait for an answer. He took his leave without muttering another word to me.

Working my tongue over my teeth, I stood and rang the table's bell for someone to come clear it before leaving. I tried to act natural, nodding at the maids who gave me their greetings, even though I was bursting with anxiety inside. I

228

slipped into my room and kicked the door shut behind me. As soon as I was alone, I rushed into my bathroom, grabbed the edge of the sink, and took a deep breath.

Dad was on to me. He was not going to let Blue Barn go down the drain because I had developed a crush. But it didn't have to go down the drain. Jonah was a wonderful woman, a strong woman. But that didn't matter. It didn't matter that her charity was successful or that it actually provided help for the community. So long as she was poor and from a common family, my father would never accept her. No one in our pool of associates would. In our world, maintaining connections was far more important than love. Maintaining partnerships has kept this society we've built alive and private. I could not only wreck Blue Barn with bringing Jonah in, but everyone else too.

Our partnerships would die right along with us, because of their association to Blue Barn, which was why my father was always so particular about the women I saw. About decisions I made. He was firm in how he raised me, and taught me the essential principles to be successful in this arena, but his strict teaching forced me to explore the reasonings *behind* his strictness. I wanted to know why he insisted on holding true to his elitism. I wanted to know why he believed success came in only one color.

Pressing a hand to the mirror, I stared at my green eyes. I hated them. I hated looking at myself and knowing that I was a *product*, not a son. Hated that for so long, all I've ever wanted was to be a son, but I didn't know it until then. Until God came

229

into my life and began ripping the blinds off every area in my life. It was the only way to face the truth.

Dragging my hand down the mirror, I dug into my pocket and pulled out my phone. I tapped Jeremy's number and fixed my white tie as I waited for him to answer.

"Hello?"

"Jeremy? Can you cover for me?"

"Sure, what for?"

"My dad's on my case."

"Why?"

I huffed. "Does my dad ever have a reason to be on anyone's case?"

Jeremy snorted on the other end of the phone. "You're right. Fine, I'll cover for you. I'll make up something good."

"Not outlandish," I warned.

"That'll cost you."

"What do you want?"

"I want to know why you need a coverup."

I paused. "I'm going to church."

He paused too. "Why?"

"I don't know. Everyone wants to get their life together at some point, right?"

"Yeah, after a midlife crisis. You're only thirty-one. You've got two or three decades before you need to start making decisions like that."

"You're literally an idiot." I shook my head. Jeremy was way too carefree.

"I'm just saying, but hey, I can't knock you. Better late than

230

never."

"Whatever, I just don't want my father to know because he isn't religious, and he'll immediately think something's wrong with the company." Because that's the only reason my father would ever turn to God.

"True again. Well, go have fun and then have drinks with me afterwards."

I frowned at my own reflection. "Jeremy, I'm going to *church*. That means I can't have drinks with you after. I'm changing."

"Goodness, then don't go."

"Goodbye." I hung up the phone with a huff and immediately checked my watch. If I didn't leave now, I'd be late.

∧ ∧ ∧

I walked into the church... late, of course. Traffic was slower than normal and by the time I arrived, Pastor Anne Marie was already standing at the silver podium with a flame on the front. I moved to an open seat in the back row. It was right by the door, so I could leave pretty quickly if things got too uncomfortable.

Pastor Anne was talking when I spotted Juanita. I wasn't expecting to see her today, or Carlos sitting beside her. Scanning the sanctuary again, I finally found Jonah. She was sitting across the room from Juanita and Carlos, which surprised me. I peeked over at the two of them and caught

231

Juanita glancing back at me. I looked away like an idiot, hoping she hadn't seen me eyeing Jonah. She probably saw me when I noisily thundered inside in a rush.

Clasping my hands in my lap, I held in a sigh so the man two seats away wouldn't hear me. *What am I doing here? Why am I trying to change? Is it all going to be worth it?*

"Yes," Pastor Anne said, and the entire room filled with light laughter. I looked around to find the joke, but Pastor Anne went on. "We are the temples of the Holy Spirit, and it's so important to remember that. Paul says in Galatians chapter two that *it is not I that lives in me, but Christ.* So, what does that mean?" She pulled the mic from the stand and walked across the stage. She was a short woman, a shade or two lighter than Jonah. Pastor Anne looked out at all of us, but it felt like she was just looking at me as she said, "We are the temple of the Holy Spirit. We house the Spirit of God. Christ lives in us through the Holy Spirit. Do you know how powerful that is?" She lifted a fist, tightening her lips as she shook her head. "We all remember when Jesus cleansed the temple, right? Matthew chapter twenty-one, verse twelve through thirteen," she paused, "write that down."

All I had was my phone. I was the idiot who came to church without a Bible. As one downloaded in the background, I typed out a note and jotted down the scripture she'd mentioned.

"Why is it so important that Jesus cleaned the temple? Because it was a replica for today. We willingly choose to sin, and Jesus comes in and cleans our temple. What we were supposed to regard as holy, we made it into a den of thieves. And what do thieves do? They don't just steal, they deceive, and plot evil. They're dishonest. That's what we become when we sin." Pastor Anne turned from her podium. "But when we're doing the righteous thing, and walking in the will of God, we begin to walk in Spirit and in Truth. And if you're walking in Truth, that means you're walking in Jesus, and you won't have to face the consequences of not walking in the Truth." She turned a few pages in her Bible. "See, we think we can just ignore the right thing to do but we can't. Because Truth is literally living inside of us. Jesus resides in us, which means we have to face the Truth every day. There is never a moment when we don't face the Truth, unless you're not saved. And even then, the Truth is still given to you with the option for you to choose Him."

I stayed still, staring at Pastor Anne. She was talking about facing the truth, the very same thing Jesus told me. I hadn't faced the truth in all these years; the bloodline of the Blues is full of racism, elitism, and disregard for the poor. We've been this way all our lives, hiding as ghosts in the system so it could operate the way we wanted it to. But we've been wrong, and I've known it for years. I just chose to follow suit, to turn my head away from the truth. I chose not to face the truth because I thought it'd be easier. But my life has been anything but. Hiding my feelings and my curiosity. Becoming someone I knew I never was, what part of that is easy? None of it, but I thought it was better than being ousted and losing everything.

But there was one thing I had to learn, and it was that in

233

losing everything, you *gained* everything. There was something different about learning the truth and applying it. I knew that if I gave up life at Blue Barn, things would turn around, but that was unbearable. How could I depart from the very thing that claimed my existence? I lived and was groomed to sit in the seat I do now, as president of Blue Barn. What could I be without it?

"We can all be a lot of things." Pastor Anne had caught me off guard, speaking right into my swarming thoughts. "But when we are in Christ, we have an assignment. We think we have one now because we've got a good job or a bad job. We've got everything we want, or not at all, but we're working on an assignment. Let me ask you, is this assignment from God?"

I watched desperately as she thumbed the pages of her Bible again. The large screens on either side of the stage displayed the small woman who looked calm and unbothered by the large crowd before her.

"In the first letter Paul wrote to the Corinthians, he talked about something very important. He talked about the Body, after talks of the gifts given. We each are given gifts and talents. Each of which is used for the Kingdom. Then we jump down to verse twelve and we see Paul starts talking about the human body." She grabbed her glass of water and took a sip. "Each part of the body has an assignment, no matter how big or small we think it is. There's no part of the body that doesn't matter because each part represents one of us. What am I saying?" She opened her hands wide. "Each of us is important because God's assignment for us is for the bigger plan. So, if for a

234

second, you're in a position and you're thinking you're better than the next person, baby quit."

She slammed her hand on the podium and shouted, "Quit! Because Satan has you ensnared with pride! The Body of Christ is about servitude. We serve for a living, and we serve together. No one is better than the other person. Not by race, not by gender, not by assignment."

I gulped, feeling exposed right there in the back of the church. It felt like she was shouting at *me*, like the inner fight I'd been battling was silly because I knew all along that racism and elitism were wrong and all people were equal.

"You can be a toenail," she pointed into the crowd, "and you can be an arm, but you're both important! There's no one better than anyone. Why? Because we are not better than the master and we make up *His* body. So how are we better than Him if we are *in* Him? Does that even make sense? Your arm thinks it's better than you, the functioning thinking human."

The crowd laughed, and Pastor Anne gave us a big smile. "Jesus came as a common man, born with nothing so that those who have a lot will realize that in having nothing from the *world* you have everything. In having no possessions tied to the earth, you gain all the blessings of the spiritual realm, God's realm. But," she pointed back at herself, tapping her chest, "it starts with realizing we are temples of the Holy Spirit, and we must keep our temples clean. So that we can function with our talents and gifts in the Body of Christ. If you're always in and out with God, you're not doing your job, and someone's salvation is on the line because of you."

Immediately, I thought of what Jonah said all those months back in the diner. She told me she came to apologize to me because my salvation depended on it, and she didn't want to hinder me. I looked up, finding Jonah immediately. She was nodding along to the pastor, and then looking back down at the Bible and notepad in her lap. Jonah was learning for herself, but I was learning just from watching her. I wondered, as my attention went back to the pastor, if Jonah realized that she'd said the same thing Pastor Anne was saying now.

"When you're disobedient, you clog up the pipes. Because now God must go all the way around and find someone else to do *your* job. That's why God tells us to be patient! Trust Him even when it doesn't look like He's on the way. He is! One of your brothers or sisters just isn't doing their job." The crowd nodded, some laughed. "But you've got to make room for Him to bring what He's coming with. You think those people felt good getting beaten out the temple? No! They didn't like that. Because it doesn't feel good sometimes to surrender your will for God's will. It doesn't always feel good to face the truth. It doesn't feel good to get rid of your ways for God's ways." Pastor Anne lifted her hands, dropping her head back and pretending to cry. When she raised her head, she brought the microphone back to her lips and said, "That's how all of you look on Sunday morning, surrendering your will to God. Swearing it felt so good to just give it all up." She lowered the mic and frowned darkly at us, grunting as she stomped across the stage. The congregation laughed, but I was confused until

236

she stopped and chuckled along into the mic. "That's exactly how every one of you look at Bible study on Tuesday when you realize God's will is not a mansion and a cushy life. It's a cross we must pick up and bear! Not to say that you won't get those things, but when you realize you might not, your face is all twisted up. Forgetting that the cross must come before the crown."

Pastor Anne moved back to the podium, a long stretch of silence filled the room before she said, "But we do it. After we realize we need that cross, we pick it up, no matter what it takes, because our brothers and sisters all around us are depending on us to do the righteous things. The unsaved are depending on us so we can shine a light on them. And most of all, God is depending on us, because He hand-carved each of us perfectly for the assignment we've been given." She walked to the edge of the stage and pointed. I know she was pointing right at me. "Once you come face to face with the truth, there's no more running from your assignment. Do what needs to be done, so that God won't have to raise up another in your place. Just think if Moses hadn't been obedient. The Hebrews would've been slaves for who knows how much longer? What if Jesus decided in the Garden of Gethsemane to tell God that He had the wrong one for the cross?"

Everyone laughed. I did too.

"See, we are all faced with something difficult because Jesus was. But Jesus chose to die to His own will so that the will of the Father could be done. We must do the same because others are depending on you." Pastor Anne Marie raised her

237

hand. "That's my time. I've got to go. But if you've made the decision today to surrender your will to God, I want to warn you that it may not be easy, but it will be worth it if you trust Him. Can you do that?"

I closed my eyes and asked myself if I could do it. Could I let God lead the way in this? Could I walk away from Blue Barn? Could I expose the horrible things we've built our future on to the entire world? Even if I said yes, how would I even do that?

I will guide you.

God … You want me to do this?

I have called you for many things that begin here.

I felt my eyes begin to burn. *I'm scared to lose it all.*

Because eyes have not seen, nor ears heard all that I have in store for you.

Why can't You just show me?

What is faith if you know the outcome? It is better to believe in the unseen as many who have seen signs and wonders only believe because of what their eyes see. Not what My Spirit tells them.

So … I have to believe?

You have to obey Me.

Obeying You is believing in You because I would put my trust in You, right?

Yes.

How can I trust You if I've never done this before?

There are examples all around you, Hudson, that will strengthen your faith. If I tell you all that I have in store,

238

you will not believe Me.

I nodded. *Ok... I want to do this. Please help me. Don't leave me.*

I am with you always, My son.

His final words felt like He was right there, breathing His life into my veins, like my heart had restarted. But this time it beat to His rhythm, not my own.

After church, I lingered in the lobby but there were so many people, I doubted I'd find Jonah. Surrendering to my growling stomach, I turned to leave the church. The warm air greeted me as I stepped onto the blacktop outside, the sun beaming down on me. I didn't want to be like the people Pastor Anne had described as feeling relieved on Sunday and angry a few days later, but I couldn't help it. I genuinely felt renewed and uplifted as I got into my car. I hoped that feeling didn't fade.

I waited in traffic for what seemed like forever to get out of the parking lot when I spotted a familiar figure sitting at the bus stop. Jonah was writing in her notepad in a flesh pink dress and matching low heels. With her ankles crossed, and her head down looking at her notepad, Jonah looked as sweet as she was.

"Jonah!" I called out my window.

She looked up and brightened immediately as she waved. She was too kind for her own good, so I had to flag her over to get her to take a ride with me.

Settling into the car, Jonah squeaked out, "Hi, Hudson! I didn't know you came today."

"Yeah. I was, uh, late."

I felt her look me over, but I kept my eyes forward. "You were the late guy?"

"Yeah."

She laughed. "Goodness, Hudson. Of course you'd make an entrance. I'm not surprised."

"I didn't mean to."

Jonah shrugged. "I'm just glad you came. Did you like it?"

I nodded, feeling that peaceful feeling wash over me again. "I liked it a lot."

"Are you coming back next Sunday?"

"Most likely."

"Let's meetup next week and sit together."

I glanced over at Jonah, she was smiling up at me, and I couldn't bring myself to ask her why she wasn't sitting with Juanita and Carlos. It wasn't my place to ask anyway, no matter how curious I was.

"I'll pick you up," I said.

She blew air between her lips. "Don't worry about it. I don't mind public transportation."

"I kind of like picking you up." I squeezed the steering wheel, bracing myself for her response to the stupid thing I'd just said. But she surprised me.

"I thought I was a burden."

"No." I shook my head and looked over at her. Jonah wore a small smile that I was certain was meant for herself and not for me to see, so I looked off at the road, wearing my own smile.

"You're not a burden at all, Ms. King."

23

Jonah King

I gave Hudson my number after his first church service. I didn't think he'd use it for anything more than replying to our church meetup spot or just telling me that he was waiting downstairs whenever he'd pick me up for church. For two months, things were platonic. We were nothing more than two church going friends who happened to be working together. Then Hudson called me one day at work, out of the... *blue*. I thought something was wrong, so I picked up immediately, only for him to ask me to lunch. Then lunch turned to dinner. Then dinner turned to Saturday outings, and church together on Sunday. Now, I think I'm dating Mr. Blue.

"You think you're *dating* him?" Izzy said on the other end of the phone. I could tell he was doing something, probably in his office filing paperwork.

"I think so." I bit my nail as I stared at my reflection in the bathroom mirror. "We have another date today."

"Well, if you're calling it a date, then maybe you are dating."

"No." I shoved my palm to my forehead, regretting using the word I normally wouldn't allow myself to say. Hudson never said it either. Whenever he asked me out, he invited me places or to do things. He went grocery shopping with me once—that time I invited him. But only because I felt like I wasn't reciprocating. But I wouldn't need to reciprocate unless we were dating. No. All relationships, down to boring work relationships, required reciprocation for things to flow smoothly.

I dragged my palm down my face as I said, "We invite each other out."

"So, you've invited him places, too?"

"Is that wrong?"

"Not at all."

"So, then, what's wrong?"

"Do you ever pay for anything?"

I paused. "Well, I've offered, but Hudson doesn't want me to pay for anything." He always flashes his hefty wallet at me and makes a joke about buying whatever facility or restaurant we're at if I wanted it… if *I* wanted it? I shook my head, ignoring the implications Hudson had been leaving that I was oblivious to—until right now. Pastor Izzy always made things so plain.

"He doesn't want you to pay because he's just a nice guy who foots the bill or because he's a billionaire. Which one is is it?"

I pulled one shoulder up in a shrug before moving to the bathroom counter. I climbed onto it, saddling up close to the mirror as I stared blankly into the sink. "He always tells me he doesn't want me to pay for anything. He says it's not right."

"Does he say why?"

"He's joked that a man takes care of a lady. Or he'll say something chivalrous along those lines."

Izzy sighed and I buried my face into my knees that were pressed into my chest. "I think he's been dating the most oblivious woman in history."

"Izzy! How can you say that?"

"Jo-Jo, he's been sending subliminal messages and you've just bounced along, I'm sure with that pretty smile you're always flashing."

I raised my head and smiled at the mirror. My eyes had dark circles beneath them, and I needed to exfoliate pronto. My winning smile wasn't cutting it right now. Not to mention my curls were tied back in a loose satin wrap so they screamed like mad out the top. Shamefully turning away from the mirror, I rested my chin on my knees as I clutched the phone.

"Israel, do you really think we're dating?"

"Ask me what you really want to ask me."

I stammered. Israel saw right through me from the moment our conversation drifted to Hudson Blue. He knew I wasn't really asking if we were dating, though this conversation made the blurred lines clearer. However, I was really asking one simple question.

"Is it okay to date Hudson?"

"Rephrase that."

"To what?"

His voice rolled out as calm as morning waves. "Is it okay to be happy?"

I sucked in a breath and held it for a few seconds. On the release, I nodded. "I feel like it's so sudden that this shouldn't be happening. Like something's about to go wrong, and I should be preparing for that and not for happiness. I'm scared, Israel."

"Aww, my little Jonah. I knew this day would come when you'd find someone you liked. All the challenges you've gotten used to, so now you're uncertain if you should feel anything but hardship."

I sniffled, fighting tears as I said, "It's been hard, Izzy."

"I know."

"I feel like none of this is real. Like I'll wake up, and I'll be opening that letter six years ago across the table from Juanita and Carlos." I stammered and I hiccupped. "I lost the closest people I knew. Somehow, the void in my heart filled with God, but then He brought someone else in to make void overflow."

"You have feelings for Hudson, ones that aren't just on the surface." Pastor Izzy stated his question because he knew I couldn't respond. What Hudson had begun to make me feel was something I didn't want to lose. But after losing Juanita and Carlos so easily, I was afraid the same could happen with him.

"What if he leaves me too?"

"I can't promise he'll stay, but I can promise there are

245

seasons in your life. Some people only come for a season, while others come for a lifetime. Who Hudson becomes in your life is up to God. You have to trust Him in all things, even love."

"But it hurt so bad to lose them, Izzy, I don't know if can do it again with Hudson."

"Then maybe you won't. Maybe God brought him into your life because of all the loss you experienced. He brought someone and planted them in your life for good."

I took a breath, wiping at the tears that fell on their own. "So, what do I do?"

"You go for it. I'll be praying for you, Jonah, but I have a pretty good feeling about this. Right now, you are equally yoked, which is good. We just need to find out from God if Hudson is planning to stick around."

"So, why go for it? What if God says I need to leave him alone?"

"Then you leave him alone. Once the sponsor ball comes and you guys are seeing less of each other, unless you make arrangements, it'll be easy. But if God says yes, then there's nothing to it."

"I should just stop seeing him," I concluded.

Izzy grunted, and I knew a disproving grunt when I heard one from him. "Why do you think God is going to say no? You think He wants you unhappy? He'd only tell you no if Hudson wasn't part of the plan. But hasn't Hudson been part of the plan for a long time?"

I straightened, staring at the chipped white paint on the bathroom wall. God had always wanted me to treat Hudson kindly, to turn the other cheek at his insults, to be a door to Christ for him to open. Could it have been that all of that was just to bring us to this point?

"This is so scary."

"Don't worry so much, Jonah," Izzy consoled. "All things work together for the good of those who love the Lord. You both love the Lord, so things will work out. Even if you part ways, things will work out."

I sighed and nodded. "Ok. But if I get hurt again, I'm coming home for good."

"Over a boy? Please, Jo-Jo, I'd report your plane ticket as fraud."

I snorted. "*What!?*"

Israel laughed. "I didn't raise a weak girl. I raised a smart young woman."

A smile crossed my lips, and I agreed. "Thanks, Izzy."

"You're welcome, Jonah."

"Speaking of raising." My nail found it's way between my teeth again. "How's Mom?"

Izzy had been keeping me updated since her boutique closed down. Apparently, Mom's business was caught in some scandal, and she was shut down. Israel finally got her to move into the apartment above the church since it was empty. In exchange, she helps out around the church, assisting Izzy in office work and whatnot.

"Silvia's good," he said. "She's still crabby most days, but we've been having dinner together every night, and she's been opening up more."

247

"Wait," I was *about* to feel relieved, but Izzy's words hit me hard. "You've been having dinner with my mom?"

"Yes."

"Are you dating my mom!?"

Israel laughed. "No, we're not dating. Your mom has a lot of things she needs to talk about, and she only does it over dinner."

I sighed. "I'm not surprised. She's always been obsessed with family dinner because we never really had it. So, whenever we did, we ended up sitting for hours talking about all kinds of things." I could feel myself smiling as I remembered the good days with my mother. There weren't many of them, but when the days were good, they were worth reliving.

"Your mom misses you, Jonah. And she regrets a lot of things."

"I know. I want to call her, but I just don't know how."

"There is no rush, but I think enough progress has been made with your mother that she may be open to a phone call sometime."

"Maybe I'll call her tonight."

"After your date?"

Snatching my phone from my ear, I blinked at the time and shrieked. "Izzy! I have to go or I'll be late!"

"Alright, I get it. No time for—"

"Ok, great! Love you, bye!" I hung and went into a frenzy, rushing around to find an outfit. Hudson and I were spending the day together at an aquarium—at my request. I'd never been before, so Hudson offered to go with me. Then we were going to have dinner at a nice restaurant.

I rushed onto the elevator wearing a pink flared skirt with a white cropped shirt. I didn't have time to make a deal of my hair, so it was pinned up in a giant bun. My hair was past my waist and thick like wool, so a bun for me with all my curls was VERY big.

The elevator dinged and I stepped out, clutching my purse as I pushed open the exit doors. Hudson was already there in his dark aviators. He was leaning against his car, a black polo that hugged his lean figure tucked into his white pants that accentuated his tight waist. The short sleeves of the polo hugged his biceps, gripping onto them and begging God to show them mercy. His phone looked small in his large hands as he focused on the screen, leaning against the car so his great height could be admired.

My phone dinged, snapping me to reality. Digging for it through my purse, I pulled it out and stared at the text.

Hudson: I'm downstairs.

I grinned and looked up. To my surprise, Hudson was looking at me. His mouth was open just the slightest as he reached up and pulled his shades off. Pushing off the car, he slipped his phone into his pocket as he came over to me.

"Hey."

"Hi." I blushed.

I promised him I'd wear something out of the ordinary today. Pink was not my color, but Juanita told me that every woman needs something pink in her closet, so she forced me

249

to buy this skirt which showed off my legs—which I hated. But Hudson didn't.

His eyes traced my frame before he said, "You look incredible."

"Thank you."

We stood there in an awkward silence, Hudson staring at me while I did everything to not freak out from all of his attention. We'd been seeing each other, but Hudson had never been so forward before. I couldn't deny I was flattered, but I was also very nervous—per usual.

"We should go," I finally said.

He cleared his throat. "Yes. We should go."

I chuckled, pushing him back as I brushed by him to get into his car.

∧ ∧ ∧

We walked into the aquarium, and I literally gagged. Hudson snorted beside me.

"It's not funny." I fanned. "It smells horrifying in here."

"You sure you want to do this?"

I sighed, dropping my hand from my nose. "Yes."

Hudson offered me his arm and, as always, I hooked on and walked beside him.

There were all kinds of things to see. Underwater creatures were hardly my favorite, but they all had interesting little details. Whether it was in their colors or the way their fins were shaped or even just the size of underwater life was amazing.

We stayed by the huge tank for the longest, pointing out fish, even some small sharks swam by. When the place started to get crowded, Hudson moved to stand behind me. He leaned forward, hunching over me to point at something. But I was watching him, the ambient blue light that reflected from the tank casting over him as he smiled and pointed. Hudson looked peaceful, like today he was experiencing true joy, until some jerked bustled by us with his loud kids, slamming right into Hudson. He grabbed onto me, hooking an arm around my waist to stabilize himself.

"Sorry," he muttered, letting me go after a few seconds.

"It's okay."

"We should move on," he said.

I nodded, and this time, Hudson didn't offer me his arm, he reached down and took my hand. My fingers had a mind of their own because, without my permission, they interlaced with his and wouldn't let go.

We walked for a while like that, hand in hand. Sometimes Hudson swung our hands, bringing mine to his lips to peck it. He made me laugh and made me warm. Hudson made me forget everything I didn't want to remember. And he made me smile, more than anyone else.

"There's a theatre," he said as we walked to blue painted doors where a sign read, *The Life Cycle of Sea Lions*. "Do you want to see it?"

"Yeah, let's go."

We went inside, finding empty seats in the back row. They were the only two left and they were sandwiched between two families with a load of kids. One of the kids was already kicking the chair in front of him, another little girl had something sticky smeared across her mouth, making her look feral. I almost sighed, but I refused to let anything ruin my day, so I took a seat and smiled at the folks around us.

Hudson checked his watch as the lights dimmed. "We'll go after this, if you want."

"I do."

He snickered. "You're not ready for kids?"

"After today," I glanced around, "not at all."

Hudson laughed, stacking our hands on the arm rest between us as he focused his attention on the screen. The movie wasn't going to be long, thankfully. I'd planned to spend the time thinking about what a future between Hudson and me could be like until I felt the prickly gaze of the man beside me. I glanced over at him, and he smiled, the movie reflecting off his glasses. Looking back at the screen, I nudged Hudson.

"What's wrong?" he whispered, but he didn't look away from the screen, just leaned closer. I think he was actually enjoying the movie.

"Nothing, I don't want to make a scene."

He snapped his attention to me. "What?"

I lifted a shoulder slowly. "That man beside me, is he looking at me?"

Hudson glanced up casually and then looked back at me. "He just looked away. Why?"

"He's creeping me out."

"I'd have you switch seats with me, but there's another

252

man on this side."

"It's okay, the movie should be over soon."

"Let's just go now."

"*No*," I whisper-whined. "Let's enjoy this, okay?"

A muscle in his jaw spasmed and he leaned forward to see the man beside me. "Yeah, alright," Hudson said as he sat back. Pulling his hand free from mine, he slipped it over the hand rest and placed it on my leg.

Every hair on my body shot to attention. I even prayed the hair on my head didn't get frizzy.

"What are you—"

"Sending a message," Hudson whispered as he looked down at me. His eyes glowed with a cunningness to them as he nodded at the man beside me who shifted and turned away from me.

"Why did he turn away?"

"Because he wasn't going to risk it. We've been holding hands this whole time, why would I suddenly hold your leg? He knew you told me."

Men are so weird, I concluded. Whatever the case, Hudson's wide hand was webbed over my thigh, caressing it every so often while sometimes he gripped it. I was about to lose my mind in that theatre when the movie ended, and the lights came on. Letting go of a breath, I noticed the man gathering his family, and taking the hand of his wife like he loved her so much. The sight made me sick to my stomach.

"Sorry about that in there," Hudson said as we exited the theatre.

"It's alright."

Hudson was blushing, red cheeks pulled back to give me an awkward smile. "Let's grab dinner."

I nodded, thankful that I wasn't the only one feeling embarrassed by that.

∧ ∧ ∧

"Today was a lot of fun," I said as we sat in his car. We were outside my apartment, stuffed with gourmet food from another fancy restaurant Hudson insisted on taking me to. Every day out with him was like a treat. Something from a book or a movie.

"It was more than fun," Hudson replied. "I think dinner was the best."

"Me too. No more aquariums."

"Or small theaters."

We both laughed before a restless silence settled.

"I guess, I'll get going," I said.

"Let me walk you up tonight."

I chewed my lip, wondering if tonight was the right night after he got grabby at the theater. "Sure," I nodded, trying to hold in my hesitation.

Hudson looked amused as he shut off the ignition. "I promise, Ms. King, I will be respectful."

"Was it that obvious I was worried?"

"Very. But I have to wonder," he leaned over, "if you were worried about me or you."

I gulped and Hudson backed away with a sly look, taking his closeness with him. Climbing out of the car, he came around and helped me out. With an arm over my shoulders, we went inside and rode the elevator up, talking the whole time about our day together. We dragged down the hall, taking a casual stroll. I was a little short to be nestled beneath him, but he still held me close as we reached my door.

"Well, this is me." I waved at my apartment door.

"Alright." He retracted his arm. "Thanks for coming out today. You looked amazing."

I fanned at him, but he caught my hand. His intense stare felt like I was locked in a dizzy sauna the way the heat kicked up between us. Stepping closer, Hudson interlocked his fingers with mine as he leaned forward and kissed my cheek. "Goodnight, Ms. King."

My voice, small and hopelessly weak, squeezed out, "Goodnight."

He held my hand as long as he could before separating and turning to head down the hall. When he was gone, my heart sang with clarity. We were definitely dating.

I fumbled with my keys, hands trembling with excitement, only stopping when Carlos's door opened behind me.

"So, are you sleeping with him or what?"

I whirled around, shocked to see Juanita in a tiny pair of satin red shorts, and a red shirt to match.

"Um, no." I turned back to my door, and she poked at me some more.

"It sure seems like it. You're dating our sponsor. How

255

low."

"And you're screwing our best friend when you knew I liked him." I snapped around to see Juanita's eyes had doubled in size. "So, who's low?" I looked her over in one tick and chuckled to myself. "Goodnight, Juanita."

In silence, I opened the door to what had once been *our* apartment, stepped inside, and closed the door behind me.

24

Hudson Blue

I kissed Jonah on the cheek two weeks ago, however, her supple skin melting in my hand was the only thing I couldn't stop thinking about. My body was on fire when I touched her at the aquarium. I'd played it cool, mostly because the lecherous man beside her kept eyeing her. She did look beautiful. Jonah was a meek woman, and I think that's why I was so attracted to her.

Every part of her was still a mystery to me, and I used to think that was stupid, but now I think it's the best thing ever. Jonah was like a gift I could unwrap every time I saw her. There was so much to learn about her, and about women in general. I never took the time to care about women, but Jonah was different. My mind had been caged for so long, letting lust lead me. But now my mind was free in Christ, and I saw things differently. Like love.

Next month was the sponsorship ball, and Jonah and I

couldn't categorize these little dates as *work*. We'd be seeing each other with everyone's eyes on us, because I was Hudson Blue, the son of an awful man. A man who'd once been awful himself. But all that only mattered if we continued having dates after the ball. If I decided I didn't care what society thought and just loved Jonah the way I wanted to. Yeah … I said love. I fell for her pretty quickly.

Jonah King would make me or break me, and I was certain she was about to do both. She'd already made me a better man by introducing me to Christ. But choosing her over everything I knew would totally break me. To me, she was worth it. And to me, she's the guidance God promised me. Whenever I'm with Jonah, I want to be just like her. Free to talk about my faith, free to ask questions about scriptures I'd read on my own. Jonah loved God so freely without ever second guessing herself or Him. She never hesitated to talk faith talk, and it was encouraging. It was fulfilling.

So, she was the full package. A woman of God, a driven woman, a woman with purpose. She was stunning and kind, too. But what made me fall for Jonah was what made me fall for God. It's odd to say that I fell in love with Him, but I did. It was a slow growing fire. One that started with a spark from coffee with Jonah, and it almost died out until His breath was blown on me through Pastor Anne Marie. Since then, Jonah, church, Erma, they've all been fanning the flames of a heated romance between God and me. I don't mean lust, I mean this unwarranted desire to do right by Him. To follow His plans and live according to how He outlined life. Truthfully, sometimes it's hard because I still haven't brought my faith into the open, but I know I'm going to do it because God forgave me and gave me a second chance. That's also why I've fallen for Jonah.

She's given me a second chance. We started over. I'd almost lost her, someone with incredible faith, and kindness. Jonah was incorruptible, just the opposite of Macey. For the longest time, I thought losing Macey was my biggest mistake in life. But losing Macey was a setup for Jonah's introduction. I needed to miss my chance with her to do things the righteous way the second time around with Jonah.

God is a God of second chances, and that's why Jesus is the second Adam. Offering us a second chance at life with God eternally because the first Adam ruined that chance. Jonah was my second chance. Not just for love, but to break down an entire secret society built on the racism of men who feared change. Men who couldn't see that God loved all colors. The very men who carried the name Blue, had no idea what our named symbolized.

God painted the sky and the waters blue, both of which take up an incredible amount of space. The earth is covered in seventy-one percent of water, while the sky expands for light years in the color blue. Our last name is a reminder that colors exist, and none should be left out. However, we've used our name to corrupt generations of people to lose out on some of the best connections. We were the ghosts in the world, haunting the systems and creating rules and regulations, pushing people like Jonah to make programs like the My

Fellow American Project.

So, today, I'd do it. I'd tell my father the truth. Tell him that I loved God, and I loved Jonah. Whatever happened after that I'd have to stand and face, but God would be with me. And when Jonah found out the truth, I'm sure she'd be proud of me.

∧ ∧ ∧

I leaned over the desk and picked up my landline. I usually called Jonah on her cell, but today I wanted to mess with her. Clicking line one, I dialed her number and followed the prompt to enter her extension. The phone rang a few times, and I leaned back in my chair and waited for her to answer.

"Sorry about that long wait, this is Jonah King speaking. Who am I speaking with?"

"Hudson Blue."

She paused. "Hudson? What are you doing?"

"I just wanted to call you at work. See how you were doing."

Her tone brightened. "I'm doing well today, actually."

"Have you gotten a dress for the event yet?"

"Not yet, but I still have four weeks."

"Very true." I twirled a pen between my fingers. "Well, if you want, I know a seamstress or two that we can visit."

"A seamstress? You mean, like, have something tailored for me?"

"Yeah. I can get the woman to do it in three weeks if we

260

go by tomorrow."

She gasped. "Hudson, no. That's out of my budget, and I—"

"Jonah, sweetheart, I want to buy you something nice."

"You're always buying me nice things. You're always taking me to nice places. I ... I feel so bad."

"Why? I've got the money to take care of you, let me enjoy it while I can."

There was a stiff silence, and Jonah finally said, "That's right, after the ball, I guess we won't be—"

"No, that's not what I meant." I sighed, sitting forward in my chair. I gazed around my office, wondering how many more days I had here. "Jonah, I've got to do something that'll likely take every dime out of my pocket. But I can't walk away, even though I want to."

Sinking my head to my palm, I took a controlled breath as Jonah said, "What's going on?"

"I don't know." I shook my head, unwilling to tell her the rest. "Jonah, do you want to keep seeing me?"

"Yes," she said quietly.

My heart tightened, and I thought it would burst from glee. "Really?"

I recognized the tension in her voice as she squeaked out, "I thought you wouldn't want to see me anymore."

Jonah had broken me. She was shedding tears for me because she wanted this to last as much as I did. She really was my second chance at love.

"Even if I go flat broke today, you'd still want to see me?"

261

She laughed, the tears passing now. "Yes, Hudson. I'm kind of glad you'd be broke."

"What?"

"Because then I won't feel so guilty for not being able to pay you back for anything."

"Sweetheart…" I adjusted in my chair to gaze out the window at the rushing traffic. "Owning the world means it's yours to give to whoever you want. You are who I want, and I want you to have the very best of what I can give you, and if it's the world, then I'll put your name on it and won't let anyone forget it. I promise."

She paused. "I don't know what to say."

"Say that you'll go with me to the seamstress."

Jonah laughed. "Fine, I'll go."

I tapped the desk and stood. "I have to go now, but Jonah?"

"Yes?"

"I … I …" I got too nervous and couldn't say it. Gripping my neck, I rolled my eyes. "I want to see you tonight."

"I'm free."

"Alright, I'll come pick you up after work."

"Ok, I'll see you tonight, then."

"See you then."

She hung up before I did. I just stood there holding the phone to my ear, listening for Jonah's voice. I knew I had to settle things with my father. My only request was for him not to cancel the ball and give Jonah's organization the money they needed.

262

∧ ∧ ∧

God, I know You're with me, I prayed as I sat in my car. I left work in the middle of the day, fearful that I'd stay too long arguing with my father and be late to see Jonah.

You will face the truth today.

I nodded, opening the door and sliding out. The manor hadn't aged in her beauty. It would always be a wonderful sight I promised myself I wouldn't forget. I didn't know how much of this place I'd be able to take with me, but I remember Pastor Anne teaching us about selling our possessions to follow Jesus. In a way, I think I was selling everything to follow the plans of God by walking in and telling my father the truth. I was tired of hiding, tired of going places no one would spot me at. I wanted to love God and Jonah freely, and today I would.

When I walked inside, no one was there to greet me. I wasn't too surprised since the maids ran errands for my father during the day. By the time I returned home, all the shopping had been done, and dinner was ready. I stood at the bottom of the spiral staircase and took a breath.

Don't hesitate now, I told myself. Shaking my shoulders out, I climbed the steps to my father's bedroom. He lived upstairs in the main house, and I lived in the east wing on the second level. The deep blue carpet that ran up the center of the steps didn't end once you reached the top. It rolled out across the floor in two directions. To the right were guest rooms no one ever used. And to the left was my father's room.

263

Coming down the hall, I was trying to calm my nerves when I heard strange noises from my father's bedroom. Whining, pleading, and grunting. I stood there for a second, hoping that what I was hearing was not what I thought.

I was going to turn back, but it wasn't like I hadn't caught my father in the act before. When I was sixteen, I walked in on him with a woman from the office. He shooed me away, but he didn't stop. And when he came to my room later, he told me that I got to witness what it looked like to handle a woman. That day has been a scar I've tried to get out of my head forever.

I knew Dad would be upset, but I couldn't wait any longer. If I did, I'd explode. This was probably the worst time to do something like this, but I was here now. So I shoved open the door, ready to put the woman out, but I froze when I saw who it was.

A bright yellow dress, dandelion sling backs, a matching purse, and a bright red thong with a lace bra lay on the floor in the front of the bedroom. My dad's clothes only featured a robe pooling on the floor, like he had been waiting for her. Father always got dressed in the morning, the only time he didn't was if he was sick. I'd caught my father in his robe before. It was early so I thought nothing of it. But now, seeing him entangled in the sheets pieced everything together. More specifically, *who* he was entangled with.

"It finally makes sense," I said as my father and the woman sprang apart. They hadn't noticed me there until I spoke.

"Hudson!" my father snapped.

The woman shrieked, gathering the blankets around her body. Skin as dark as night sky, skin that had once glowed like an ember was now dull and lackluster.

"Erma said your appetite had changed, and all this time," a tear ran down my cheek, "I thought she was crazy." I leaned against the door post.

"Erma!" my father shouted bitterly. He was nearly screaming her name, spittle flying as he hid the woman behind him. "Why are you here? I can explain, Hudson."

"I thought you were different."

"Hudson," my father's voice sounded apologetic. His panting had finally calmed and the pillow he held to his lower body crinkled in his hand as he gripped it. "This was just—"

"Stop it," I said quietly. My focus shifted to the woman beside him, cowering and holding his shoulder. "How could you do this to them?"

She didn't answer, turning her gaze away to the room around her.

Backing up, I tripped out the door and into the wall, coughing as I felt more tears spill down my cheeks. My father moved hurriedly from the bed, grabbing his robe from the floor. But I didn't want to hear from him or speak to him. Before he could reach me, I pushed off the wall and raced for the stairs while he called behind me.

"Hudson! Hudson!"

Erma's eyes widened when I ripped open the front door. "You knew." I pointed at her. "You knew all along."

"Hudson, I was sworn to secrecy." Her voice cracked like

she might cry. The sound only annoyed me. She didn't get to cry over this. She wasn't the one who'd been betrayed.

What would Jonah think?

"I couldn't say a thing!" Erma insisted. "Please, Hudson! I'm sorry!"

I shook my head, words erupting from my chest in a bark. "You could've told *me*!"

She stepped back and I shoved by her and out the door, tears stinging my eyes as I realized, *today, I really faced the truth.*

25

Jonah King

Normally, I sighed whenever I left the office for the day. Tired, cranky, hungry. It was a routine I worked through regularly, except for today. Today, Hudson was picking me up from work. He'd done it before, but we were going to see a seamstress today, and he was getting me a tailored dress.

I was squealing with joy as I twisted my doorknob, double checking it was locked. The office door beside me squeaked and Carlos stepped out alone. He reached in and clicked the lights before catching me gaping at him. Since the day of our youth event, when Carlos and I shared a silent laugh over Juanita, we've been casual. Head nods in the morning when Juanita wasn't around. Waves, if we caught each other leaving. Like tonight.

I raised a hand, and he nodded, adjusting his backpack on his shoulder. There was once a time when just a touch from Carlos could start my heart again if it stopped. Now, I don't know what it'd do if he was the only person around to restart it. I'm certain he'd have to beat my chest with a crowbar to get me to feel anything again. But honestly, I did feel something for Carlos, and not the same something it used to be… or what it was for Hudson.

"Carlos," I called out. He was halfway down the hall when he looked back over his shoulder. The same stale gaze that sometimes wavered between broken and angered met mine. "Have a good night."

A corner of his mouth ticked up in the slightest bit, and he said, "You too, Jonah."

Maybe things could be mended between Carlos and me. I'm not sure if Juanita and I will ever recover, especially after the little spat we had a few weeks back. With a sigh, I started a slow walk down the hall until I was certain Carlos was gone. I decided to take our fancy staircase instead of the backstairs, so I could peer out the front glass doors and see if Hudson was already waiting for me.

Descending the stairs, I stopped midway when I saw Hudson sitting on the floor in the corner of the room. His hands covering his face, his head hung low. My heart skipped a beat, but I made sure my feet didn't skip any steps as I burned them up getting to the bottom of them. My heels clacked loudly, and I tried to stay calm as I crossed the lobby.

Jess, the receptionist, was packing up as I approached. She gave me a tight smile and said, "Ms. King? Everything alright?"

"Yes!" I turned around, trying to block the view of Hudson. I wasn't sure if she'd seen him yet, there was a chance she didn't if he came in while the crowds were rushing out.

"Do you need something?"

"No." I gave her my best smile. "You can go home. Thank you."

She nodded, hanging her purse on her wrist. Her smile was uneasy, and her expression spoke to her confusion, but she said nothing as she offered me one more head bob and headed out the door. When I was certain she was gone, I made a beeline over to Hudson in the corner and knelt beside him.

"Hudson? What's wrong?"

He looked up, and I had to take a steadying breath. Tears were rolling down his cheeks, green eyes no longer able to hold back the flood.

"Jonah, everything I've known has been a lie." He hiccupped, clutching his arms. "He always told me that we were different. That people who weren't like us weren't good people." He laughed nervously before letting his watery eyes meet mine. "We were *racists*, Jonah. Elitists. People who hated anyone that wasn't perfect. My entire world was ruled by color and money. I became someone I hated, lost someone I once loved, and almost lost you." He choked. "All because I was told this was wrong."

"*What* is wrong?" What is *this*?

He gulped, his throat bobbing with the noisy sound. "Us."

A simple word sent a swirling feeling into my chest. I knew Hudson had once said some nasty things to me, but I thought he was just being that way because he was angry. Not because he was *supposed* to behave that way. Not because he was bred

269

and groomed to believe there were differences between us so great they could not be overcome.

"I'm so sorry, Hudson," I said, placing a hand on his knee. He eagerly reached for it. Pulling it to his lips and kissing my hand.

"I love you so much, Jonah. I don't want to lose you," he whispered.

My mouth slammed closed, and I chewed the inside of my lip as I blinked at him.

Hudson loved me. He loved me when he wasn't supposed to... now it all made sense. His odd conversation about losing things and losing his fortune. He wanted me to still be here if he lost it all, because he was risking it all *for* me.

"You shouldn't love me." I pulled my hand from him. "You shouldn't love me if you're going to lose it all." I clutched the hand he'd been holding, "I can't ask you to do that, and I don't want you to be unhappy." The words stuttered on my tongue, wanting to be out there for him to hear but also wanting to stay close, because I was afraid. "I ... love you too. And that's why—"

Hudson moved, crushing me in his embrace. He cleaved to me, holding on for dear life as he whispered into my hair. "I once thought you were identical to the first woman I loved. But little by little, I began to see that you two were nothing alike. Now, I know for certain you're nothing alike. Because she asked me to risk it all for her, but you asked me to lose nothing for you." He squeezed me a little tighter, forcing the tears out of my eyes. "Thank you, Jonah, for being more than enough for me. For forgiving me and introducing me to God. You've given me a second chance at a lot of things, and I will always owe you for that."

Slowly, I wrapped my arms around him as I rested my head over his shoulder. We stayed that way for a while until Hudson retracted and sat down in front of me again. His tear-stained cheeks and look of misery almost made the waterworks start again.

"I need to tell you something." He looked away. If it was anything like what he just told me, I didn't think I could take anymore. But I nodded anyway.

"My father was a man I thought believed in his own words. The words he raised me by."

His sheepish demeanor told me this was as cruel for him as it was for me. Listening to the man I fell in love with confess to being a racist, growing up in a household ruled by bigotry, was uncomfortable. But this was a conversation Hudson needed to have.

"My father told me that women…" he paused. "Women like you—"

"Black women," I said boldly.

He swallowed and shocked me by shaking his head. "Not just Black. Any woman of color. Any woman who was poor. Any woman who was disabled. Any woman who was uneducated. They were off limits." He chuckled. "Jeremy said we were all raised the same way, but my father was the only one who took it seriously. I…" he sniffled, "I took it seriously too. Especially the race part. Because of a woman I once loved.

A woman who was poor and uneducated and Black. Everything my father said was bad for me."

This confession had taken a turn I was not ready for, but I took a breath and nodded as he went on.

"Macey was her name." He stopped to look over at me. "We slept together, and I fell in love with her. But I knew it would be impossible for us to ever be together, so when she asked me to tell everyone about our relationship, I didn't—I *wouldn't*—and she walked away."

"I see," I said. "Is Macey the woman you thought I was like?"

He nodded, his eyes finally leaving mine so I could breathe again. "Yeah. But that was six years ago. I've been over Macey for a long time. But because I was angry with myself for letting her go, I started forcing myself to be someone I wasn't. Someone who pleased my father ... but not God ... and not you."

I let him take my hand when he reached for it. It would've been silly to be angry at him for a past relationship, especially since Hudson was not the man he used to be.

"God wanted me to do the righteous thing. He didn't want me to be that man anymore. He didn't want me to pretend I didn't know the way I'd been raised was wrong. But He also didn't want me believing the lies I'd been told." He squeezed my hand. "Jonah, I walked in on my father with a woman today. A woman who... is like you."

It was weird that Hudson always said '*like you*' when he meant a woman of color. But I suppose it was difficult to admit to the things he'd been taught. Not any more difficult than it was to admit to walking in on his father and another woman.

I gasped. *Olan? He's so old!*

"My father raised me against the very woman I caught him with," Hudson said.

"That's awful."

"It's worse than that." He hung his head and inhaled a shaky, wet breath. I could hear his tears choking him. I could see his shoulders bunching. I could feel his pain drifting from his very body. "It's worse than that," he said again. "I caught him sleeping with your friend, Jonah."

I was still reeling from the thoughts of Olan sleeping with *anyone*. It didn't matter to me if they were young or Black; just that fact that he was still sleeping around had shocked me into silence. But now Hudson's words caught me off guard, and I was left blinking at him with a stupid look on my face.

"Did you hear me?" he said.

"What friend?" I asked.

Hudson's eyes faltered before he regained his focus on me. "Juanita."

I flinched. Glanced around. Shook my head. "That's not possible. Juanita was at work."

Hudson didn't look away, his hardened gaze raising the temperature.

Ripping my hand free from his, I unbuttoned the first buttons of my shirt and stood to pace and breathe, fanning myself. "No," I shook my head. I knew she'd slept with Carlos, but that was a *mistake*. Honestly, those two had been a ticking

273

time bomb since I'd known she liked him. But *Olan?* No ... Juanita wasn't like that. We had differences, but not different lifestyles or beliefs.

"Jonah..." Hudson came up behind me, and tried to grab my arm, but I snatched it away and stumbled to the side until I hit the floor. I whined as I shifted onto my hands and knees, feeling new tears burn my eyes. These weren't tears of pity like I had for Hudson, these were tears of anger and betrayal.

I heard Hudson beside me, felt him pulling me to sit up. But I didn't want to, I just wanted to cry it out. "It's not true!" I yelled, thankful that the office was closed, and Jess and I were always the last two to leave so I was certain no one was there to witness my breakdown. That was a small mercy.

"Jonah," Hudson pulled me up and into his lap. I gripped his jacket, the expensive material nearly melting in my hand. With a shake of my head, I looked up at him. His expression was apologetic, brows close together, his mouth curved into a deep frown.

"How do you know it was her?"

"I saw her."

"No ... What if you didn't see her? What if you saw someone who just *looked* like her?"

"Her clothes were on the floor." He swallowed. "A yellow dress and shoes with a purse."

My heart came to a halting stop, and I gripped onto Hudson even tighter. That was her outfit today. I remembered because I bought her that dress last year for her birthday. She was born in the winter, but she loved yellow and bright colors,

274

so I got her a dress the color of the sun. She was our winter warmth. Sunshine in the dreary cold. The dress had been on sale, and I was able to afford it… she wore it to church a lot… and now she wore it to cheat on her faith. To cheat on *God*.

I could feel myself breathing heavily, could kind of hear Hudson saying things about calming down, but everything was muffled as I sat there staring ahead.

Why would she do this? First Carlos, now this? I should've said something. I should've stopped her. But I didn't.

"Carlos," I whispered finally.

"What about Carlos?"

"They've been sleeping together. I should've stopped them, removed them from the organization but I didn't know how. I didn't know what to say because I didn't want to deal with it. I just—"

"Jonah," Hudson squeezed me, "it's okay. We can deal with it now."

"We can?"

He nodded. "What do you want to do?"

My eyes traced down Hudson's chest where I'd wrinkled his suit pretty good from clinging to him. Just to distract myself, I began to smooth out the fabric over his chest as I said, "I'll talk to them."

"Ok." He nodded.

"What are you going to do?"

He shook his head. "I don't know yet."

∧ ∧ ∧

275

Hudson and I never went out to dinner, neither of us was up to it after that. We never went to the seamstress either, and now we were just one week away from the ball, and I still didn't have a dress. But a dress was the last thing on my mind. For the last three weeks, I've been quietly observing Carlos and Juanita. When she came to work the day after Hudson told me about finding her and Olan together, Juanita seemed distant. Like she was wondering if Hudson had told me anything. But when I didn't confront her, or treat her any differently, she eventually mellowed out. By the weekend, she was all over Carlos again.

I sat in my apartment rubbing my hand over the scratch in the wooden table. It seemingly showed up one day without notice. None of us knew how it got there. We called it the table's scar. I laughed weakly as I felt tears stirring. How had we moved so far from where we started?

Rubbing the scar again, I whispered, "This is the storm, isn't it, God? The one when I'd have to hold up the lamp for Juanita and Carlos." I pressed my hands to my eyes. "Why does it have to hurt so much?"

God didn't answer today, but He didn't need to. I knew what He expected me to do. The only way to light a torch is with a match. And you've got to strike the match first, which means friction is required.

Pushing from the table, I looked around the apartment, the place had never felt so empty. It was like no matter how wide I opened the curtains, I couldn't get any light or warmth in here. Not until I turned on my own light.

With a deep breath, I left my apartment and stepped across the hall. *Give me strength God.*

I am here.

My fist shook as I knocked on the door. There was no answer. I knocked a little harder until I heard Juanita's voice pierced with anger, "Who is it?"

"Jonah."

It was silent for a moment before I heard footsteps carrying her to the door. When she pulled it open, she was wrapped in a blanket. I stared at her smirk for a second, like this was all a game for her. Then something else clicked in me, an old rage I'd buried.

Without thinking, I shoved Juanita back a step. Her hand slipped from the door, and she fell into her apartment. I didn't bother looking around because I wasn't there to stay. Kicking the door closed behind me, I marched over to her as she backed along the floor from me.

"What is your problem, Jonah!"

"You are!" I snatched her up by the blanket and snarled in her face, "You're spreading yourself way too thin, and I want you out of my company."

Her eyes stretched, and then she shook her head when she realized what I'd said. "Who do you think you are? *Your* company? It would be nothing without *me!*"

"Then let it fall," I said darkly, then I shoved her to the floor.

Apparently, the noise summoned Carlos who stepped into

the hall. He was shirtless, wearing only his boxers. "What's going on?" he asked, eyes wide.

"After the ball, I want you both to pack your things from my company and leave."

He squinted and glanced back at Juanita who was still on the floor, gathering her blankets. "Jonah, what's—"

"We are a Christian organization, and until you've made yourself right with God again, I can't allow you to sit as leaders of my company. Leaders should represent us in a positive, righteous way, not cause drama and scandal."

Carlos looked pained, his eyes lowering to the floor. "I understand."

"What?" Juanita snapped. "Carlos, we built that organization." She placed a hand on her chest. "We moved across the country with her! She can't put us out!"

"I'm asking you to step down. If you won't, then I am willing to go to the courts to have you removed for breaking the contract you signed to uphold an honest Christian lifestyle—which would not include premarital sex."

"We *are* Christian! Making mistakes doesn't take away our beliefs!" Juanita yelled.

"That's true. But sneaking around behind everyone's backs makes you a liar and I can't work with dishonest people." I paused and glanced between them. "That applies to both of you."

Carlos opened his mouth like he wanted to speak. I turned my attention to him and said, "I thought you regretted it all?"

Juanita threw her head back in laughter. "Well, he lied.

278

Carlos loves making love to me."

"But you just like screwing around. Doesn't matter who it is."

Her brows lowered. "What are you talking about it?"

"What is she talking about?" Carlos's defeated look slowly eased into anger.

"While you're working late, Juanita's sleeping with the senior advisor—or whatever Olan is—from Blue Barn. Hudson told me he caught them together. In bed." I folded my arms. "Even described what she wore to work. How could he know that, Juanita?"

"You're lying!" She turned to Carlos in desperation. "She's lying, baby. Don't believe her."

"I don't care what anyone believes." Juanita was desperate, and Carlos was broken, but that wasn't for me to figure out. "I just want you both out of my company by the end of the week. The Monday after the ball I will be sending out a memo explaining your sudden resignation as respectfully as possible." I turned for the door but stopped. "You two were my very best friends, and I lost you both." When I glanced back, both of them were looking at me, eyes filled with apologetic tears, but this had to be done. "My door is always open for you both, and the doors to the project we started together will never close to you. But until things change," I fought my own tears, lifting my chin, "this is goodbye."

And just like that, I closed the door on the two people in my life I thought would always be there.

279

26

Hudson Blue

I looked in the mirror at myself, fixing my hair. It was a long rectangular mirror that I'd set up in my new apartment. It's only ten minutes in traffic (three minutes if I walk) from Jonah's place, so I get to see her more. I moved out of the manor, took only my clothes and essentials. Furniture, and relics from the house I left behind.

The only important thing I took were my grandmother's pearls that had been entrusted to me, and a painting that was worth a fortune. My mother left it for me, so I hung it here. It wasn't anything fancy, just a tree. But that tree was painted by a blind man who simply visited the field the tree was in, touching it over and over, listening to the way the wind brushed through the leaves to figure the height. It was a stellar work of art, the detail he'd put into the piece over a century ago. My mother acquired it when she was pregnant with me and said what the man actually captured was the tree of life.

That's what he saw; though blind to the world, his eyes were open in the spirit.

I was nervous for the event tonight. I couldn't wait to see Jonah, to see what dress she'd decided to wear since we missed my seamstress. Jonah didn't care, of course, but I still wanted to get her something nice. So, on the last dime I was willing to spend from Blue Barn, I bought Jonah a ring. It was a diamond worth six million dollars, on the shiniest silver band I could get it on. I wanted Jonah to have the nicest ring she'd ever seen. I wanted Jonah to have the *world*, but this little ring was the only piece of it I could give her.

I felt the nerves boiling in my stomach as I flattened out the wrinkles in my perfectly starched blue suit, paired with a silver shirt beneath, and a navy tie. It was customary for Blue Barn associates to wear blue at special events. I had no idea what color Jonah was wearing because she wouldn't let me see her for the last week, like we were getting married or something. She said I'd be more surprised when I saw her if it'd been a while. Then she stopped returning my calls after Tuesday. She texted me with the same concept. I didn't mind, especially since that gave me time to really hammer over what I wanted to say to my father today. I was going to see him before the event so things wouldn't be awkward for us. It's been almost four weeks since we've spoken. I left the day I found out he was sleeping with Juanita and didn't come back for a week when I was certain he was gone. I did that until I retrieved all my things, but now I had to face him, and I had something to tell him.

Jogging down the stairs, I slipped into my car and took a breath. This was the last ride I would take in this car before I returned it to my father's garage. Everything I had was from him. I hadn't really earned much myself. Blue Barn was given to me, my name as a Blue was given to me, everything important was simply placed in my hand. Not to say I hadn't earned it, but I hadn't earned anything that I could call my *own*. Except my apartment, but that was still being paid for with Blue Barn's money. Until I found a good job, it would remain that way. But I promised myself I'd start weening off of Blue Barn, I just didn't want it anymore. I wanted to sell all my possessions and start over again for the sake of righteousness.

I opened the door to the manor and went straight up the stairs. There were no maids here, to my surprise, but I let the curiosity roll down my shoulders as I knocked on my father's door.

"Who's there? Erma, I told you to leave."

He fired them… because they didn't cover for him.

Shaking my head, I opened the door and stepped inside. Olan whirled around, ready to snap, but when he saw me, his mouth zipped shut.

"Hi, Dad."

"Hudson, where have you been? I've been looking all over—"

"Why? Are you afraid your secret is going to get out?"

My father swore darkly, spittle flying before he turned away in frustration. "What do you want me to say? That I'm sorry?" He turned back, his chest rising and falling quickly. "Well, I'm

283

not sorry." His expression turned dark, a wicked grin crawling across his face. "Juanita was the best screw I've had in a while."

The comment was meant to sting but it only made him more of a fool.

"You don't get it," I said, shaking my head.

"No, *you* don't get it! You say something and this whole place falls! You hear me?"

Of course I did. If I opened my mouth about what I saw in that room, the public would crucify us. Blue Barn had already suffered one scandal with the My Fellow American Project. To hear that Olan Blue had been sleeping with a woman from that same company—a woman of *color*, after being accused of racism when the project first pulled out of the sponsorship program—would ruin us.

Shockingly, I didn't care.

"That's the plan, Dad."

He stepped back, eyes darting over my frame. "What did you just say to me?"

"I said, the plan is to make this place fall." I waved my hand around. "Make Blue Barn crumble. Down with the Barn." I shrugged. A favorite line of mine from a book I'd read popped into my head, and I made it my own as I deadpanned, "The Barn must fall. Get it?"

"You get this, and you get it now—"

"I'm going to expose you," I said flatly. "I'm going to write it all down and get it printed in the news."

"I will shut every door in your face, Hudson. No one will ever print your story! And no one will ever believe it! Not even the desperate reporters." My father's shoulders bounced in laughter as he began to feel satisfied. He was triumphant, but only for now.

"Please make sure a few investors buy into the charity tonight," I said. "The check is already written and signed. Postmarked for today." I reached up and grabbed my tie pin engraved with the letters 'BB' and unclipped it. The weight of it in my hand felt both heavy and light. I held on to it a moment longer before setting it on my father's dresser.

"My resignation letter is already in the mail. Thank you, for everything, Dad."

He swallowed. "Hudson, stop it, alright?" Nervously, he began to pace the room wearing his silk robe and slippers. The memories of him and Juanita tangled together flooded back into my head, making me wobbly.

"I know what you saw was surprising, but we can work this out," he said. "There's no need to draw attention or alarm everyone."

I shook my head. "I have to walk away. Sell my possessions and pick up my cross."

"What?" My father frowned.

"You've never been religious but, recently, I found something to believe in. *Someone* to believe in. And He's bigger than Blue Barn. So I want to walk away for Him. And I have to forgive you for Him." I nodded. "I forgive you, Dad."

He frowned. "Goodness, is that what this is about? You believe in God or whoever? Fine." He shrugged. "I don't care. You think I'd care about that?"

"No, I don't think you've ever cared about me. I was just the son who was born to you, the one you were taught to groom as your successor. But I have a Father who loves me now, and I found a woman who loves me, too."

My father clenched his jaw, his nostrils flaring as he grated words between his teeth, "I don't know what's gotten into you, but I know if Jonah—"

"Don't you *dare* say her name." I snapped, taking a step forward. "I don't want to hear you say anything about her."

My father stared at me. For a moment, I would swear he looked guilty. Like he'd finally realized I was protecting Jonah from him because all of this was ultimately his fault.

After a heartbeat of silence passed between us, my father's face erupted in anger, but I cut him off before he could speak. "Don't be late tonight."

"You think you're going to make me run into hiding and listen to you?"

I walked to the door, resting a hand on the knob. "You should be listening to me because I've done things you have no idea about. I've planned this. That was the only thing you taught me that I cherish. To make plans for the future." I smirked as I turned back to him. "I didn't make plans with Macey, but I have with Jonah, and I plan to follow through on them."

It took a moment for the words to sink into my father's mind as he tried to recall Macey. The moment he remembered her, his eyes popped, and his mouth dropped open.

"I've told things and I've done things you have no idea

286

about," I reminded him, then, without another word, I left my father's room and the estate for good. The car keys sat on the dining table for my father to find later. There were no words spared for a goodbye with Erma. I was done with that place.

I caught a taxi to the event. No one was expecting me to step out of a *taxi*, so that was the first stir of the night—the first stir of the new story I wanted written. Everyone will be wondering why I arrived separately from my father in a plain cab, instead of in the sleek car I aways drove. Then everyone will be knocked off their feet once my resignation hits the news, and the woman I'm dating is revealed. God said He would guide me, and this is a plan only He could've authored.

People will believe the claims I make, and they'll begin to dig deeper. And every news outlet that has something against Blue Barn will have a goldmine of scandalous secrets to dig through. The reign of The Blue Barn Company was about to end. The world was about start making its own decisions, having its own mind, not the mind that for so long, me and other people at Blue Barn and in our circle have told them to have. We've produced lies and scandals just to feed people things and keep them under our control. Now, people will be able to think for themselves… I wonder how the world will look.

I waved at the photographers outside the event as I climbed the royal blue carpet into the lavish facility. Red, white, and blue were the colors of the night and the theme was, of course, the American flag. Soldiers were invited to march in

287

with the flag, and there was a camouflage table in the center decorated for them to sit at. The rest of the tables followed the red, white, and blue color pattern. Each had a tablecloth, theme-colored glasses, and a bouquet of flowers that were multicolored. Jonah didn't want us to forget that every color is welcome at God's table, and since this was a Christian organization, tonight we'd be feasting at *His* table.

I could hardly wait to find Jonah. I spotted Carlos first. He was standing with a few people from Blue Barn, chatting in his blue suit. He looked shy, like he was forcing himself to smile and be polite.

"Hudson," I felt a warmth on my back and turned to see Lolita stepping beside me. Her Spanish curls were pulled to the side with mini flag pins holding them together in a bun. Her iconic red lipstick and a gold necklace popped against her baby blue dress. My soon-to-be former secretary looked stunning. We'd made up long ago. It was actually the day I reinstated the charity. She wanted to know why I was sending the woman I'd been sleeping with a breakup message. I told her everything and she laughed then issued me an apology I wouldn't accept because it wasn't necessary.

"Lolita." I turned and hugged her.

"I'm proud of you," she said as she grabbed my hands. "You've grown more in these last few months than in the past seven years."

I chuckled. "Is that a compliment?"

"Of course, it is, Mr. Blue." Lolita paused and looked around. "I wanted this so badly, and I'm glad I got to see it before I retired."

"You're retiring? Why?"

"I think it's time that I begin to do things that I really love."

"And what's that?"

Lolita grinned. "Work for the My Fellow American Project. A little birdie told me there's going to be some openings soon. I want to give back since I helped in ways I shouldn't have. I helped keep this community separated, and now I have a chance to help put it together again."

"I'm glad you're getting to do this, but I'm sorry that I was the reason for both your retirement and putting your hand to the flame to do things you regret."

She waved a hand. "I was grown, I could've said no. But I wasn't grown enough, and now I am."

I leaned forward and pecked the top of her head. "Then I guess this isn't goodbye."

She smirked. "Oh, I know it isn't."

With that, Lolita left me in the center of the room to slide over to the food table. There was an assortment of desserts and a buffet of typical American foods, along with foods from dozens of other cultures. I was enjoying watching my staff drool over foods we've never had before until Juanita stepped out in a white dress. She didn't glow like usual. She stood off to the side, looking around like she was searching for someone. I hoped it wasn't my father.

With a sigh, I slipped my hands into my pockets and turned before she could catch me, walking right into my little lady.

"Jonah," I gasped as I stepped back. She was beautiful in

her long red gown with a train trimmed in red lace. The bodice was fitted like a mermaid, hugging her hips and pushing her chest out of the strapless top. There was an American flag pin on her dress, and her curls were free. Big and bold like they were meant to be. "Jonah," I said again.

She giggled, chewing her bottom lip. "Hudson, you look amazing," she said, but I still couldn't speak. I was staring at her, frozen like I'd never thaw. "Stop staring." She covered her mouth. "You're making me blush."

"Sorry," I finally forced out. Jonah had taken my breath away.

"I have something for you—"

The crowds outside erupted and I turned to find my father making his grand entrance. I was supposed to be with him, but I'd already walked the blue sea alone. Turning back to Jonah, I noticed she was holding a little blue box, and I only had half a second to wonder where she pulled that from.

"What is this?" I asked as I took the box.

"You said you were getting rid of everything, so I thought I'd help you get off to a new start."

I smiled as I opened the little gift. "Jonah," I looked up, and her brown eyes were shining with uncertainty.

"You seemed attached to the other one, so I just thought I'd get you a new one."

I took the silver tie pin out; it had a scripture engraved on it. "Jonah chapter two, verse ten," I chuckled, "that's when God spoke to the fish and it vomited Jonah out."

She nodded. "That was Jonah's second chance."

"And you are mine."

Jonah smiled, taking the pin from me, and clipping it onto my tie. "There, now you really look amazing."

"Thank you for this." I held up the box.

"You can thank me properly with a dance after I give this introduction speech."

"Yes, ma'am." I nodded.

She squeezed my hands before whisking off to find her way to the stage. Juanita and Carlos climbed it with her, and they all stood in order, so they looked like a human American flag.

Throughout the speech, Juanita and Carlos struggled. I wasn't sure what'd taken place between the three of them, but it was obvious that this was all an act. Except Jonah, she was genuinely happy. Smiling bashfully at the investors. And when she stepped down from the stage to shake hands with people from Blue Barn, she simply extended a hand to my father like she didn't know his secrets. Smiling like he was the man he pretended to be.

"I've got to say," I said as Jonah came over to me afterward, "the investors look very interested."

"Good. Because we'll need it." She looked around at the crowd, smiling and bobbing her head. She had to be the most beautiful woman I'd ever seen, and also the strongest and most faithful to God. That's exactly why I admired her. Why I loved her. After all we'd been through, Jonah King and I had fallen in love.

"Jonah?"

"Hmm?" she hummed. Big brown eyes only glanced at me

291

for a second as she watched the crowd of people.

"Will you marry me?"

That got her attention. She snapped her vision to me, a frown on her face. "What?"

I held up a pink box and opened it. I would've made a scene of getting down on one knee, but I didn't want this to be for the tabloids. I wanted this to be real, because what I felt for Jonah was real, not some romantic story. Jonah wasn't part of some big plan, she was *my* plan, and my backup plan. I planned to live this life of second chances, loving God and her until she was tired of me. And even then, I wouldn't stop loving her.

"I have something for you, too."

She gasped and glanced around. She was speechless as she stood there blinking at the ring.

"Let's skip everything else, and just get married," I said.

She placed a hand on her chest, sucking in deeply. "Are you sure? You want to *marry* me? Have you thought this through?"

I snorted, placing my hand on her back to pull her small frame against my own. "Who else would have me?"

"Lots of women."

"But you're the only one I want to have me." I slipped a hand to her chin and tilted her head back. "Jonah King, will you marry me?"

She smiled, that bright one that made every man melt and every woman jealous. "Yes, I will marry you."

My nose bumped hers as I leaned forward. This time, I wouldn't kiss her cheek. I'd kiss my future wife right on her puckered lips, enjoying the pleasure and happiness she brought me.

But truthfully, the pleasure was all mine.

Epilogue

Jonah Blue

1 Year Later

"So, how's Mom?" I asked as I sat in Hudson's little car. He bought the car because he refuses to take public transportation.

"She's doing really good. You and Hudson are still coming for her baptism next week, right?"

"Yes." I tapped the wheel. "Our flights are booked."

"Good," Izzy said on the other end of the phone.

Mom and Israel were engaged. She started calling me once he asked her to marry him, and we talked for hours about the way our relationship went downhill. How things got dark because Mom never thought she could be happy again. She let the darkness she felt inside seep into every part of her life, poisoning the joy we'd once had. She envied me because I'd found something I loved and had people to do it with. After Dad died, Mom was heartbroken. She did what she could for me, but it wasn't enough. Now, however, she's found God, and she's fallen in love, and we've begun to mend our relationship.

Israel had always been like a father to me, so I didn't mind him becoming my actual stepfather. It was just weird to think that Pastor Israel was marrying my mom. I shivered at the thought again as Izzy said on the other line, "I spoke with Carlos a few days back. He's doing well. Got that job we've been praying for at that office. He'll be the director of volunteers."

"Nice." I nodded. "Good for him. I'm glad he's doing well."

"Any word from Juanita?"

I sighed. "Nope."

"I haven't heard anything either. I'm sure she'll be okay."

"I hope so."

Carlos moved back to Texarkana, and he rededicated his life to Christ. Izzy relayed the message that he was welcome to come back and work with me, but he kindly refused. He said he wasn't ready to come back just yet. He was still figuring himself out. Juanita, on the other hand, completely disappeared. None of us heard anything from her. Knowing Juanita, I was sure she was doing fine, but that didn't mean I wasn't worried.

"It'll all work itself out," Pastor Izzy said. "Now, I've got to go. Say hi to Hudson for me, even though I'm still upset you married him before I got to meet him."

"Please get over it, Israel," I joked, and he laughed.

Hudson and I got married at the courthouse. We didn't want anything fancy or flamboyant. We just wanted to be married. The night he asked me, the night of the sponsorship ball, I'd given him a pin I'd had engraved a week before. Izzy told me that God had brought me into Hudson's life as his helper on this second chance journey, and he was there to stay.

Before all this happened, I was honestly just like the real Jonah. Angry that God would give Hudson a second chance, that He would forgive him, just like Jonah was angry that God would others in the Bible. I didn't get swallowed by a fish, but when I tried to avoid doing the righteous thing, I was swallowed by my problems. Now, I'm thankful I went to that diner, that I was obedient, because I'm happily married to the very same man I wished nothing for.

Hudson thinks that pin is just about *his* second chances, but it's also about mine. I lost a lot, too, and now, Hudson and I are starting over. Together. We're going to do things the way God wants us to, and we're going to do it as one.

When Israel's laughter calmed, he said, "I've got to go, but I'll see you next week, Jonah."

"Alright, I'll see you soon."

After we hung up, I stepped out the car into the high sun. I blocked the sweltering rays as I crossed the parking lot to a shelter. There was a candidate here for the My Fellow American Project. Casey, the shelter's case worker, whom I've worked with for three years now, called me three hours ago about a woman who showed up in distress. Casey said the woman was scheduled for an abortion later this afternoon. I'm not sure why she showed up at our headquarters to tell us such a thing. Maybe that was her way of asking for help.

Unfortunately, Casey couldn't convince her not to get it. She was determined to do this, but she was still at the office. Maybe there was time for me to step in, though I wasn't sure how much help I'd be. The woman said her mind was made up and that she was only there to sign up for one of our programs afterwards. She wasn't doing good. That was why she wanted to abort her child.

I wish I could've gotten there sooner. All we could do was deal with things from this point forward and pray that would be enough.

I pulled open the doors to the My Fellow American headquarters. Casey met me at the front. "Afternoon, Mrs. Blue."

"Afternoon, Casey. Where's our girl?"

She nodded toward her office. "She's in there."

I thanked her and headed over. Most women from the shelter liked to do these consultations alone. It wasn't until I stepped inside that I realized why this woman wanted to speak privately.

"*Juanita?*"

She looked over her shoulder, eyes wide and misting already. Her belly was big and round beneath her hunter green sweat jacket. She had the hood pulled up, and she looked tired.

"Nita," I whispered as I closed the door. "What is going on?"

"Jonah—" a hiccup clogged her throat.

I stood at the door just blinking at her until she spoke again through her falling tears. "He got me pregnant," she said, "but he won't help me. and I don't know what to do. I was so stupid!"

"Nita." I knelt beside her chair. "Hey, we can figure this out. We can put you through the program and get you help." My heart ached as I stared at my friend… my very best friend. So much had transpired between us, but Juanita came back to the one place she knew she could, and I really felt like a light because of it. The torch God said I would be.

"I was supposed to get an abortion, but I just can't do it," Juanita whispered.

I nodded.

"Please," she wiped her eyes, "can you please help me?"

"Yes," my voice was pinched with sorrow. I took Nita's hand. "We're going to help you. Can you stay here over the weekend? I'll come get you first thing Monday morning."

She nodded stiffly. "Ok."

With a gentle smile, I stood and pulled her in for a hug. My old friend had returned, and now I had to help her. The woman who made me almost lose my mind, was right here in front of me, her own mind nearly gone. The woman who took the boy I thought I wanted was asking me to help her. The woman who had become my enemy was right here, but I wasn't angry. I wasn't bitter. I wasn't sad either. I was happy—but not because I had the chance to gloat or look down on her. I was happy because she'd come home. She was finally here, and, despite everything, I didn't want Juanita to be anywhere else.

∧ ∧ ∧

298

"Hudson?" I called as I stepped through the door of our apartment. He moved in with me, though I liked his apartment more than mine, but Hudson wanted to preserve the memories of where our journey began and stay here a little while longer. After running into Erma, he asked if *she* could have his apartment. She was holding down a janitor's job at a burger joint and was between apartments. Of course, I said yes, but only if she agreed to be my future nanny. She was a pro at raising the Blues, but she wanted a second chance to make things right with the next generation. We were all about second chances.

"In here!" Hudson called from the bedroom. He'd painted it himself, a fresh coat of white, like I requested.

I stepped into the bedroom to find my husband holding a book in his hand. *His* book.

"They're here!" I squealed, tossing my bag down. I practically ran across the room, smiling so hard my cheeks hurt.

Hudson hugged me, passing me a hardcover book. "Here's your *signed* copy."

I snorted. "I'm glad I know the author."

He pulled me a little closer, exhaling slowly. "The author is glad he knows you."

Hudson kissed me deeply, standing in the middle of our small apartment, surrounded by stacks of his own books, his hard work. Over the last year, we'd been doing well financially, but now we were about to do *really* well.

After quitting Blue Barn, Hudson started blowing the

299

whistle on his own company. Not even a week passed before he was offered a tell-all book deal, plus a job at a local newspaper. He enjoyed writing articles by day while writing his story by night. He'd told his father that he had prepared ahead of time for his departure from Blue Barn, which was in the tabloids for six months straight. But Olan did pretty good with blocking Hudson, fighting the headlines and calling his son a liar until he couldn't anymore. The tabloids were never Hudson's goal, he only used them to get attention for the main event.

Hudson Blue wrote a book about elitism being a ghost in our society. It was the leading force for so many wrongs in our world. People ate his story up. He was set (after our trip to Texarkana) to appear on television after selling one million physical copies and over two million digital copies in his first week of sales. The money was flowing in, and we were about to make a fortune off the plan God gave Hudson one year ago.

Somehow, my story became Hudson's story, and when he sat down to write his book, he asked me to recount things and tell him about my own struggles. Initially, I thought it was odd, since the story was his. However, one week after he began querying agents, he shared the title he'd come up with. The title that would glow on the cover of the best-selling book in America:

My Fellow American.

ACKNOWLEDGEMENTS

A big thank you to Jesus Christ for getting me through this! This book was filled to the brim with faith, politics, and social injustices. However, I am forever grateful that God blessed me to pen this book for such a time as this in a very divided America. To my fellow Americans, thanks for reading.

Follow me on **social media!** @awritingbean to get updates on new releases, pre-orders, and reduced prices on my books. You can also subscribe to my Patreon for access to my book club and special "behind the scenes" looks at characters, world building, and more.

More books by A. BEAN & TRC Publishing!

Christian Fantasy
The Scribe

Cross Academy

Christian Post-Apocalyptic Fiction
The Barren Fields

The End of the World series

MAGOG saga

Christian Science Fiction
I AM MAN series

Christian Romance
The Living Water

Withered Rose Trilogy

Beautiful Lies

The Gap

Decipis Trilogy

Fractured Diamond

The Woof Pack Trilogy

Singlehood

Christian Children's Fiction
Too Young

The Rebel Christian Publishing

We are an independent Christian publishing company focused on fantasy, science fiction, and romantic reads. Visit therebelchristian.com to check out our books or click the titles below!

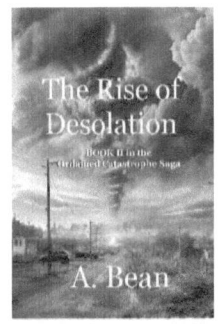

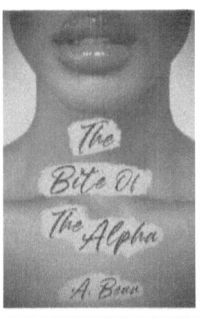

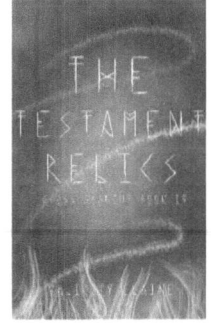

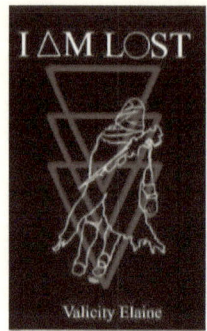

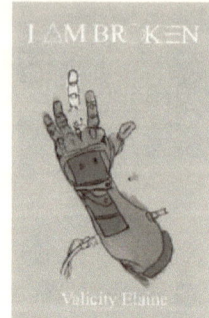

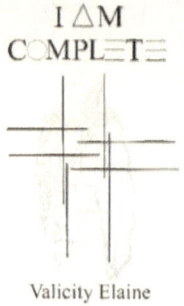